# MAFIA KING

paige press

# MAFIA KING

*New York Times* Bestselling Author
# CD REISS

Copyright © 2021 by Flip City Media Inc.

All rights reserved.

*CD Reiss is a trademark of Flip City Media Inc.*

No part of this book may be reproduced in any form or by any electronic or mechanical means, including information storage and retrieval systems, without written permission from the author, except for the use of brief quotations in a book review.

This book is a work of fiction. I made up the characters, situations, and sex acts. Brand names, businesses, and places are used to make it all seem like your best real life. Any similarities to places, situations or persons living or dead is the result of coincidence or wish fulfillment.

Paige Press
Leander, TX 78641

Ebook:
ISBN: 978-1-953520-32-6

Print:
ISBN: 978-1-953520-33-3

Editor: Erica Edits
Cover: CD Reiss

# ABOUT THE BOOK

*An epic mafia romance trilogy that sets a new bar for just how dark a hero can get, from NY Times Bestselling author CD Reiss.*

Santino is my king. My lover. My husband.

He's the head of the Cavallo crime family and the moment he choked my vows from me, my life was bound to his.

I'm done fighting my fate, until I hear two rumors, and I'm shaken to the core.

One rumor about the past—that I wasn't the first bride Santino took.

Another about the future—a new bride is about to be taken.

Changing the old ways is like dousing the flames of hell with tears.

But I married the devil himself, and when I vowed to obey, I lied.

# PROLOGUE
## SANTINO

When I lay eyes on Violetta in her uncle's hallway, it's not a woman I see. She is a child clawing her way up the far side of the cliff to adulthood, like the sun just cresting the horizon line, casting a new glow on the world.

She is an unfinished transformation. I'm aware of the pressure of her adolescence pushing against the child hard enough to break it, but in that moment, the change setting upon her is not what moves me.

On that day, in the hallway, she is not a human with a body rushing through the stages of life, rising sun after rising sun, changing with the persistence of a ticking clock. She is something more.

I'm at that house to bind myself to a treasure I promised to secure and protect. Every black-veiled *nonna* and hot-barreled soldier will murder and die for it. It is our power, and it's been left to me. I've come for what's mine.

But when I see Violetta, the womanchild with more

power and darkness in her eyes than I've seen in assassin or priest, I know she is eternal darkness and everlasting light.

Fate has sent me there to protect a treasure, and it is not hard stones or cold metal.

It is Violetta Moretti.

## 1

## SANTINO

Under the cluster of three pines, right after the hard left, the tree's roots have broken free of the cliff and reach for passing cars. Even if you get around them without getting the driver's side door ripped off, you still have to be alert, especially at sunset, because that's where the hill turns into a mountain. You have to change gears, get the fuck out of the way of the roots, and avoid oncoming cars silently hurtling down an extreme grade, in neutral, with their headlights still off.

I've driven this road unscathed many times at every time of day, but for no good reason at all, its treachery has never felt more dangerous than this evening. Bringing the car to a full stop—at the risk of getting rear-ended—to peer around the corner like a student driver seems like the only way to reach the top.

As the bumps under the tires *thp-thp-thp* and my mind molds three words into them, I realize why I took such care. I don't want to die with the words *la tua bella* in my thoughts, sounding like Violetta's acid-laced voice.

They're the only words she's spoken to me in five days.

We eat dinner at the same table. I compliment her dress or hair, and she replies with *la tua bella*. When I say good night, she says *la tua bella*. When I tell her to look at me, she whispers *la tua bella*. The only time she's said anything different was when I asked her if she wanted me to tell her about Rosetta.

She said yes.

But I couldn't give up my position. I demanded she speak to me in full sentences first. She cast her eyes down and repeated the same three words, and I walked away rather than give more than I was taking.

Even then, I knew it wasn't a good decision, but I was unable to change it. I'm a car with broken brakes, speeding ahead in the half hour between day and night when you can get away without headlights, whipping around curves on blind faith.

*La tua bella la tua bella la tua bella.*

My job is to protect her. All she has to do is obey me.

But what's driving me to madness is wanting what I was never entitled to and never expected.

Her love.

I need her to love me but, because of how I took her and what I've hidden, she's incapable of opening her heart.

I slow down and drop into a familiar driveway on the side of the hill, pulling up to the house I signed over the day after I bought it. All the lights are on and Loretta's already waiting for me in a jacket, slacks, and bare feet.

"*Ciao.*" I kiss her cheeks. "Your shoes."

"I just got home from work." She goes inside. Once I close the door, we fall into speaking Italian. "You still have perfect timing."

"I won't keep you long."

"Too bad. Will you take an espresso?"

"*Si, grazie.*"

We are in the kitchen now. She's put on slippers. Our habits together are the same. I'm leaning against the counter and she's filling the Moka with water, not looking at me, as if my presence functions as audience to her femininity, not a participant in the scene.

"You know where the sambuca is," she says with a jerk of her chin toward a familiar cabinet. "If you want to correct it."

"No." I *tsk*, softening the refusal. It's one of the ticks I never thought about until Violetta.

"You're such a good boy now." She scoops dark brown powder into the Moka pot, baiting me, then glances over with a shrug. "So what brings you, at this hour, to my house on the hill?"

"A favor."

"Of course. What is it this time? More clothes to burn in the fireplace?"

"Easier."

"How exciting." She's droll, turning the knob on the stove. It clicks, but no flame appears. She sighs, tries again.

"I have it," I say, getting the stainless steel Zippo from my breast pocket. I turn on the gas and flick it. The burner flame appears with a whoosh and I step out of her way.

She doesn't move though. She just stands there, looking at me.

"I heard what happened in Amalfi," she says. "With Siena."

"Women gossip too much."

"I heard it from a man." She adjusts the pot on the burner. "You should have told her, you know."

*La tua bella*

"Why should wives know everything?"

Her scoff is so slight, I would have missed it if I didn't know her so well.

"What good would it do?" I add when she takes down two cups instead of answering.

"What's the favor?" She places the cups on a tray.

"I want you to talk to Violetta. Woman to woman."

"About?" She grabs a lemon from the fruit bowl. "*Limone?*"

"*Si.*" Telling her seems redundant, and the request itself is humiliating. She can't refuse me, but the danger is Loretta will tell one too many people he has no control over his wife. The Moka spits steam. "She needs to know why."

"Why her sister was first? Why she was in Italy? Why she died there?" She peels a curl of skin from the lemon. "Because no one knows the real answers to these questions."

"She needs to…" I clench my jaw so hard against the list of humiliating answers, I can't finish.

Talk to me? Listen to me? Love me?

Did I come all the way up this mountain to ask this shameful favor? I'm not going to beg any woman or man to help with my own house.

"She wasn't raised right," I say, forcing my jaw loose. "She doesn't know the way things are."

"Does she not know? Or not accept?"

Loretta picks up the tray and takes it outside without another word. I grab the full bottle of sambuca and follow. Despite my earlier refusal, I'm going to need to correct the espresso.

When I get outside into the humid night air, I smell the roses around the patio and the rosemary from the herb garden. I hear crickets calling to get laid. All of it is to be expected, but knowing the smells and sounds of the place makes the difference more clear.

There's cologne. A man. And it's fresh in the air—not the stale remnants of yesterday's guest.

Loretta sets out the cups and we sit, overlooking the lights of the city. I drop the licorice aperitif in my coffee and hold the bottle over hers. She nods, and I use it to correct hers, then I set down the bottle and lean back. When the breeze flows from the west, the cologne smell disappears behind roses.

"I'm not asking a lot," I say. "Tell me the problem you have now that you didn't have the last time I brought her."

She sips her coffee. I don't touch mine. I don't even rub lemon on the rim of my cup. It would be too strong in my nose and mouth. I cannot lose the advantage of knowing a man lurks in the shadows.

"The problem," she says, "is nobody asks you to

explain anything. We all just jump. Meet me here? Like this." She snaps her fingers. "We do it. Keep my wife in your house? Done. Throw yourself off this cliff?"

"I didn't ask you for that."

The breeze changes direction, and the cologne comes up from the east. Behind me and a little to the left. He is wide, whomever he is, likely to attack from my non-dominant side. I cap the sambuca.

"Not yet." She sips her espresso and does not look behind me even for a moment. "You need to talk to her. Tell her you're still mourning her sister."

"I'm not." The air changes again, but I don't need it. I feel him breathing. He's in the bushes of the terraced yard, heading up the concrete steps to the patio. If there wasn't a man present, I would explain that I married Rosetta because I promised to. But Violetta? I didn't need a promise to marry her. I needed a reason to stay away from her. She scares the hell out of me. "Violetta is my wife now."

The sound of his feet on the stones is hidden by the wind, but I feel the air move and the electricity from Loretta. Grabbing the sambuca bottle by the neck, I stand, spinning around and swinging the bottle in a heavy arc.

I manage to override the torque of my swing about an inch from his left temple because my eyes deliver two pieces of information to my brain.

One, the man is Damiano.

Two, his hands are up to show they're empty.

"*Cazzo*," I bark, snapping the bottle back. As I do, I notice the bulge in his jacket. Hands up or not, he's carrying.

"*Cristo*," Damiano says. "Little jumpy, no?"

"What the fuck, Dami?"

"I was just coming to say hello."

"Like a cat going to bacon." I sit down again and sip my coffee, an indication that I'll stay. "That cologne stinks like a fresh asshole."

Damiano sits across from me, not hiding the gun. I won't hide mine either.

"He didn't think you'd meet him." Loretta stands.

"So you let him wait in the bushes?"

She winces in reaction to the anger in my voice. Good. She should flinch, and yet, I shouldn't blame her. She has little power to choose her path.

"You know I don't like being played with," I add.

"It's on me," Damiano says, then adds a formal nod. "*Chiedo perdono.*"

I'm being placated, but tonight, my curiosity is stronger than the insult.

Loretta folds her arms. "He has something important to tell you."

"Thanks, babe." Damiano pats her hand, then turns to me. "You're so paranoid. What the hell was I going to do? Kill you? For what? This one?" He jerks his thumb toward Loretta. "She'd fucking shoot me for touching you wrong. Ain't that right?" He looks at her with affection, which she returns.

"Shooting would be too good for you." She goes inside.

Damiano watches her ass as she walks back toward the house. "You gave up a good woman."

"I had duties elsewhere."

"Sure." He drops into her seat and pours the liqueur

into the cups. "Speaking of. How's that spark plug you married?"

He could be asking an innocent question to make small talk, or he could be taking my temperature to see how hot I'm running at the mention of my wife.

"Ask Siena."

"Oh, yeah, I heard she came by your place in Amalfi to say hello."

"Did you send her?"

"Why would I do that?"

I don't know why he'd send his sister to cause trouble with Violetta and me, unless he didn't know if it would be trouble and he wanted to find out.

Loretta comes out of the kitchen holding two cups with ice and sets them on the glass tabletop with a click.

"Look at her," he says to me, talking about Loretta as if she's not there. "Good as bread."

"Tell me if you need anything." She glances at me, then pats Dami's shoulder.

The door clicks behind her. He pours sambuca for each of us and holds up his.

"*Salute.*"

"*Salute.*"

We touch glasses and drink.

"Now," I say. "You can tell me what you want."

He fixes his cuffs, rearranges his legs, lets his eyes wander like a bored child in summer school. "Your uncle Marco. On the other side."

Marco is my zia Paola's husband, and while my aunt raised me when my mother couldn't, Marco allowed her to take me in, and I'm frequently torn between gratitude and disdain for the fact that he did no more. He was never a father to me, and not much of a father to Gia and Tavie either.

"What about him?" I ask.

"He got himself into a little bit of trouble with my dad."

I try not to laugh and fail. Marco Polito has no business getting into trouble with Cosimo Orolio, who runs Napoli like our old boss, Emilio Moretti, ran territory ten times the size.

Damiano refills his glass and tops off mine. "He borrowed some money to cover a bet, couldn't make the payments, this and that, my father picked up the loan—"

"You're speaking to your father now? Since when?"

Damiano pauses by drinking. The ice topples into his upper lip. He wipes the cold water away with his fingertips. "Not at the moment."

"That's a shame."

"They say blood's thicker than water, but when I was thirsty, what did he offer me?" He pours a third cup of sambuca. "Nothing. *Sa*-fucking-*lute*." Damiano slaps back his sambuca.

This is not how we do it. We are not children or animals. He's either been spending too much time with the college kids on the other side of the river, or he's trying to calm his nerves.

"I'm gonna bail him out." Damiano clicks his glass down. "Marco. Your uncle. I'm taking care of it. All I need is your blessing and it'll be paid."

I don't give the blessing right away, because once I do, I'm responsible for it, and I'm not interested in crossing Cosimo Orolio right now.

"And your father agrees?"

"Through an emissary, yeah. He don't care."

"How's Marco paying you back? All his pants have holes in the pockets."

Damiano shrugs and looks away, and I know—finally—loosened by conversation and sambuca, he's getting to his point. "I figured it's an act of good will. Between you and me."

"I have no ill will toward you."

"Yeah. Sure. I know. It's fine. But see, I gotta tell you. Man to man." He puts his elbows on the table and clears his throat. "I miss it. Being inside, you know? With a… kinda… family, I guess. Not as payment so much, but so just saying… in good faith, I can get some of that back. Here. Me and you."

"You want to work with me?"

"Yeah." He shrugs a little as if he wasn't ready to answer a direct question but might as well, since I asked. "And maybe I can climb the ladder, then… some time… we can be like it used to be, on the other side. On a personal level. You're in charge and I can be… once I prove myself… like a right-hand guy."

Back home, Damiano and I were partners and equals. That's what he wants, and if I were the same man as I was then, I'd give it to him. I'd embrace the past and make it the future. But right now, I don't trust him on either side of the ocean.

"If I say no?"

He throws himself back in his chair, arms out,

palms up, as if my answer renders him innocent of any consequences. "Like you said. Marco's got holes in his pockets. He's a bad investment."

"He is."

"So that's a no?"

"I'll bless you cashing him out. Not the repayment schedule."

"*Bene.*" He nods with a rueful press of his lips—like a parent who didn't want to have to punish his child but now has no choice.

"Is there a problem, Dami?" I stand.

"No, no."

"You sure?"

"I was just remembering that day." He backs toward the door. "In the hospital with Emilio. Just us and that fucking consigliere. Nazario Coraggio. When he gave you Rosetta, and he gave me—"

"What about it?"

"Who knows *why* he did it, besides us?"

"And Franco Tabona?"

"He knew shit." He shakes his head and *tsks*. "I never told him. I never told anyone. Tabona went after your wife to get to you. Man, if he knew? Shit. It woulda changed the math real quick. But it was fun watching you wipe them out."

I should have killed Damiano the first time he implied my wife was a target, but he's still Cosimo Orolio's son, and I rule a small, peaceful corner of the world. Cosimo would have sent a hundred men from Naples. The resulting war would have raged for a day —maybe two—before he crushed us.

When Emilio died, I was nineteen and officially, I

was no more important than a loyal soldier. Cosimo filled the vacuum without shedding a drop of blood, but he couldn't maintain the scope of Emilio's territory, because no one believed he could. Within six months, his boundaries were as tight as a fist, but about as small—without America, and I was sidelined within his organization.

I was worried about the Tabonas. This was a misdirection of myself.

"Doesn't matter the reason," I say. "Franco Tabona sends men for my wife, Franco Tabona gets wiped out. That math never changes."

Loretta watches us from the kitchen, arms crossed like a big sister letting her brothers fight it out.

"You think I told them," Damiano says, "but I didn't. If any of them knew? What would they do with her?"

We both know exactly what would be done with Violetta if everyone knew the nature of my promise to her father.

"After they take what you married her for? They gonna just kill her or take a day to give everyone a dip in her sauce?"

I'm standing before he's even finished, hands on the table, leaning in his face. "Don't talk about her ever again."

Loretta comes outside with a bowl of fresh ice she knows we don't need. She's there to make sure whatever happens is witnessed.

"I kept the secret," he says, seeming unafraid. "Even kept it from my own father. And you won't even offer me a taste of friendship."

Loretta puts the bowl on the table. I sit back and jerk my chin toward her in a dismissive motion. Damiano flicks his wrist at her. She goes inside.

"You stole what was given to me." He jabs his thumb to his chest. "For once, I was first in line and you stepped over me."

"The crown wasn't meant for you."

"Violetta was given to me."

"She was always mine."

"You took her." Damiano pounds the table. "Ripped bread out of my mouth. I come here and ask for crumbs in return for saving your uncle, and you won't even give me that."

I cannot discuss who owns Violetta for another moment, because there's more than a promise to a dying man at stake here. Damiano's either baiting me to take out his eye, which would start a war, or he's sincere and is willing to start a war over his version of the truth.

"My friendship can't be bought," I say, standing slowly, ready to leave.

"And my silence hasn't been paid for." He drops two cubes of ice in his glass.

"You want a war, Dami? You don't remember the last one well enough?"

"You owe me." He pours himself more sambuca. "All this time, not telling every capo in the four corners how to get at the treasure he gave you. Peace ain't cheap, and the note's gonna come due before her birthday."

"Enjoy your sambuca."

I leave him there and give Loretta a quick goodbye before tearing down the hill.

The way home is deceptively less treacherous.

## 2

## VIOLETTA

The mountains shudder when Santino speaks.

"*Vai.*"

He holds his paper between us, asking nothing else of me for now. I'm hungry and he can fuck himself, so I sit down to breakfast.

"*Buongiorno.*" His greeting rolls off his tongue like marmalade dripping off burned toast.

I'd like to know where he's been spending so many of his hours, but since Italy, I've only said three words to him, over and over. It's losing its power, and at this point, it's more of a habit I'm revving up to break.

"*La tua bella.*" In our new language, this can be loosely translated as "go to hell."

The bread in front of me looks like a crumbling bathroom tile.

Santino's not exactly cowed by my anger, but he isn't trying to break me. Either he understands what he did to me, or he doesn't care. No matter how disrespectful I am, nothing makes him tell me what happened with Rosetta.

Did he love her?

Did he ever love me?

Does it matter?

Yet I've been too angry to ask directly. I'm starting to think my three-word strategy is backfiring.

"You should go out today," he says from behind his newspaper. "Do some shopping."

Me, doing anything he suggests, is self-harm. Disobedience is a reflex, not a choice, but it's a choice I would make even if I thought about it.

When I started my most recent semester at college, I had no idea I would end up married to the most powerful mobster in Secondo Vasto, living in his dollhouse, helplessly and carelessly ripped apart in body and mind. In a beachside bedroom on the shore of the Amalfi coast, I finally let myself believe my husband had chosen me. That when he took me from my family, it was as much for love as honor; as much about what he was owed for my father's debts as what he would have wanted anyway. A desire no less intense for being poorly expressed and cruelly implemented.

I gave him my body and my pleasure. I let him rule over me, and I let myself love being ruled by him, opening the fingers that had clenched around my own desires—relaxing into an unturned palm to show him the shards of ancient clay, fired in my false freedoms, broken in my protective fist, and I said, Take it. Take it all.

Like a man making a wish over his birthday candles, he blew the shards and dust away, leaving me with nothing to hold. He took nothing for himself because he didn't want what I had as much as he wanted me to offer it all to him.

*I understand why he'd bring her here to marry her since she wasn't quite eighteen.*

Santino DiLustro had been engaged to my sister, Rosetta, long before I was ever in the picture. He didn't want me. He didn't desire me. He wanted my sister, my beautiful sister, who had been stolen from me once when he took her to a festering misery of a country, and again when he let her die ruined and alone—wearing the same ring he won't let me take off.

I turn the stone toward my palm so I don't have to see the way the sun hits it, and I eat my tasteless toast.

I am a woman of precious stone and solid honor, and when I pushed him away our first night back, screaming those three words—*la tua bella la tua bella*—his lack of violence or threats spoke volumes. He knows he fucked up.

Good.

He knows I hate him.

Even better.

I don't know the thickness of the line I'm walking, or what I'll do in the moment before he does something violent enough to push him to reach for a cigarette. And that danger has its own buzz of electricity. I'll say *la tua bella* as long as it fucks him up, even if it fucks me up.

I want him to hurt. I want him to struggle.

I want him gone.

I can't wish him dead. Death is too good for him. And all this wanting and wishing does nothing. I have neither money nor friends. I have no choice but to make him as miserable as I am.

"Violetta," he says, and I realize the unchewed toast is putty in my mouth.

"*La tua bella?*" I say with a lilt that could mean, "yes, dear?" or "how can I help you?"

When the women gossiped that he was a whore-maker, they weren't talking about Loretta. They were talking about Rosetta.

"Please don't do this anymore," he asks softly from the other side of a stone wall of silence.

Did he woo her, I wonder? I'm *Forzetta*, but she was *la tua bella*. Did he bring her flowers and trinkets to show he was thinking about her? When the debt came due, did he ask for her hand and think he was getting the better of the deal? How does he like the interest on the loan now that he's stuck with me?

Did he steal me the way he did because he didn't really want me?

Was she taken like I was, by surprise and against her will? Did she sleep in the same dollhouse room, overlooking the pool he slices into every day? Did she spend the first nights huddled in the same corner, wishing her life was over?

I remember she was excited to go to Italy, and I was jealous that she got to go. Did he meet her there? Did he steal her there? Did he drop on her like a surprise? Or did he afford Rosetta a loving kindness he's never extended to me—cherishing one sister and abusing the other?

The more corporeal questions practically ask themselves.

Did they share the same room? Was she willing to open her heart and so much more to him as soon as he took her? Was he gentle with her? Or did he rough her up like he did with me? Did he stick those powerful thumbs up her ass and bring her to gasping orgasms?

Did we really ever share the same man?

I can't breathe. I can't think. I can't stop hurting.

I thought I could change things. I thought I could carve my own path.

I was wrong.

I'm the same trapped, scared girl I was in the wedding chapel. How it is possible to go from so blissfully happy to terrified all over again?

The answer sits before me, wrapped in a custom suit and brooding eyes.

*Santino.*

This is all his fault. All of this. Anger scorches a trail through me, hot and sharp, leaving blackened, smoking dust from heart to mind to toes. He could have saved her. Siena said he wasn't there when Rosetta died, leaving her with strangers, instead of safe with me and the Zs.

Of all his sins, this last one should be the one he burns in hell for.

I may not have the power to escape this nightmare, but I have the power to live it on my own terms. He can no longer just take what he wants.

"You will talk to me," he states like a cold fact.

Is that all he wants? *Me* to talk to *him*?

Well, I had a speech class where I did nothing but talk, and his demand that I talk to him opens up new opportunities to confuse and hurt him.

"We hold these truths to be self-evident," I say, slowly at first as I dig deep into my eleventh-grade curriculum. "That all men are created equal, that they are—"

"Wait," he says. "Slow down."

"Endowed by their Creator with certain unalienable—"

"Violetta." He leans forward. "What are you saying?"

Of course he doesn't recognize the Declaration of Independence. In context, it's outside his experience. The real problem however, is that the *content* exists outside the context of his will.

"Unalienable rights, that among these are life, liberty, and the pursuit of happiness—that to secure these rights—"

"I speak four languages," he hisses. "Not this gibberish."

"Bummer."

"What does it *mean*?" He growls, thrusting himself in my direction, as if he wants to insert himself down my throat.

"Life, liberty, and the pursuit of happiness means you must return the first thing by giving me the second, or the third will never happen for either of us."

He doesn't get it, and he wants to. I can see it in his face. He's trying to break it down and find some clear course of action in my words that doesn't involve him letting me go.

"It means," I continue, "go fuck yourself." I enunciate each word in English. Fuck him and his Italian. That world already chewed me up and spat me out. It's not getting back in through my mouth.

"There are things you don't understand," he says.

"Because no one tells me anything."

"That's the way it is."

"What part of 'go fuck yourself' do you need translated?"

"I am protecting you."

"You. Are. Killing. Me!" My shout scrapes the walls of my throat, louder than I intend, weaker than I want. The wall around me doesn't even shake, and neither does Santino DiLustro.

When I clench my fingers into a fist, the diamond indents the tender skin of my palm. It belonged to Rosetta first.

Is it bad luck to wear someone else's ring? Did I miss that particular superstition? It wasn't passed down through a family as an expression of eternal love. This ring claimed a woman—*one woman*—as his bride. For the other, it is a locked metal cuff.

Jumping up, I pull off the engagement ring and nesting wedding band and throw them onto the table in front of him. They skid and slide over the edge. He catches them.

"Did you force her? Did she know she had no choice?" I croak with a voice unused to new words. "Because Zio and Zia sent her to Italy. They took her shopping before she left. I went with them. They never mentioned dressing up to meet her husband. They never mentioned you at all."

He puts the rings in his pocket. "I took her to the other side to get things for the wedding. Lace and almond confetti. Please sit."

I can't even believe what a different world she lived in with him.

"So she knew?" I decide to go for his jugular without thinking too long about it. "Or did you just rape her outright?"

"Shut your mouth." He bolts to standing as if ejected from his seat.

"You did," I say with one finger up in his face.

"Never. And don't you ever even say it again."

"Then you killed her, and took me to get your debt paid."

"You do not know!" He leaves the sentence without specifics, as if to say it's not that I'm missing any particular knowledge, but that I—Violetta Moretti—just don't know.

"*You* do not know, Santino." My voice hits the ceiling and bounces back twice as strong. "You do not talk. You do not explain. I don't want to hear it." I jut my arms forward and push him. He barely moves, as if he knows I'm lying. I *need* to hear it. "You can justify yourself to God."

"I will." He takes my wrists in a tight grip. "I will be judged by God and sent to hell by Him. Not by you."

"Fuck you."

I try to knee him in the balls, fail, twist, and wind up on my back on the floor with him straddling me at the hips and pinning my wrists above my head. His chest heaves. His eyes are feral. I can hear his pulse roar in his veins.

I am an animal under him, freeing my left wrist for a moment, but he catches it and stops trying to restrain me while his attention is on my clenched fist. He lets my right arm go and reaches into his pocket to retrieve my rings.

"You took these off."

I say nothing. I have nothing new to add.

"Open." He shakes my wrist, but I don't obey. "Violetta." My name is a warning.

"You stole my sister from me." The words come out in a spitty, hissy mess. Angry, hot tears well up in my eyes. "You stole my family from me. You stole my life. And you had the audacity to act like your hands were clean this whole time. Fuck. You."

I spit in his face with the same strength I used to spit on the picture of him and my father, leaving a stringy K from his eyebrow to his upper lip.

He looks as if he's going to send me to meet my sister.

Instead, he growls one word through clenched teeth. The line of spit moves with his lips. "Open."

My defiance is used up, and I open my left hand so he can jam the rings onto the fourth finger.

"The only way these rings come off is if someone cuts off the finger. Do you understand?" He leans down so close to me that, if I wanted to, I could lick my spit off his face.

"I'll keep Rosetta's ring to remember her."

With a jerk, he stands over me—one foot on either side of my chest like a highway viaduct over a barren field of rage—slips a handkerchief out of his pocket, and wipes his face.

"You were not the only one on this planet to experience grief."

Lying on the dining room floor with throbbing

wrists and heavy breaths, I stare at the flat white ceiling with the unlit, dripping-crystal chandelier in the center. Sunlight creeps in through from the south, where the glass patio doors face onto the pool.

"But it's mine," I say. "She was my sister, and it's my grief."

"It's mine too."

This truth colors him like a dye that seeps from the inside out. His grief is mine, but it's not just for Rosetta. It's for the father he never knew and the mother who abandoned him, for his own disappointments and brokenness.

"I am sorry for your loss, Violetta. I am truly sorry." He reaches down to help me up.

I don't want any part of this anymore. How did I even get trapped here? I don't want grief. I want to be as mad as I deserve to be.

I take his hand and let him help me stand. He leans his face close to my head. My scalp tingles at the closeness of his lips, but I remain ramrod-straight, my own lips tight and my body unyielding. I expect a kiss, but it never lands.

Instead, he whispers, *"Forzetta."*

He pulls something out of his pocket and lays it next to my plate. Its glass is a shimmering mirage—a portal back into my old life.

My phone.

"I know you've been lonely," he says. "This house isn't meant to be a prison for you. But make sure Armando is with you."

"For my protection." I touch the hard glass. It responds by lighting up. The wallpaper is of me and a stranger I once knew named Scarlett. He's kept it charged.

I look up at him. He seems hopeful, like a dog offering a thrown stick and expecting pats on the head or a big sloppy kiss. But he's just returning what's rightfully mine. I cannot arrange my features into the look of gratitude he's hoping for. I can't even thank him.

A few months ago, I would have already been texting Scarlett and calling the Zs, eagerly scrolling through Instagram to see what everyone had been up to in my absence. Now the phone feels as though it belongs to someone else—the carefree American girl I was at the beginning of the summer. She's gone. But I'm not the fulfilled Italian wife either. I'm stuck somewhere between, and this phone won't do a damn thing but remind me of who I'm not, and never will be again.

There's a long, awkward pause as all my apps glow under my fingertips, crying to be the first one open. I can't bear it.

Santino rakes his gaze over me, and for an instant, the heat between us returns. I remember with aching clarity why I gave myself to him, and the tidal force with which he took that gift. Will I ever be strong enough to withstand the riptide of his eyes?

He did a decent thing, but that does not mean he is decent. A kind gesture does not make him good. A kiss from him does not mean he is loving.

Just because he is Santino does not mean I have to revere him.

No matter how badly my body wants him. How badly it wants to rip him out of that fancy suit and beg him to pleasure me as punishment for the horrible things he's done.

I turn the phone glass-side down, tap it, then push it away a few inches. "Anything else?"

"Celia will be out tonight," he says. "So you will make dinner."

Was this supposed to be the bargain? Giving me my phone so I'd cook for him, like this marriage is something other than blasphemy and parody?

He doesn't wait for me to agree, because I don't have a choice.

Every step he takes to the foyer is a poem to grace, power, and desire.

I hate him and I want him, because I am a profoundly fucked-up woman.

# 3
# VIOLETTA

The phone gives me no joy. The emails are all business, internships I can't apply for and opportunities for other students. Social media makes me sad. Scarlett and the few other friends I have are far away. None would understand.

If this were a different marriage, preparing a traditional dinner for my husband would be one of my great joys. But how can I square that with my desire to never give Santino pleasure of any kind, ever again?

My zia taught me how to stem herbs, string *braciole*, and balance a sauce. On our last day together in the basement kitchen, surrounded by friends and family, the comfort of our hearts, she knew she was about to lose me. She made a feast anyway.

And I think: I will do this for me, and the countless Moretti women who have loved men who can only love darkness.

Maybe my mother thought this too. Maybe—without options—she never had to think of it at all.

I get lost in practical tasks. Mixing and pinching and chopping and stirring, I make everything from scratch. Santino doesn't deserve it, but I want it, so I will have it. Everything I want that it's possible to have, I shall have.

Upstairs, I thumb through the closet, looking at the shapeless, matronly clothes Gia picked out for me because I'm a wife, not a whore. I try on a green striped dress, but my own reflection makes me flinch. *He already knows I'm not the beautiful one.*

The meal I prepared got me out of my head and back into my body, so I put on a pretty blue dress I bought on Flora Street the day I was almost kidnapped.

Better. And it's what I want. If it's what Santino wants too, or if he likes what he sees, that's none of my business.

Is this how I will live from now on? Doling out pleasure to myself and keeping it from my husband? Starving myself in the hope that his hunger kills him before he kills me?

The front door alarm chirps to let me know someone has entered the house. I quietly make my way into the kitchen and pull on oven mitts.

"You're here," Santino says in a tone touched with surprise.

"Didn't you tell me to make dinner?" I snap open the oven and take out the eggplant parmigiana.

When I stand with it, I find him staring at me with a curious expression. Part surprise. Part relief. A little of something like muted triumph.

"*Si*," he says. "And you did."

I almost laugh when I realize he thought I was

going to use the phone to escape. As if I'm some kind of child, jumping all over myself to go from frying pan to fire.

"You thought I was going to leave you hungry?"

"You've starved me of everything else," he says with a shrug.

"Boo fucking hoo."

He smirks as if he's enjoying my utter lack of sympathy for the pain I've caused.

Passing close to him, I take the hot pan to the dining room, where I've laid out the settings. The wine breathes in a decanter next to the bread and butter.

Santino sits and shakes out his napkin. Like a good wife, I pour his wine and fill his plate before I sit. His mood is high and his manner is relaxed. He's in exactly the element he expects. Everything in his world is in its place.

"This smells good." He picks up a fork and waits for me to say something. He thinks this meal is an olive branch. He thinks I've forgiven him.

I put my hands in my lap and stare out the window, where the sky dims from blue to orange. When he finally begins eating, I do as well.

"Is this Celia's recipe?" he asks.

Back into my lap go my hands. I say nothing.

"Of course not," he mutters as if apologizing for an insult.

I neither confirm nor deny.

We do this the entire meal. He says something or asks a question. I don't respond, putting down my fork until he starts eating again. I can feel his frustration grow with every pause, but he's audacious in his assumption that repentance is for losers and it's possible all past sins can be forgiven without any work on his part.

His plate's almost clear when he's simply had enough. "What is it you *want?*"

I scoop up our plates and take them to the sink. That's where he goes for it, coming behind me with his murdering hands and kissing my neck.

"Do you want me to just take you?"

*Yes.*

*No!*

Christ on a ladder. He thinks I'm playing a sex game.

But yes, I want him to just take me.

"*Non toccarmi.*" I elbow him off, figuring he'll believe me if I tell him not to touch me in Italian.

He grabs my arm with enough force to make my middle damp with heat, and enough force to let me know he's done playing my silly games, and turns me around to face him. My entire body lights up with promise. It's more of a struggle to resist his seduction than it is to keep silent.

"I hate you," I lie. I want him more than I hate him. God, I am so, so broken.

"Hate me as much as you want. Spit on me. Fight me. Whatever you do to me, Rosetta's not coming back."

"Fucking you won't bring her back either."

"But maybe it will bring *you* back."

"It won't." I mean to be definitive, but the words that are supposed to go directly from my brain to my mouth get rerouted through my heart, and there they're turned into an invitation with his name engraved on the envelope.

Santino reads the tone loud and clear, scooping me up and hauling me upstairs before I can tell myself to protest. For my sister. For my self-respect. For any amount of power I want to maintain in this sick marriage.

But I can't work myself into the lie, because my whole body sings for his as he takes me into the bedroom I refuse to share with him and sets me on the floor.

"Run or lie down," he says. "I won't chase you, but if you don't leave now... if you stay in this room... I'm going fuck you."

I believe every word he says. I can leave right now and he won't stop me. I can go be alone in my room with this hot ball of throbbing desire breathing between my legs like a living thing.

I walk to the door, more sure of my choice with every stride. One, two, three, four steps. I put my hand on the doorknob, pause, reaffirm my decision to myself, then without looking at him, I slap it shut.

"You were saying?"

It takes him only two steps to come within reach.

"You," he says as he pulls my pretty blue dress over my head. "Are first." He tosses the dress aside as if it offends him. "You." He yanks my underwear down to my ankles with one stroke. "Are the only." From behind, he unhooks my bra, then pushes the straps over my arms, leaving me naked. "It's you, Violetta. Only you." His hands come around me and thumb my hard nipples. "There's no other woman I want. No other tits." A hand drifts down between my legs. "No other pussy. You are mine. First and always."

That's when I remember what I'm pissed about. I'm the Second Sister. The Left Behind. The Lesser of Two.

"Fuck you, liar."

Before I can draw another breath, I'm airborne, landing on the bed like a pillow. He jerks his clothes off as if they're on fire. I sit up on the bed. He's naked over me. His cock is a life force—maddened and engorged and demanding.

He puts a hand on each of my knees. "This what you want?" Roughly, he pulls up my knees and I fall on my back. "I was gentle before." He yanks my legs open and I'm exposed meat to a hungry lion. "Now I'm going to fuck you the way you want." Without preamble, he pierces me with two fingers, pushing as deep as they go. "I'm going to unlock the bitch and find the kitten." He twists his hand and expertly flicks my clit with his thumb.

I groan.

"Purr for me." He thumbs harder, but I'm not taking orders without a fight.

"You disgust me."

I take him by the throat, but my grasp seems to have no effect. His eyes narrow, and a smirk threatens one corner of his mouth when he presses down his thumb and makes a circle. My thighs tighten and my hips push his fingers deeper.

"That why you like this?" He moves his thumb against my nub, and I tighten my grip around his neck.

"I can't stand the sight of you."

"Then don't look."

In one move, he flips me onto my belly and pulls me half off the bed by the ankles. He spanks my poor bare ass with his palm, then the back of his hand, then spreads me apart and wedges himself along the slit between my legs.

"This better for you then?" His cock presses against my folds as he holds me down. The forced immobility triggers a rush of desire.

"What do you care?" I want him to take it without me giving it.

"I don't." He rests his cock where I'm wet, pausing his movement. "Tell me to stop. Tell me no."

The opportunity to disobey and submit at the same time is not one I can turn away from. I could say I'm emotionally disengaged from what's happening. I could tell myself there's a coldly calculated plan underlying my resistance and the pleasure I get from it.

But those are lies. I've never been more fully present.

"Yes."

He jams his cock into me so hard I bite back a scream of both pleasure and pain. The emotional gratification of complete physical surrender pushes up against my mental resistance. The friction between them is electric. He holds me down, pulls my hair, and fucks me as if I'm his property. His plaything. His birthright. Every thrust gets harder, asserting his dominance over deeper and deeper parts of me.

This isn't a culmination of love, but the power to split me open and rip me apart—and I love it.

"Come on," he grunts, riding me as if I'm a stubborn horse, grabbing my hip hard and pulling it into him while yanking my head back by the hair. "You going to be nice now?"

His reangled shaft goes deeper, rubbing new places, and all I can do is cry out when he reaches around and runs his fingertips against my swollen clit.

"That's right," he rumbles, going faster and deeper. "What I give. You. *Take.*"

Fuck him, but I can't make words, just gasps, then whimpers, then finally a long groan as I shudder and come around him. He explodes so deep inside me, he's writing his name on my soul.

Spent like his last dollar, I drop into a flat puddle. Without a word or moment to breathe, Santino pulls out while he's still half-hard. I flip over, sore, used, empty and full, leaning back on my elbows, and watch him gruffly put his clothes back on.

"You are my wife." He tucks his sex-slick cock into his pants. "You will cook for me. You will talk to me. You will trust me or you will be punished."

"Being married to you is the punishment."

Not impressed by my insult, he shrugs into his shirt. "You will suck my cock and you will open your legs for me."

My knees relax apart as if obeying a command that my brain can't filter out. I stop and consciously press them together.

Santino sees this, fixing his cuffs with a frown. "You *will* forgive me."

"You going to open my heart for me too?"

With the quickness of a cat, he takes a knee in each hand and pushes them apart as far as they'll go. As if he's flipped an invisible switch, I'm lit up with desire.

"I will fuck you so blind you will never look at me this way again. I will fuck you so hard you won't be able to speak another word of defiance. I am your husband. Do you understand? I can take what I want."

"You can rot in hell."

"I will. Every day I pray to God and the devil answers. You want me to rot in hell, but I don't have to rot to know where my death will lead." He lets me go, but my legs stay open for him, because I'm broken, and maybe I'll rot with him. "We will go to mass tomorrow. Maybe you can light a candle for me."

"Maybe you'll get struck down at the door."

Santino smirks and leaves.

I wait for the click of the lock, but it never comes, because despite my intentions, I've let him take me to his bed in his space.

The prison is no longer the house, and the warden isn't Santino. It's me, and I'm captive to the space between my legs.

I go to my own room to sleep. There, I dream that choices made are promises kept, and they have the power to overcome my body's longings.

# 4

## VIOLETTA

In the early morning, I am sore. The ache reminds me of that last morning in Italy—how I felt well-fucked. Like a woman. Like I could feel safe and satisfied being plundered. Now all it tells me is that I'm not as numb as I want to be.

The pool glimmers outside my bedroom window. How many summers did I spend sweating in my old bedroom, wishing I could go for a swim? Summer made me feel claustrophobic in a sheath of sticky skin. In front of the bedroom fan, I'd hitch up my long skirts and swing my bare legs or bend low, pulling down the neck of my shirt to dry the sweat between my breasts.

Santino's palace is perfectly temperature-controlled, and still, I long for the sensation of managing my body's own heat. So I slip into a bathing suit, hoping the chlorine or the cold will shock some sense into me. I doubt it though.

Dropping my towel onto a chaise, I stand at the

edge of the pool. My shadow bends along the built-in steps, not quite touching bottom.

The pool is, inescapably, Santino's domain.

When I step forward, the shadow follows, hitting the underwater floor. For this moment, I'm marking his place as my own. I submerge myself, and in the gurgle and whoosh of sound, I'm immediately flooded in memories. How he pressed me against the wall of the pool. Kissed me. Left me unsatisfied. How he teased me, tormented me, and denied me, knowing I wasn't ready to surrender fully.

And then when I did, the pleasure. The frigid kiss of gelato on my tongue. His finger brushing my lip when he fed me oranges. That same hand under my clothes.

I surface with a gasp.

My phone is buzzing where I left it on one of the lounge chairs, and my heart leaps into my throat.

Santino. Who else texts me anymore? What could he want?

I get out of the pool and check it. To my surprise, it's not my husband. Even better, it's from someone I'm allowed to love. Scarlett.

*—Finally home from Iceland! It was amazing!! Can't wait to swap travel stories. I'm leaving for Monaco with my dad in a few days. Can we hang on Monday? —*

My heart leaps a little. After weeks of isolation and terror and confusion, I can see Scarlett. I can finally get my head straight. I don't let myself consider what I'll tell her, how I'll explain what my life is now.

But before I can respond, another text comes in,

and this one is from the man himself.

*—Wear what's in the bag—*

What bag?

As if to answer my question, Armando emerges from inside the house, a huge man with a gun under his jacket, carrying a girlish white shopping bag with pale pink tissue paper tufting up from its insides. Did Santino send an old-lady monstrosity fit for a pious wife? Or something sleek and slutty red, to remind me that even my blood was never my own?

With a thrust of my legs, I push myself out of the pool, water cascading down my shoulders and hips, so much more tender with me than my husband has ever been.

"You can leave it," I tell Armando.

He drops the bag and retreats.

I take my time drying off, then I snap the bag by the handles, stomp up the stairs, and drop it on my bed.

With a *ding*, he's in my phone again.

*—The dress is for church—*

So he was serious last night about church. Is it even Sunday? I look out the window again, as if the clouds could tell me. I lost time in Italy—lost my footing and my bearings. My phone says it's Sunday, so it must be.

From the bag, I pull a pair of white stockings, a matching lace bra, and a garter.

*—The rest is for me—*

The dress is far more demure. It's a classic navy blue jacket dress with gold crest buttons that—unlike the underwear—is appropriate for church. It's not as dumpy as the things in my closet though, as if Santino has a more nuanced vision of what his wife is supposed to be.

—*The rest is for you? It's not exactly your size*—

Santino's response comes quickly, and I flush at the knowledge that wherever he is, whatever he's doing, I've captured his attention, if not his sense of humor.

—**God owns what the world can see, and I own what the world cannot**—

Getting dressed in the clothes he sent for me, I forget that I'm angry. I forget that he betrayed me with my sister before he knew me and with lies after he married me. But that's wrong. I can't ever forget it.

—*You talk a lot about owning me. You can't own people*—

—**You are Italian and my wife. You are mine. Be in church at 11:45am**—

He has an answer for everything, but I call bullshit.

I can't escape Santino, but that doesn't mean he controls my every move. If I'm not his prisoner, then I don't have to go where he tells me to go or wear what he tells me to wear.

This life I've been living is the life of my mother, my

sister, my aunts, my nonnas. The women in my family have all sat idly by as the silent partner, the quiet backbone of a family often torn apart by violence committed by men like my husband. I may not ever really escape it, but I can remind myself of who I once was.

And I can hurt him. If I can't hurt his body, I'm going to break his heart little by little. Piece by piece. I'll chip away shards of his control until he tells me everything I want to know.

I text Scarlett.

*—Happy jetlag! I don't know about you but mine is totally worth it—*

That last part is questionable, but I leave it and continue.

*—I miss your face and I have so much to tell you! But Monday is bad. Are you free today?—*

**—I can be!—**

Before I leave, I check the mirror, trying to guess whether I'll look normal enough to pass muster with Scarlett. She's only ever seen me dressed like a normal American college student, never so Sunday-formal or well-pressed. Well, she's about to see a new side of me, because no matter how good I look, I'm nothing but a designer dress stuffed with secrets, and even the softest fabric can't soothe the riot of conflict under my skin.

That's just another reason to skip church.

CONVINCING Armando to drive me to The Leaky Bean, our favorite off-campus coffee shop, involves a lie about a change of mass time and another about how long I expect my coffee date with Scarlett to last.

I get caught up in the surreal moment of going across the river where the streets are full and people my age are goofing off, shopping, living the lives they imagine for themselves. In this world, if there's a man whose job it is to drive you places, he drives you where you want to go, not where your husband demands.

The town center is everything I remember from a lifetime ago. The telephone poles flake with layers upon layers of flyers in every color.

ROOM FOR RENT
LEARN GUITAR
HOMEWORK HELP!
LSAT STUDY GROUP

Bicycle racks crammed with pastel cruisers and speeders outline the edge of the sidewalk. A row of mopeds lean on their stands, perpendicular to the curb. What catches my breath are the people walking in the sun with a cup in one hand and a phone in the other, their shoulders and legs exposed, and their voices humming in the air. It's just as it's always been, and just like Italy.

Armando parks and I get out, waving him away with a promise that I'll be back soon.

There are no black cars except ours. No black suits

or men sitting with their arms crossed in judgment. It's burgers and coffee and hacky sack and skateboards.

This is freedom. This is *life*.

"Violetta?" Scarlett's voice squeals behind me. I turn just in time to be mauled by my best friend, sporting a very nice, very new tan. "Why does it feel like I haven't seen you in years?"

"Because it's been too long." I want to cry, I'm so happy to see her, and when we get into the coffee shop with its blackboard menu, student art, mismatched wooden tables, and constantly hissing milk steamer, I almost do.

When we order, I have to stop myself from asking for the things I've been drinking in Santino's kitchen—because I don't have to. No espresso. No cappuccino. Instead, I get a strawberry Frappuccino—which has the distinction of being the least Italian drink with the most Italian name—and Scarlett orders an iced green tea, because though she's been trying for years, she just can't quit caffeine. We chatter about her move from coffee to tea, Icelandic men, and her new hairstyle that's subtly different from her last hairstyle, barely stopping as we pay for our drinks and secure a table.

"Hold the phone." Scarlett is in the middle of describing a lost suitcase fiasco, but stops as if she hasn't seen me this entire time. I'm convinced she's going to comment on the dress, but instead she points at my hand. "Is that… is that what I think it is?"

My cheeks heat up and my heart races. Even though my best friend is the most self-centered person I've ever met, the diamond is too huge to miss. I had a story prepared, but now I can't even remember it.

"Oh… well, you know it's… I wasn't sure if you'd, uh…" I'm desperately looking for something to say that sounds casual and mature, but my mouth is moving and nonsense is coming out.

"Not notice?" Scarlett's eyes almost bug out of her head as she reads my thought. "Have you *seen* the rock on your finger? You could see it from Mars."

She grabs my hand to get a closer look at it.

"I guess." I blush, fully embarrassed, because now I have to tell the entire shocking story and I don't want to. She'll never understand.

"Which Greek prince stole your heart?"

I have to tell her something, but what? I have to tell a horrifying story without the horror, and I have never felt so far outside the world I aspired to be a part of. "Um, Italian actually."

"No shit. I guess you weren't kidding, huh?" Her face is pure awe, recalling some string of words I wasn't kidding about.

"What?"

"About how serious Italian men are?"

Had I told her anything about living on the other side of the river?

I had to cancel plans to attend Novia Gardiamo's last-minute wedding.

And maybe I told Scarlett about Mariella Casella, who married a man she didn't seem to like, but who insisted.

What did "insist" mean then? And what does it mean now?

Did I know all along that girls were being forced into marriages? Did I not pay attention to it because I assumed it wouldn't happen to me? Did I tell Scarlett these stories as if they were funny anecdotes about a faraway culture?

We're sitting, and Scarlett is talking right through my self-doubts.

"I mean, my god, we're only apart for, like, seven weeks and you got engaged?"

"Well, married actually."

She looks genuinely hurt. "You got married without me?"

Thankfully, she's drawn the attention back to herself and I have to nod *yes*, biting my tongue to keep from spilling the details she can't hear. That it might have been dangerous for her to be in the church that day. That I didn't even pick out my own wedding dress, or have a real reception, so of course I wasn't responsible for the invitations.

Scarlett is still talking. "You didn't let me plan your bachelorette party or your wedding shower. We didn't go dress shopping! I feel cheated from this entire experience!"

I want to shout, "Same!" Instead, I grab her hand. "It all happened so fast there wasn't time for any of that." That's true enough anyway.

"Violetta," Scarlett purrs. "Are you... you know...?"

"Am I...?" I leave space for the answer. When she arches her eyebrows and looks at my belly, I realize I must be the dumbest person in a hundred-mile radius. "No!"

I deny it as if I'm offended, which I don't have to be. I'm married after all.

"I'm not pregnant," I add less defensively. "It was

just so emotional." True. "And in-the-moment." Also true… for me. "But I promise you, if I ever have a make-up bachelorette, you'll be the only one in charge."

"If?" Scarlett snorts. "Like this husband of yours could stop me."

Could. Would. Can. Will.

"I can't wait for you to meet him."

Lies. Not only can I wait, I will prevent it from ever happening. If she ever meets Santino, she won't believe or understand him. Even now, watching one of the most familiar faces I know, I can see the mistrust. Scarlett never understood my obligations, and she won't understand them now.

How could she? I still don't.

"He must be that fucking wonderful to scoop you off your feet like that."

My friendship with her is over. She just doesn't know it.

Instead of being rescued, I've been caught. Spending an afternoon with my old life was supposed to help me remember who I am, but instead, it's telling me I no longer fit and never did. I was playacting the entire time.

"Yeah," I say.

Something—or someone—over my shoulder catches Scarlett's eye.

"What?" I ask, hoping to shift the focus back to her.

"A *man* just walked into this place," Scarlett says. "By the board games. Dark jacket. Little older. Definitely a prof or grad student."

"Glad to see you haven't changed," I say, trying to do

a casual stretch-and-glance so I can at least scope out this hottie.

"Right now, I am so glad you're married, because I'd fight you for this one."

I see him. He's neither professor nor student. Not a hunky athlete coming back from the practice field, scruffy and sweet, or a dreamy philosophy major hoping to find answers inside inscrutable textbooks. Instead, my eyes land on broad shoulders, a wicked mouth, and a sharp suit. My pulse races, because of course.

Of course.

Santino DiLustro, who's supposed to be in church and seething that I didn't show up, and who employs the man who drove me here, is standing by a flyer for a one-bedroom apartment.

When he sees me, he smiles like a new husband, and he walks to our table with the confidence of a lover. I want to tell myself I'm just playing along, trying not to start drama in public, but it's not that. He's absolutely magnetic. Everyone's watching him with lust, aspiration, or envy, and he's mine.

All mine.

I stand and let him draw me into the heat radiating off of his powerful body. He kisses me tenderly on the cheek before smiling at Scarlett with the beneficence of a saint.

"Scarlett." I hear myself saying polite words, and I'm grateful I have an autopilot function. "This is my husband, Santino. Santino, this is my best friend, Scarlett."

She stands and offers her his hand. I can't help

marveling at the sight of this powerful man shaking hands with an American girl in cutoffs and flip-flops.

"We were just talking about how you swept Violetta off her feet," Scarlett chirps. "I'm so sorry I missed the wedding."

"It was a very brief engagement and a small ceremony." Santino tucks a strand of hair behind my ear, his fingers lingering at my neck. Though I can't guarantee he feels my pulse pick up, I am sure his touch was meant for this purpose. "We couldn't wait."

"I can see that." Scarlett is smirking at me, and it's hard not to get lost in the fantasy of this moment: that Santino and I really did meet on some normal day, some-normal-where, had a normal series of conversations, and instantly fell in normal love. That he's as enamored of me as his touch suggests. That there's nothing for me to fear with him, or from him.

"I'm so sorry to interrupt," Santino says, "but I forgot to tell Violetta we have somewhere to be this afternoon." I expect a subtle threat of violence, some reminder that I'll come with him whether I like it or not, but his face stays calm. When he turns to me, he's every inch a man besotted, who merely wants his new bride by his side as often as possible. "Do you mind?"

Do I mind? Yes, I mind, but no, I do not. Talking to Scarlett wasn't the escape I thought it would be. I nod, because I want to go with him, even if he demands it.

"Depends where we're going," I flirt.

"Remember my zia Paola, from the other side?"

"How could I forget?" I try not to sound sour, but I can't keep the tartness from my tongue.

Gia's mother, Paola, brought Siena Orolio to the

beach house long enough for me to find out Santino loved my sister first. I'm pissed off right now because of her. Paola witnessed what Siena said to me. She saw the color drain from my face because I didn't know about Santino and Rosetta.

"Marco—my uncle—he has business here. Unexpected things... anyway, he brought his wife and they're making a trip of it." Typically vague reasoning for a sudden transatlantic journey. Marco and Paola just hopped on a plane from Italy and showed up for an undisclosed amount of time.

Actually, that's only unusual for the kids strolling the grassy square by St. John's University.

For us, it's perfectly normal to fold space and time where family is concerned. Our houses are often split into smaller units for long-term guests from the other side.

"Where are they staying?" I hope it's not at our place.

"Anette and Angelo's, on Porto Street, and it's going to be a long Italian dinner, so..." He turns to Scarlett again. "I have to steal her."

"I could use a nap," Scarlett says with a glance at her iced tea. "They say this has caffeine, but I think they're lying."

"We'll walk you out then," Santino says.

The arm that was around my waist slides down, and to my surprise, he laces his fingers through mine. On the sidewalk, he lets me go grudgingly so Scarlett and I can hug and kiss goodbye, making promises to see each other soon. But I'm lying to save her feelings.

I'll be surprised if I ever see her again.

5

## VIOLETTA

Santino holds open the passenger door of the Alfa Romeo. As soon as it slams closed behind me, the summer students in shorts and tanks seem like children, and University Square seems like a movie set. It's all real to them, but to me, it's no more than a tangible dream I'm cut off from ever living.

Santino gets in beside me and drives away, his wrist dangling over the top of the steering wheel. Will this be the rest of my life, I wonder? Will I always be seduced by a man I despise? Will my body, mind, and heart always be at war?

*Rosetta, tell me what to do here.*

But no response comes from her or anyone else, dead or alive. There's only Santino.

Finally, I say, "Did we miss church? Sorry about that."

He shakes his head. "Don't lie to me."

I didn't lie exactly, but pointing that out won't do

me any favors. He and I understand each other. I'm playing a game and he'd rather I didn't.

My phone buzzes with a text—Scarlett.

**—YOUR HUSBAND IS SOOOOO HOOOOOTTTTTT!!!!!**
**—**

Don't I know it.

*—I was afraid you'd think it was weird—*

I don't clarify what "it" is.

**—*I would have snapped him up too. You need to have his babies now. Like, now—***

I shake my head and put the phone back in my bag.

"What?" Santino asks, navigating the light street traffic to the bridge over the river.

"She likes you."

He slows at the merge to the bridge entrance and gives me a glance.

"Scarlett. She thinks you're handsome."

"And what do you think?"

The wood boards clap under the tires, then quiet as we get to asphalt.

*I think God Himself made you specifically to torture me as penance for some grievous sin I haven't committed yet.*

Instead of saying that, I shrug. "Genetic lottery, I guess."

There's a pause. He doesn't seem inclined to comment on his genetics or Scarlett's thoughts.

But I can't help myself.

"My sister got all the best genes too." I say it, and despite my better judgment, I complete the thought out loud. "Didn't keep you from killing her."

His silence gets stonier, and I wonder how far I have to push him before the hardness shatters into a deadly hail of information, each confession a shard hot and sharp enough to end us both.

---

BEING MARRIED to the capo may come with privileges, but as Santino pulls the Alfa Romeo into the driveway, I'm hard-pressed to list them. The duties and obligations are more clear. I've already missed a mass I was apparently obligated to attend so I could meet up with Scarlett, but if church is to ask God for indulgence and forgiveness, the meal afterward is where the sins are gossiped about.

Which is why—even though I'd rather chew glass—I get out of the car to go upstairs to freshen up.

I'm curling my hair when Santino appears in the bathroom doorway as if I invited him.

Which I didn't.

His jacket is unbuttoned and his elbow is high on the doorframe, exposing the shoulder holster.

"You're carrying," I say. "Why?"

"Five minutes." He drops his arm and walks away.

I turn off the curler without confirming this countdown, and I unzip my makeup bag. My stomach may be in knots, the world may feel like a rollercoaster. Santino can keep his guns and his bulletproof windows. I will not leave this house without armoring myself with blush and lipstick.

My mother once said something about women's defenses being vastly different than men's. She never said it to me. I was five when she was killed.

Rosetta used to tell me about things our mother had said, when I was younger and asked questions. Her words didn't always make sense and I forgot most of them, annoyed Rosetta was trying to assert herself as the one in charge of our parents' adult quips and adages. Now, I'd give anything to hear a word from either of them.

"What would you tell me?" I ask the mirror, envisioning the two of them standing behind me, their hands resting on my shoulders.

"That it's time to go," Santino answers.

"I wasn't talking to you."

"You're beautiful." Santino sounds bored having to state the obvious. "That's enough. Your face needs no more preparation."

"I'd believe you if I knew why a woman we saw a week and a half ago didn't mention she was taking a trans-Atlantic flight to our doorstep."

"Business happens."

I dust my cheeks and nose with pink, just enough to keep me from looking like a china doll, not enough to need to blend. "She bring Siena Orolio with her this time?"

Santino steps into the bathroom and puts his hand on my shoulder.

"Don't," I say.

What I expect is a reassertion of his power over me,

and I'm ready for all the pleasure and surrender that comes with it.

What I get is confirmation that Santino DiLustro knows when to back off. Our eyes meet in the mirror.

"You were always…" He looks at his shoes and rolls his hand at the wrist as if he can form the right words from the air like cotton candy. *"Dai, dai, dai, come si dice."*

He can't jog the expression. His frustration is painful to watch.

"I was always a pain in the—"

"No! *Sempre.* Before Rosetta. Before I was a man. Before we were born. You were always. Always. I…" He looks at the ceiling then closes his eyes. "Right after I took control of Secondo Vasto, I came to your uncle's." He invokes that day when I saw him in the hallway as a reminder. He has no idea it's a cornerstone of my life. "To tell him I would marry Rosetta when the time came. And I saw you there. This connection, it was so strong…" He holds up his hands as if he wants to stop my thoughts. I've never seen him so unsure. "You were a child, so I didn't hold it in the same place. I had no idea of you as a woman."

"So you married my sister because you couldn't marry me?"

*"Porca puttana."* He exclaims *for fuck's sake* in irritation. "Violetta, no. But I met her, and we spoke, and… yes. She was beautiful and… how do you say… *incantevole?"*

"Lovely?"

*"Si.* I thought, I could not walk away. I had to

protect this woman and her little sister, like I promised."

"Wait. Protect?"

"My God, just listen."

"The debt? What about—"

"There is no debt!" Santino clamps down, having said more than he wanted to. "Your father was the most powerful capo the *camorra* ever knew. How could he owe some lowlife like me a debt?"

"My father was a grocer," I say, turning away from the mirror. "He had a store he named after my sister, and my mother worked behind the register. He loved us. That was all I ever knew until very fucking recently."

"I know." He puts his hands on my arms and leans down to look into my eyes with seriousness and warmth. "I know. And you're right. He did love you both. But everything else is a very small piece of truth."

I have only this slim, unguarded moment to extract more from him. I should ask why now, why me, why this, but another question muscles past those and into my mouth.

"Did you love her?"

His hands slide down my arms and rest under my hands, leaving the ring I shared with my sister nested in his palm. He thumbs the stone as if asking it for strength.

"You were a child." He raises his gaze to meet mine. "A future sister. The thoughts I have for you now didn't occur to me. Then…" He glances at the ring. "I saw you as a woman, and that changed."

"When?"

He drops my hands. "We should go."

"Santi! Was it when I saw you in Zio's office?"

"Every day," he says as he backs out of the bathroom, "I fail you."

"He was kneeling and weeping."

"Every day," Santino continues as though I haven't said a word, "I push you away."

"Was it gratitude? Is that why he was crying at your feet?"

"When I finally lose you"—he goes on as if I haven't built the scene for him—"I'll be in hell, and I'll deserve it."

He leaves before I can ask him another question. The moment of revelation is over, and I'm to perform my social duties with scraps of information. I'll have to see Paola for the first time since her guest dropped the world from under me.

The jewelry box on the vanity plays a tune when I open it to remove the red seashell brooch carved with three dancing Furies. I slide the pin through the navy fabric, clip it closed, and check the mirror to make sure it's straight. The fashion statement is 1970s old Italian woman, and it's accurate.

I am a shrewd Italian woman out for answers.

# 6

# VIOLETTA

Angelo and Anette's house sits in a neighborhood one step above the one I grew up in. The garages are in the back, and the houses are separated by narrow driveways. The front yards aren't deep, and all have painted plaster shrines where the Virgin Mother presides over patches of grass and rosebushes. As the sun sets, the altars are bathed in yard lights.

I always thought the Virgin shrines were showy piousness. But as we pull up, I see them for the first time as a way the residents connect with each other by a common thread of faith.

Santino pulls into the last spot in the driveway, behind a row of luxury cars. The block is lined with them.

"Why didn't you tell me?" I ask. "About Rosetta?"

"You want to talk about this *now*?"

"No, I want to talk about it before she died, or when you married me, or any time in the last month."

He sighs and clicks the car into park. "You think I keep secrets."

"Uh, yeah. It's a compulsion with you."

"No." He smiles and clicks his tongue. "My compulsion, as you say, is I make promises, and I keep them."

"Oh. Too honorable. Sure."

"Your sister was all you had."

He's stated such a core truth, I twist in my seat to face him. "So?"

"She wanted to wait until you were older. She said you two only had each other and I was taking her away. She didn't want you to hate me. Obviously, that couldn't be avoided."

His comment isn't glib. It's stuffed with regret and sealed shut with surrender to things being the way they are because that's just the way they are.

I believe him for all these reasons, and because I knew Rosetta. This request to protect my feelings is exactly what she would have done.

"And now," I say, following his gaze to the house, "it's Sunday dinner as husband and wife." Two young men with an arrogant bounce in their step and bulges under their jackets mount the front steps. "Look at these harmless church folk."

"They're only harmless inside a church."

One of the men turns just enough for me to see the left side of his face. I recognize him from the photo I spit on.

"Is that Damiano?"

Santino leans forward and peers up the steps. "It is." He relaxes back into his seat, tapping his fingers on the gear shifter.

"What are you thinking so hard about?" I ask, and he gives me a quizzical look. "I smell wood burning."

"There's a fire?" He looks around.

I laugh. His command of English is near perfect, but throw an idiom his way and he turns literal. It's kind of charming.

"It's an expression. Your head is wood, and when it thinks too hard… never mind. Just tell me."

"No one knows you're learning Italian. They don't know how much you understand."

"They know my zia and zio. I don't think anyone would be surprised."

"You're mostly American." He nods toward me in an assumption that his words are beyond nuanced disagreement. "Don't persuade them otherwise."

I exhale in a half-laugh. "After all the effort you put into turning me into a good Italian wife, you want me to keep pretending you failed?"

The insult doesn't land. He knows what he wants and what he's done to make it happen.

"Their ignorance is our advantage." He unlocks the doors. "Keep your ears open."

"Okay, I guess."

Santino's supposed to trust these people, but obviously he trusts me more. That's also charming, and damn me for being charmed. I can't help it.

"*Bene.*" In the moment after we come to an agreement, he's still. I know by the tilt of his body that he's thinking of kissing me, but he thinks better of it and gets out.

We walk into the house together, with his hand on my lower back, and greet everyone as if the Sunday meal is here every week and we're just a regular married couple, visiting the family. I meet Angelo, the man of the house with a shirt-stretching belly. His brother in-law, Marco, has an epic comb-over and a nose that looks as if it's been busted sideways a few times.

"You know my daughter," Marco says, waving Gia over.

She shines in a yellow dress and strappy sandals, her hair in a stylish bun caressed by a dainty headband. She embodies a radiant summer and I can't help but love her. My feelings about dinner immediately improve.

"Gia!" Santino greets his cousin. "*Come stai?*"

"*Va bene assai!*" Gia kisses his cheeks and hugs me. "I've been dying to see you ever since you got back!" Her English has already improved from when we met. "You have to tell me everything. Everything!"

Gia gives me a knowing wink and my stomach takes a nose dive. Up until our last thirty minutes in the beach house, I would have joyfully turned our trip to Italy into savory gossip. The house, the food, the wine, the sex. All crushed with a few words from Siena Orolio. Now I'd be gossip of a different sort.

"Come!" Gia grabs my hand and tucks it around her arm. "You'll be so much more comfortable in the kitchen than out here with the horrible men."

I let her lead me deeper into the house. It's smaller than Santino's, but most are, and decorated with the same level of stuffy tradition. Ornate furniture, knickknacks, still life oil paintings. Lots of gold paint. But the farther in Gia drags me, the more the whole scene shifts. A room off to the side, the door ajar, looking refreshingly modern. Sleek white couches square off with a massive bean bag chair. In one side room, a TV the size of the pickup truck sits on a wall with every recognizable gaming console below it. Instead of heavenly miracles in oil and canvas, there are movie posters with busty women.

"Oops!" Gia dances around me to snap the door shut. "Tavie's room is such a mess."

With me on her arm, Gia sashays toward the upstairs kitchen, which is populated with women's voices.

"Violetta!" Paola catches us before we go in. "Gia, go." She shoos her daughter into the kitchen, then when she's out of earshot, Paola's shoulders drop and she holds out her hands. "I am so sorry. What happened with Siena, it was... I didn't expect it. I would never have brought her if I knew."

"Knew that I didn't know?"

She nods slowly, then gradually, the movement turns into the shake of a no. "I wouldn't have brought her if I knew she would say things like that."

So she was aware of my ignorance that day, and she's admitting it now.

"Thank you for being honest," I say.

"If this makes you feel any better, Santino looks happier than I've ever seen him." She puts her hand on her chest and taps her gold cross. "I swear it's the truth."

"I believe you," I say, but don't mention the rest—that I wish he wasn't happy.

"You're wearing it." She taps the brooch with the Furies. "It suits you."

"Is this Santino's new bride?" A woman's voice comes from the other side of the archway leading to the kitchen. She's in head-to-toe beige that matches her hair dye. "Guglielmo's niece?"

"Anette," Paola says. "This is my husband's sister. The woman of the house."

In a moment, I'm pulled in with the women. They smile and greet me. I recognize many of their faces from church and the pork store. From funerals and weddings. They're the adults in my world, and only now have I graduated to live among them.

"You look so tan!" Francine says. I scour the dark corners of my brain and remember her waiting outside St. Barnabas to walk her son, Aldo, home from school. "I hear you just got back from Amalfi!"

"I did."

"How was it?" a young woman with meticulously ironed hair asks dreamily. A quick glance at her finger tells me she's engaged. Her face is bright, open, expecting. Friendly.

An old woman shelling peas breaks in with a thick accent. "It was her honeymoon. How do you think, Lucia?"

Lucia blushes and turns her attention back to cutting slices of bread.

"It was great." I'd probably get more piqued interest if I said it was terrible, but a generic reaction is the correct prize for my generic words.

"She married Santino DiLustro," a woman says, and by the M shape of her hairline, I can see she's the engaged girl's mother. "You'll be lucky to go to a Motel Six on what Lorenzo brings home."

Lucia sticks out her tongue and everyone laughs.

They think my marriage is perfect. They think I'm lucky.

What can I say? I was kidnapped and forced to marry? I didn't get to choose my bouquet or dress?

They either know already or they don't, and if they know and don't mention it, I shouldn't.

Across the kitchen, a little girl no more than six drops a heavy can of olive oil. Everything comes to a screeching halt. We all run to help mop it up, which saves me from having to defend my sham wedding.

"It's all right, sweet." A gentle *nonna* kneels beside the girl, limbs creaking, and wipes away her tears. "It's too many acts in a comedy in here."

I smile.

"Do you speak?" Lucia asks, suddenly at my elbow.

I jump from surprise. "Sorry, what?"

"Italian."

"Forgot after years of disuse." I shake my head with a guilty smile. "You know how it goes."

She points toward the little girl. "You laughed at *Fare troppi atti nella in commedia.*"

Right. I'm not supposed to understand that. "I was thinking of something else."

"I bet you were." Lucia's mother winks at me.

Standing in that kitchen, the fullness in my heart pushes it into complicated shapes. This is not my family, yet this is my family. I don't know these women, yet they're my people.

Once the floor is cleaned, I pick up a job seeding peppers.

"I can't believe Re Santino's cock will stay tamed," someone murmurs in Italian loudly enough for me to hear it.

I'm sure they don't intend for me to understand, so I keep my eyes down. Everything runs very still. Slowly, I turn to see who spoke and find Lucia's mother with her head lowered, talking to another woman with dyed black hair who's trying not to laugh.

"Santino is a whoremaker," Black Dye replies, looking at me as she fills a pot with water. I pretend to smile and go back to the peppers. "That poor girl. Does she know everyone else knows?"

I work to keep my face even and nonplussed, but inside, everything feels as if it's dying.

They think I'm a whore? Of course they do. Elettra got shaken into butter and told in no uncertain terms that an attraction to a whoremaker turns a girl into a whore.

My face is hot, my heart races, and I need to get out of the kitchen before everything inside my rib cage explodes. I don't know if I need to cry or scream, but whatever I do, I won't do it in this kitchen.

"I-I'll be right back," I say to no one and walk numbly in search of a bathroom where I can get behind a closed door.

The house is tight with people. By the time I find a bathroom, my brain is churning mush and all I want to do is vomit.

*Everyone knows. Everyone knows. Everyone knows.*

Lucia didn't want to know about my wedding; she

wanted it confirmed I was stolen and forced. Everyone knows, and I'm definitely going to vomit.

The bathroom door flies open, and I almost fall into the guy leaving it. I jump back and find myself staring up at the scarred mouth of Damiano Orolio. He carries himself like a typical Secondo Vasto gangster. He doesn't look like the kind of guy Santino would have around. Too brazen, too cocky, too built like a locomotive.

He looks me up and down in a way no man has dared since I stepped foot into the world as Santino DiLustro's wife.

"Excuse me," I finally manage.

He pushes past me with a look of supreme entitlement. I slip inside the bathroom, lock the door, and slide to the floor with my back to the cabinets, trying to still the internal churn.

*I am a queen.*

*I am a queen.*

What do queens do when they've encased themselves in a stony majesty and still get stabbed in the back?

I kneel at the porcelain altar to hurl, but I do it like royalty.

"*Ciao,* Damiano!" A man on the other side of the door sounds as though he's hit the wine hard and it's hitting him back. "I'm fuckin' starving."

"You drink too much." It must be Damiano who answers.

The rest is muddled in murmurs. They've moved down the hall. Since my stomach seems to have settled on its own, I put my ear up to the door.

"… parades her in here like some damn race horse…"

"… looks just like the…"

"… those the rings?"

My breath dies in my throat as I look at my hand. The rings. Rosetta's diamond.

"… engravers…"

"… Theresa says…"

"… she Enzo Rubino's …?"

Their voices fade into the white noise of the house, and they're gone. I drink a paper cup of water. Santino's fascination with my rings and under what circumstances I am allowed to take them off may be more intense than I think is reasonable. But he's my husband, and he's from the other side. He's possessive.

But how many random guys ever talk about a woman's wedding rings?

None of them, that's the answer. No Italian mafioso is going to gossip about diamonds unless he's fencing them.

Maybe it's because they know I'm wearing a dead girl's promises.

I pull the nesting wedding and engagement rings off and look inside, where an engraver would leave a mark. It's just a serial number or something. Fuck this. I put them back on, cursing.

Fuck Santino for putting me in this position. I head for the front door and blessed fresh air, but I knock into Gia and almost send the bread she's carrying to the floor.

"I'm sorry!" I manage to catch a loaf before it falls.

"Can you set these out?" She's obviously totally

overwhelmed. "I'm supposed to get the wine, but the glasses are all wrong, so I have to fix them before—"
"I have it." I take the bread. "Shoo."
"You're a lifesaver."
She's off to fix the glasses. I set the bread on the long table. On the other side of the room is a hallway. I hear men's voices rising and falling in a way that suggests formality, like something serious is taking place.
Nothing's more serious than how much I want to go home, and the only way out is with Santino. I follow the voices down the hall, betting he's there. I'll claim I'm not feeling well. Between what I overheard in the kitchen and the stench of cigar smoke coming from the room to the right, I can vomit on request.
"Violetta's a special case." I freeze when I hear my name in Santino's voice, and I flatten myself against the wall. "The *'mbasciata* was blessed by her father."
I know that word. *'Mbasciata* is an arranged marriage.
There's a window opposite the arched opening, revealing the room in the reflection. Santino sits with three men—Marco, Damiano, and Angelo. All are smoking cigars and drinking iced, amber liquid. Other men stand in the corners, present but not participating, their movements dictated by hierarchy and choreographed by generations of tradition. I try to catch Santino's eye in the reflection, and as if he can hear my needs, he sees me, but motions, quite clearly, that I am to leave.
I'm about to give him merry hell in front of all of his merry fucking friends, who all clearly know about

my sister so intimately they can recognize the goddamn rings on my fingers, when I hear Gia's name tucked in a blanket of Italian.

I can't explain it, but something is harrowingly, hauntingly familiar about what's going on. It's like déjà vu, or the way you remember a dream, or a memory—not of something the eyes witnessed, but an event described and constructed in the mind, which the mind filed as if it actually happened. The way they all stand. The solemnity of their voices with an undercurrent of excitement, almost.

A transaction is taking place, and though I never saw such a thing, I recognize it.

My stomach bottoms out and I do the only thing I can think to do—eavesdrop, breathing in baby spurts and praying none of the women feel the need to personally call the men for dinner.

"I was there," Damiano says. "You cut out a step. Twice."

"This is a problem for you?" Santino's tone is a dare to the scarred man I met outside the bathroom.

"No. But I never heard of a capo refusing if the father agreed."

"And the father agrees." Marco tips his glass toward Damiano.

Wait. Marco is the father? That makes his daughter the bride.

Gia.

Holy shit. They're selling Gia.

I clench my fists. The palms are already wet.

"But did you consult me about this deal?" Santino asks Marco. "No. Did you ask me to find a good match on this side? No. Did you ask me about Damiano? What kind of man he is? No. You did not. Anyone else in the four corners of my territory offering a bride in payment without coming to me first would wake up spitting their lungs. But you think you can get away with it because you're my uncle?"

"You're denying him?" Damiano asks.

"Have I refused you, Dami?" Santino's gone from threatening to patronizing in under a minute. "Have I even asked you why you're paying this debt from under your father's nose? Eh?"

"No."

"No." Santino gets up and walks around the room, pacing the circumference of the table as the men wait. He stands in the archway, facing the window.

Our eyes meet in the reflection. He rubs his chin then flicks his hand again, shooing me away.

I hold up my middle finger.

He turns to face the table. "I did not refuse my blessing, but you forget why the blessing is necessary in the first place. It's my job to ask questions."

"She's not with child," Marco assures them. "She's pure. Clean. Nothing."

"She works for me," Santino says. "I'm better aware than you of what she's doing all day. I question why you"—he looks at Damiano—"don't want to tell her."

"He doesn't want to get her hopes up," Marco says.

Santino doesn't move his attention from Damiano. "I didn't ask you, uncle."

Marco jabs his cigar in his mouth. I'm surprised by how little power Gia's father seems to have at this table.

"Maybe I'm turning American," Damiano says. "I want to get to know her a little first."

"You don't trust she's what her father says?"

"Sure, I do. But I don't want to end up with a mouthy fishwife." He looks Santino up and down, and though the reflection isn't sharp enough to reveal every detail, I can tell it's a bold, insolent stare. "It happens to the best of us."

Santino's pause weighs four tons. It's a knife cutting through time, splitting it and filling it with dark unknowns no one is willing to uncover with an interruption. I don't know how he does it, but I hold my breath until he speaks.

"Did you want to say something about my wife?" he says.

"Please…" Marco squeaks, wringing his hands.

"No?" Santino says. "Yes? Say it plain, for Gia's sake… so I can cut your dick off before the deal is done."

"Do it!" a younger voice chimes in. Brash. Angry. One of the men standing in the shadows comes forward—Gia's brother, Tavie. My God, he's watching these talks? He's hardly a damn man.

"*Mi dispiace*," Damiano apologizes, stroking his hair back so everyone can see he's not dismissing his own apology with horned fingers.

"And your bride's father," Santino says.

"Forgive me, Mister Polito. I am sure Gia was raised correctly."

Marco *hmphs* with a nod, as if the half-hearted apology is powerful enough to erase an offense to his daughter.

Oh, my sweet Gia is trapped from all sides.

"My wife's name won't cross your lips again," my husband says.

"Of course." Damiano turns to exhale a cone of cigar smoke. I see his full face in the reflection. He looks past me as if I don't even exist, straightens his hair, and turns back to the room.

"Do you bless the *'mbasciata?*" Marco asks.

Santino is the only thing standing between Gia and the horror I went through.

He doesn't answer right away. For the first time in what feels like an aching eternity, I don't despise my husband. Then he speaks.

"Here are the terms. Damiano Orolio. You have one night, chaperoned, to decide if she's a match for you. You decide yes, you wire the money to Cosimo. Marco…" Santino turns toward his uncle. "You tell Gia as soon as the debt is clear, and you tell her *why*."

"But, Santi…" Marco objects.

"You look your shame in the face, Marco Polito, and you tell her." Santino turns back to Damiano. "If you decide no, the deal is off." He steps close to Dami and mutters, "Don't talk to me about a repayment schedule like the first one you came to me with. Understand?"

"Yeah." Damiano looks away, as if regretful, but in the window, he glows with vengeance. "But looks like we're gonna be family anyway."

Santino takes a deep breath. Holds it. Clenches and unclenches his fists.

"Finish drawing the papers," Santino says. "This *'mbasciata* has my blessing. My cousin gets hurt"—he points at Damiano, then Marco—"I'll skin both of you like rabbits."

I slide my back to the wall and close my eyes. All of them are animals, Santino included. Well, fuck him and fuck that. I'll just walk home. Maybe I'll take Gia with me and we can run away together.

I slink down the hall and around the corner before daring a look back. Damiano's the first out of the room, and I see him full in the face.

He's hulking—as tall as Santino and as wide as the doorframe. A deadness slicks his huge, brown eyes, and when they land on me, I remember that he doesn't like me. I'm a fishwife. A harridan. A threat.

In the marrow of my bones, I am afraid.

Then Santino's voice rises from the walls, the windows, the mighty air of America itself.

"*Coniglio!*"

Damiano freezes when Santino calls him a rabbit, but though Damiano's still for a moment, he does not turn around. His dead eyes are on me as the man who rules us both lays down the law.

"*Caveat emptor.* You better be sure you like what you've bought before you bring it home. I've blessed the marriage, but not your life."

# 7

## SANTINO

We are not Sicilian. There is no—and never has there ever been—head of the *camorra*, but Emilio Moretti came as close to being a true king as any man. He ruled an underground empire in Naples and, through a business in transport, held power that reached the shores of America.

I rule a small Italian enclave in America. No capo before, and none since, has had the same reach as the last Moretti.

In Napoli, they said Emilio benefitted from divine intervention and that those angels had set a boundary inside which he would suffer no rivals, no challenges, and no interference from the law.

"My boys," Emilio croaked, still in the hospital with an infection in his lungs after surviving his first assassination attempt. Damiano sits next to me, and on the other side of the bed, Nazario Corragio, a.k.a. *Il Blocco* —the Cavallo *consigliere*—takes notes in runic shorthand. "You see how even I am not above death?"

"*Sì.*"

I'm seventeen, and I understand this talk of Emilio's invincibility is a load of bullshit. But I also understand that everyone else in the room smells incense instead of *stronzata*, so I know why he needs to make the point.

"But that's why you're alive!" Damiano says. This big man is an old woman at heart. It's one thing to believe in miracles. It's another to think they're an entitlement.

"Today," Emilio objects. "Maybe not next time. And I need you both to be ready."

My friend and I exchange a glance. If Emilio dies, Cosimo will take control, and anyone who stands in his way will not live long. Dami may move up in rank in that exchange of power. I have nothing to gain.

"I have no sons," Emilio continues. "I have two girls. Good girls. And they will inherit everything I own."

Damiano leans forward with his lower lip hanging like a piece of raw liver, because he knows what's coming. Both of us do. We're not stupid. At least, I'm not.

"Capo," I say, partly because I don't need confirmation that this man I respect feels as close to death as a grandma, "this is unnecessary."

"Hey, *bastardo*." Dami flicks my cheek, and I swat him away. "Let the man talk."

"*Shh*" the *consigliere* hisses.

"The doctor says you're going to be fine," I say. I don't want to hear about his daughters and what they'll inherit, because I know this powerful man isn't going to demand I protect them and their husbands after his death, which I would gladly do. "Like new all over."

Emilio ignores both of us. It's taking all his energy to speak. "No woman can inherit what the oldest of my girls will."

*Not this.* My young brain races ahead. *Don't do it. Just give me the crown. Don't sell me for it.*

"We got this..." Damiano murmurs. He wants it. Money without work. Power without respect. It's all more important to him than the most important choice a man will make—his own wife.

"The first husband must be strong to wield it. He must be a man of character." Emilio wheezes while I pray so fast I haven't had time to inhale. "Damiano," our boss says, and I breathe with relief. "I need you to protect—"

"You got it, boss."

"—Santino."

Now Dami stops breathing, because he gets it. I don't.

"Don't worry," I say. "You can trust him. He won't turn on me when he's in charge."

"Santino. Should I die, you will take my oldest living daughter in marriage before she's twenty. And you, Damiano, will have the younger. Be good to her. She will test you."

Nazario writes it down.

That's when it clicks into place. Santino is taking the older one. That's me. I've been promised in marriage to a ten-year-old. It's finished. Life's been mapped for me in front of witnesses.

Damiano's face is drained of blood. If I asked him to, he'd deny I was promised to Emilio's oldest daughter. He'd take her. But the consigliere isn't called *Il*

*Blocco*—the lock—for nothing. He wrote it down and I'm finished.

"What about me then?" Damiano objects. "I just get the second? For what?"

I kick him, but he's too insulted to get a bride without assets to pay attention.

"She'll have..." Emilio takes a difficult breath. "Something. The house in Sciacca." He waves to Nazario, who writes it down.

"That's in *Sicily*," Dami says, now fully humiliating himself. It's not even worth kicking him anymore. His best bet is to catch our boss when he's healthy again and make a damned argument.

"Santino," the consigliere barks. "Do you have any prior commitments to marriage?"

I don't. I haven't been promised. No bride's been arranged for me. Unless I'm ready to run into the void and become an invisible exile, I cannot reject this order from the man who's been a father to me, yet I cannot make the words to accept it.

"Santino DiLustro." Corragio snaps his fingers at me. "There are people waiting. Speak."

Emilio's face is gray. His mouth is slack. But he will live another thirty years. He will see his daughters fall in love. They will marry good, strong men who will take their inheritance and I will be free.

Until then, I have no choice. I get on one knee at the side of the bed and take Emilio's limp hand. The gold ring inset with a crown of diamonds is on the end of his finger, loose on the second knuckle, where the doctors allowed it.

"I will, Capo." I kiss the ring.

Emilio closes his eyes. "Corragio, note what was said here."

"*Si, si,*" the consigliore assures him, as if he hasn't been noting it the whole time.

I get back in my chair.

"And make arrangements for Santino to collect if I die. No one must know. Until the day comes, let them think it was lost. You are each sworn to silence."

"Capo—" Damiano starts.

"He has spoken." Corragio gives Damiano a withering look, daring him to make a case for himself and suffer the consequences. "Accept or don't."

Damiano looks like a man torn between murder and death.

"Go," I murmur with a kick to Damiano's leg.

He doesn't react. His mouth doesn't move from the tight line he's made to keep from saying one way or the other. His eyes go from side to side, reading an invisible text.

Corragio clears his throat.

"Kiss the ring, *stronzo*," I hiss.

"No." Without a word of respect or regret, Damiano walks out.

I may have killed before he did.

I may have always been quicker and more callous.

But that day, his courage put me to shame.

---

The rules are simple.

If you want to arrange a marriage for any reason, even love, you come for my blessing. If there are any conflicts, I refuse. Same as the last man who sat where I sit now. You asked him—except, no one did.

Vittorio Saponara was the capo of Secondo Vasto when I got here. He was a weakling with a team of soldiers stealing from right under his nose. He couldn't keep his son from running books out of the back of his bar or even keep a Jamba Juice off his own block. It took me three weeks to figure out how to get rid of him, then ask Cosimo for his blessing to do it—which he didn't give, because Saponara was his nephew—and another week to take care of business anyway.

I didn't set the Jamba Juice on fire with Vittorio Saponara in the toilet so my uncle Marco could fly all this way to arrange my cousin's marriage without my blessing.

I didn't apologize to Cosimo for taking over Saponara's business before he was even cold in the ground, then manage to not get killed by the seven guys Cosimo sent over that first year, so that his son—who he's not even speaking to—could set up this deal right under my nose, a few weeks after I refused the first one.

Over dinner, when I take my attention away from Damiano's flirting with Gia, I think about how this deal was set up without me knowing. Where's the hole, and how will I plug it?

"Vino?" A carafe appears in my sight right after Violetta's voice asks if I want wine.

I follow the arm up to my wife, who's leaning over me with a sour puss.

The rules are simple.

Wives do the job of being wives. Her frown is what

happens when they're busy doing things that will get them into trouble.

"No." I cover my glass and catch Damiano watching us.

He was telling a joke about a construction worker and a thirteen-cent prostitute a minute ago. Now he's staring at my wife as though she's the punchline. He should act like a guy caught ogling his sister and move his eyes somewhere else, hoping I didn't notice, but he tips his glass at me.

You know who wouldn't have let any of it get this far? The secret deals and unblessed matches?

Emilio Moretti. He could see through bricks in a church wall. Some said he had ancient magic powers, and he didn't say otherwise, because if they knew it was as simple as not letting your guard down, they would have shot him sooner.

I had had plenty of reasons to decline to bless Damiano's union with Gia. His refusal to tell her. The offer he made on Loretta's patio and the consequences when I refused. But that threat to expose the truth about my wife to people who would destroy me to get to her had hung over the meeting.

She'd be used and killed, and I'd be too dead to protect her.

I had no choice but to approve the wedding.

"Violetta," I murmur to her before she pours for Lorenzo.

She looks back at me. I take her carafe and put it in the center of the table, then I bring her outside, to the front of the house. On the front steps, I tap out a cigarette. I don't crave one as much as I want to keep my hands from doing something more impulsive.

"What?" She stays at the top step as I go through the motions of putting the pack away and lighting up.

"You stayed after I told you to go."

"I thought you were swatting a fly. Was I not supposed to hear you sell Gia?"

"I sold nothing."

"I'm sorry. *Mi dispiace*. Pope Santino the First had to *bless* the sale."

I laugh. She's going to put me in my grave, but I will die with a smile on my lips.

"It's not funny." She crosses her arms. "It's wrong. Deeply fucking wrong."

"This is how it's always been."

"You can take your traditions," she says with one disrespectful finger raised at me, "and you can shove them right up your ass."

"You trying to get me in the mood?" I grab her hand and move it away from my face. "You don't have to work this hard, *Forzetta*."

"Why?" She wrestles herself free because I let her. "Why are you letting this happen to Gia?"

"Why do I let it rain?"

"Because the clouds kiss your fucking ring?"

"No. It's going to rain whether I allow it or not. I keep everyone from getting wet."

Her arms are crossed. Her ring is turned around with the stone against her arm. She taps it. "You're full of shit."

"Am I?" I flick the cigarette into the street. It lands

in a spray of orange sparks and rolls away. "Maybe. Let's see how wet I let you get."

She's not amused or aroused. Yet.

"But let's say you knew Damiano wanted to steal something from you?" she says. "Would you let him marry Gia then?"

My mind flips like a coin. In a heartbeat, a conversation with my wife where I try to teach her the ways she never learned turns into a matter of life or death.

"What?" I say, climbing a step to get closer to her.

"I overheard…" She stops. Breathes. "Damiano talking about my rings to someone else, because everyone in the fucking world knows I'm not your first choice."

I barely hear a word after "my rings." The rings are irrelevant to anyone but my wife and me, unless they want what I have. Then they're everything.

"What did he say?"

"He mentioned them to someone else. A man. I don't know who. It was through a door."

"What *words*?" My neck is getting hot as the fire consuming the rest of my body rises through my collar.

Her brows knit. She's trying to remember. I want to shake her, but any memory loosened that way will be lost.

"I don't…" She stops, tilts her head. Listens to a sound on the street or in her mind. "They said you paraded someone in like a race horse, and I guess that had to be me?"

"But the rings?"

Her hand rests on the railing, and she looks at the diamond resting on the fourth finger. "And they confirmed between them... one asked like, 'Those the rings?' and the other guy confirmed. So I guess, yeah. That's it. Why are you looking at me like a bear is eating me?"

A bear is not eating her.

A bear is standing over her, licking his chops, dreaming of the feast before him, and the only thing standing between him and my wife is what's inscribed inside that ring.

You know who would have seen this danger coming? Emilio.

"What happened?" she says. "You're white as a sheet."

"Listen to me," I say, trying to sound serious, but calm and in control. I am neither. "If anything happens to me, you take this ring off my finger." I hold up my left fist, pushing out the fourth finger with my thumb. "You understand? If I'm dead, you get it off my body with your own hands."

"Can you stop? It's just jewelry."

"You must promise me this, Violetta. Swear it." Hands on her shoulders, I squeeze, bending to eye level even though I'm on a lower stair.

"What is it with the rings?"

I'm a fool to think she'll stop asking, but I can't tell her here. She's not ready, and her knowing will put her in danger.

"If anything happens—"

"The rings. I know." She nods slowly, looking me in the eye. "I swear it. You can trust me."

I take her face in my hands and kiss her, because I do trust her.

# 8

## VIOLETTA

In the car home, silence gnaws at the edges of the tension between us. I don't know what's on Santino's mind, but I've settled into a gritty despair. He never promised to free Gia after what I heard, but it affected him. I'm pretty confident the wedding's going to get unblessed or whatever. Then I have to work on making sure every other girl in this town is safe.

Without a groom ready to steal from him, I don't know how I'll do it. I'm not a superhero or a saint. It's all too big, too old, too ingrained to fix. I'm just a woman. A mouthy fishwife. A thorn in the side of His Highness.

"You didn't eat," Santino says as we turn down the road to his house. The headlights bounce off the fog, creating ghosts that whoosh away as we pass.

"There was a lot of wine to pour."

He pulls up to the gate, and it opens for us. "Stay away from Damiano when I'm not there."

"Why? Because of the rings?"

"He's a man without a master." He stops and puts the car into park.

"Italians shouldn't write fortune cookies." I open my door. The dome light goes on and I should leave before I say another word, but I have no strength to maintain filters.

I get out and step up the gravel walk to the house, hopeful that greed for a diamond has saved Gia, and fearful that even after the cut lip and the infighting, the spark of friendship burns brightly enough to allow Santino to believe Damiano's eventual denials.

"What happened after my father died?" I ask when Santino catches up to me at the front door. "With you and Damiano?"

"A king doesn't rule more than his kingdom."

"For the love of God. Skip the fortune cookie bullshit."

He smiles and unlocks the door. "We're Neapolitan. We are *camorra*. We beat the fascists because we had strength without a center. Is it fortune cookie bullshit to say I'm not the only capo in the Cavallo family? Your father was a true king." His sigh is heavy, loaded even, as he swings open the door and steps out of the way for me. "It's truth. Damiano can serve any of us, or he can fight me for territory. He can seek power without denying my authority."

We stand in a house of windows, lit from the outside. Neither one of us turns on a light.

"I thought you worked for the same master," I say.

"You mean, of course, your father."

"Yes, I mean my father." I set my jaw. "My father the grocer. And the only really-for-real king, apparently."

His silence is heavy. I can't view my father as someone like Santino, someone who plays violence like an instrument.

"Sometimes I forget you lost him so young and didn't get to know him like we did."

Why am I standing here in the dark, listening to him tell me who my own father was? And why doesn't he just take out a fucking knife and stab me while he's at it?

He was my papa, a memory relegated to a ghost of a man on all fours, roaring like a bear and laughing with his tiny daughter. A thick gold cross necklace dangled from his neck. His hair was dark and slicked back, and he had so many bright teeth in his smile.

"I'm going to bed," I say, heading up the steps. "I don't want to fight about which one right now, please."

"I am the man I am because of your father, Violetta." Santino grips the banister, but doesn't come up. He is no longer cool and collected, but fervent and emotional.

My newly-minted sadness shatters against the surface of his sincere passion. "Who are you then? Who are you that I should look at you and say, 'Good job, Dad! Because no matter what you stole or who you killed, you made Santino DiLustro into the man he is today, and...'" My armor is customized to keep me from crying over my husband, not my father, and the sobs burst through at high speed. "'And I'm so proud to be your little girl.' Is that what I'm supposed to look at you and say? Because, honestly...?"

The rest of the sentence is built like a weapon of war and aimed straight for my husband's heart, but my sobs are too thick to aim through and my breath is too thin to pull the trigger. My knees cannot hold the weight of my heart's ammunition.

What if I hadn't overheard the conversation about my ring? What if I'd puked instead of putting my ear to the bathroom door? Or if the men had been more careful? Or knew I understand Italian?

I wouldn't have been able to tell Santino what Damiano has planned, and then what?

I collapse, sitting on the stairs, holding the railing as if it's the only thing that can save me.

But it can't.

Neither can the strong arms around me, tightening into a shell of bone and flesh. On the stairs, I cry into Santino's shirt, saying meaningful words in meaningless sentences. *Gia, Gia. Don't. Wrong. Please. Can't. Gia, no.* I started crying over my father, but now I'm bawling because Gia was sold right in front of me and I don't know if she's saved, while Santino weaves meaningful sentences out of meaningless sounds. *Shh. Si, si. Va bene. Va tutto bene.*

He lays me back and I'm on a bed, racked in delusional sobs that keep me from remembering how I got up the steps or even seeing which room I'm in. All I know is that he's here, wiping my face, kissing the salty streaks from my cheeks, whispering soothing lies I need to believe. My fists clutch his shirt and skin, and my crying turns to pleading.

I kiss his lips, the source of my comfort, and the lies are silenced, because everything isn't going to be okay. It's not fine and good, and I'm not going to hush. I'm going to grope at his clothes, push his hand under my skirt, and beg him to hurt me.

"Please," I whisper into his mouth.

He is forceful but tender, pulling away the layers of fabric between us only as much as necessary, leaving his shirt and my dress over the shoulders, until his fingers can comfortably reach between my legs.

"Violetta," he says, mouth open against my cheek in a groan.

"Please," I repeat, wrapping my legs around him. He needs to do this before I cry again.

The head of his cock is smooth along my seam, sliding inside me without much effort. His thrusts are as gentle as his kisses, and when he's finally deep inside, I shudder with relief and move against him.

I want to feel as if I'm breaking in body as well as soul, but he refuses to hurt me.

Instead, I punch his chest, slap his face, and claw at his back so hard I feel wetness under my fingers.

He doesn't stop me until I grip his throat. Still rocking gently, he takes my hands away and pins them over my head.

That's all I need. In a rush of pleasure, I stiffen and arch in an orgasm made of my tears and his tenderness, blinded with a poisonous mixture of elation and anguish. But when he falls on me, breathing heavily, it's all gone.

My grief. My fear. My despair. Gone.

I'm left with blood under my fingernails and three Furies in their place.

Righteousness. Ambition. Justice.

# 9

## SANTINO

I cannot take my eyes away from my wife long enough to sleep, because when she's awake, I see her father in her features, but when she sleeps and the moonlight casts a triangle-shaped shadow across her cheek, I see her mother.

Rosetta looked more like Camilla Moretti, soft and rounded at the edges, with a heaviness to her form that was beautifully solid. Emilio was known to grab his wife's bottom behind the grocer's register, and she'd smile and slap his hand away. Camilla ran that store, and as far as we knew, that was all she did, besides raise two children and keep the house.

With my blood violet breathing softly on my chest, I remember her mother in the back room, punching an adding machine with a pencil and yanking the crank. It made a racket of clicks and creaks. But what had my attention was the piles of cash on the desk.

"*Che c'è, Santi?*" she greeted me without looking up.

I didn't know how to react. She was a woman—my

boss's woman—and so was afforded a certain kind of respect from a sixteen-year-old boy.

Yet the way she asked me *What, Santi?*, along with the contents of the desk, confused me into a fit of nerves. I'd only met her twice, and she disarmed me on the third time.

"I have to drop this for the capo." I held up the paper bag of cash Dami and I had extracted from a parking garage, a shoe repair, and two bars on Via Torino. The paper ribbon dropped down the other side of the desk while the clicking and creaking continued. "I'll come back."

"Leave it here."

"I'm supposed to give it to him."

The sound of the adding machine stopped. She looked at me with big brown eyes, round as Rosetta's and as piercing as Violetta's. "Leave it here, Santi."

No man in this part of Naples ever took orders from a woman.

But Camilla Moretti wasn't going to say it a third time, and if Emilio had put her behind that desk with that much cash to count, she did more than run a grocery store.

I put the bag on the desk.

"*Grazie,*" she said, running the paper tape through her fingers to check the numbers. "That everyone on Via Torino?"

"Everyone who owes, yes."

"Good job."

I stand there as if I can't leave without something, but I couldn't have named it if you put a gun to my head.

"You can go," she said, penciling a number into a ledger.

Once she dismissed me, some cord was cut and I could leave.

In bed with Violetta, I smile at those few minutes with Camilla I'd forgotten. I remember her as hostess for all the big dinners for the men who worked for Emilio, and at packed weddings in crowded courtyards, dancing with her husband. I remember her with customers at the store, and gossiping with the women. But my one glimpse into a life that wasn't so obvious had been stuffed in a box and put on the topmost shelf. Out of mind, out of sight.

Camilla knew what was in my bag down to the street I was working that day. Those piles of cash were not from the grocery register. She knew her husband's business. Maybe not every nuance or relationship, but enough to keep a ledger.

The moon dips below the roofline of the garage, and the shadow across Violetta's cheek folds into her jaw, disappearing like the hand of a sundial. I wonder if her mother's knowledge protected her, or if it made her a target the night they were both killed. I wonder if she had to fight for it too, or if Emilio brought her into the business right away. He'd never had a chance to train me for his job. When they were shot, Cosimo Orolio took over, filling a power vacuum in a quickly contracting territory.

Damiano, who claims to work for no one. Who set up the *'mbasciata* with Gia after I refused to bring him onto my team. Who came to *Mille Luci* after my wedding and asked for friendship. Whose sister dropped bombs of information on my wife.

If he marries Gia, he will find a way into my life through the women.

If he doesn't, he will threaten to expose Violetta again, and once he does, the incident on Flora will look like a child's game.

If he marries Gia, I have time to correct him.

If I refuse the match, I have until Violetta's birthday.

It's both very late and very early when I slip out of bed.

I swim, shower, dress, and leave without waking the woman in my bed.

## 10

## VIOLETTA

Last night, I let Santino's intensity run my reactions. I let him break me down over my sister and my father when what I should have done was demand he guarantee he'd remove his blessing from the arranged marriage.

At dinner, Gia had sat next to Damiano and giggled like a little girl. She'd played with her hair and batted her lashes. She wants to be American, but it's not about handbags and shopping and saluting the red, white, and blue. She was never cursed with the freedoms of America. The high-stakes choices. The hard-won victories.

But the freedom to try is close enough to touch, and I can do at least that.

After Santino confirms he's stopped Gia from being sold for her father's debts, I have to work on ending every *'mbasciata* before it happens.

I wipe the dried spit off the photo of Santino, Damiano, and my father and place it on the mantel with others. A woman with her gaze fixed in the middle distance, holding a bundle of joy that may be my husband. Santino young, holding baby Gia. Him with Paola and Marco. I place them in a kind of order —like a family tree. I will learn it. Memorize it. Internalize his relationships as if they are a new inheritance.

Celia and I cook dinner and talk about the garden she's put in the back. The grocery shopping. The expected arrival of the man of the house.

The water works itself back up to a rolling boil, and the bloated white gnocchi pop to the turbulent surface like bodies scarred with little slits. Their names are known to me. My mother, my father, Rosetta.

Santino appears as if called by them, coming behind me to plant a kiss on my cheek. "The sauce smells good."

"It's Celia's." I don't turn to him. I just watch the scarred blobs roll in the heat.

"The gnocchi are hers," Celia says. "Hundred percent. And perfect."

"*Bene*," he says and starts to leave.

I'll see him at dinner. I can say something then. But I am impatient. I need to be soothed immediately.

"You freed Gia, right?" The words exit my mouth before I think about them, cut through the air and stop him in his tracks. "From the marriage?"

"You can go," he says to the space in front of him, but we know he's talking to Celia.

She swipes the countertop with her palm to pick up nonexistent crumbs and says good-bye. Thirty seconds later, Santino and I are alone, staring at each other over the kitchen island with the water boiling between us.

I scoop the softened balls out of the pot and lay them on a paper-towel-covered plate.

"She doesn't need to be 'freed,' as you call it," he says finally.

"Why? Her father stopped it? Or Damiano walked? Or did you unbless it or whatever?"

He turns toward me and rests his hands far apart on the island's counter. "There are things you don't understand."

My arms lose their strength, and I drop the spoon. My face is too weak to stay on my skull. I'm going to turn into an empty, gelatinous mound if he means what I think he means.

"Tell me something," I whisper. "Anything."

"I can't accuse him of wanting to steal from me."

"But I *heard* him."

"You did. But the wedding has to happen anyway."

Quickly now, I scoop the gnocchi from the water, trying to jump-start my brain with repetitive action.

"Gia isn't built for this," I say.

"They said the same about you."

My body runs cold. "Who said?"

"Don't you know?" He cocks his head to the side.

I think back to Zio sobbing at Santino's feet. Either pleading for my freedom or weeping in gratitude. It doesn't matter. The couple who raised me to have a normal life because my sister was the one who was sold thought I couldn't handle it. Too young and independent. Not built for this.

"You should have listened." When I dump another load of gnocchi into the water, I'm careless because I'm angry, and it splashes. "I was almost kidnapped and murdered the first fucking week you had me."

"She'll learn." He takes my face in his palms. "You learned."

"Because you're only half an asshole."

"Thank you?"

"This is not funny."

"Inside that steel chest, you have a soft heart."

"It's *wrong*, Santino. Marriage is supposed to be a sacrament, not a 'get out of debt free' card."

"Isn't our marriage a sacrament pledged before God?"

He cannot think that anything about our marriage is valid before God, the law, or any kind of moral authority, and yet, he and everyone else I can swing a stick at thinks so.

"No, Santino. Actually it's not." I pull his hands off me, set out the plates, and fill them with pasta and sauce as if each gesture is a fine fuck you. "*You* were married. *You* had a ceremony. But I wasn't there for it. It's was a transaction on our wedding day, and it's a transaction now. You made a vow to my dead father. I'm just the one who got fucked."

"Be that as it may, it's the way these things go. Gia knows this."

"She's a kid." I slide his plate over to him. I'm in no mood for the dining room. "We already lost Rosetta to this tradition, and *you* killed her." Everything builds to a crystal-clear point in my head. "It wasn't pneumonia. It was *you*."

Man, that feels good when I say it, but it doesn't feel

good having been said. I think I've been fair until the cruelest of words can't be unspoken.

I'm not going to apologize. I'm high on righteous anger, and if he comes at me, I'll need the adrenaline.

But he doesn't come at me.

"I was going to eat first." He rubs a spot of sauce from the edge of his bowl and kisses it off. When his lips pucker over his thumb, I can't decide which I want between my legs more, his hand or his mouth. "But you're going to give yourself *agita*. *Vai*." He indicates I should follow and walks out of the room without looking back.

My judgment is totally damaged, because I trail him through the house and down the basement stairs. In my bored hours, I explored down here, checking the locks on the doors and the boxes on the shelves. Santino opens a door with a code and opens it to a room with walls of gray sheetrock. The nails have been smoothed over with joint compound and the seams have been taped, but the rows and rows of shelves shoved full with boxes went in before a painter could even start.

Santino brings down a shoebox to a white plastic table and flips open the top, reaches in, and pulls out a gun. He lays it on the table without a second thought.

I pick it up and inspect it. It's the kind with a carousel of bullets, like you see in westerns.

"Whoa!" He snatches it away and puts it back where it was, still within my reach. "This is loaded."

"Sorry, but… if you don't want me to get it, don't leave it in a random box."

"Take it. Just don't point it at me." He flips through

the box. It seems to be full of documents and photos. On paper. He's too old school for a digital camera.

I pick up the gun. "It's heavy."

"My grandfather shot at a few fascists with it." He takes out a folder and drops it on the table. "Supposedly."

Opening the folder reveals more pictures, and when I see them, I lay the gun down, disinterested.

Rosetta was seventeen the last time I saw her, and that is the Rosetta I see in the 4x6 glossy rectangle, sitting on our Zs' stoop in wide-leg jeans and a tank top. No makeup. Hair coming out of her ponytail as if every strand was intentionally set free.

The chronology in the box must be random, because the next picture is my father, Rosetta, and me outside the market that I thought was his primary place of business. He's in a suit no grocer would wear to the shop. She's on the cusp of puberty, and I'm as tall as her elbow.

"Why am I frowning?" I say.

"Your father denied you a second lollipop."

"Man. I am not happy."

"Violetta is *buona come il pane*, he used to say." He chuckles, describing my father's belief that I'm as *good as bread*, which is pretty solid as Italian compliments go. Then he twists it around, "But the attitude on her is *brutta come la fame.*"

"Ugly as hunger?"

He shows me another picture of myself at about four with my arms crossed and a sour puss from here to next week. Yeah. Daddy was right.

"Where did you get these?"

"Your father gave them to me in his will. He thought I'd give them to Rosetta, but…" He shrugs and lets the rest of the sentence say itself. "I was a kid too. The first time the Tabonas tried to kill him, they threw him into a water tower with cinderblocks around his waist."

As he speaks, he takes out pictures one by one, and I'm blindsided by my first few years of life. The people in the square at the center of the apartment complex, the little stores, the tight streets, are all completely different than I expect and yet, exactly as I remember.

"I fished him out. Cut him loose but…" He shakes his head. "The water was dirty and he had an infection in his lungs. Said where Franco Tabona failed, bacteria could succeed. But that's why he trusted me with his daughters."

"Didn't know you so well, did he?" I say slyly.

"I was almost eighteen. Plenty of time to disappoint him, but I did promise, and I kept that promise. I made sure you both were sent to America, and I came here, established my business, then introduced myself."

"And you fell in love with her."

"She was beautiful, and I loved her."

How can I be angry at him? How can I hold this grudge so tightly when his remorse is loosening my grip? We both loved the same woman. I shouldn't hate him for that, but I do.

"But no," he continues. "I never loved her the way you think."

Instead of triumph, I'm enraged. How dare he not love her?

"We said we were going to the other side to get things for the wedding." He flips through the box, tossing random photos on the table, but he's looking for something in particular. "That was the story we told, but it wasn't entirely true."

"You were going to marry her there because she was too young to marry here." I pick up a Polaroid of Rosetta leaning over a white cake and blowing out two candles in the shape of a 1 and a 3.

"When I took her to Italy, she was seventeen. I was already too old for her, but it was what it was, and then..." He finds what he's been looking for and puts it on the table, tapping the corner. "This."

I gasp. It's an ultrasound, which is enough to be shocked over. But there's so much more to it.

"Not normal," I say. "This is ectopic."

"Fine, yes," he says with anger that's not directed at me. "An ectopic pregnancy. We leave here with a blood test to get married on the other side, because her child will not be a bastard. And the doctor in *a casa del diavlo?*" He sneers when he says *the house of the devil*—it means the *boondocks*—as if he had the chance to set fire to it, but didn't. "That doctor missed what a nursing student can see right in front of her."

"Oh, God."

"I was in the city for a few days taking care of some business," he explains more calmly, because now it's on him. "She said she was fine, so I went, and when I came back, it was over."

I put the sonogram down next to a photo of them in the strange place made of old stones. It's not exactly the same piazza where Santino fed me orange wedges, but it could be any of the hundreds more in Napoli. There, he looks a hundred years younger and a hell of a lot happier, in a sport jacket and shirt open at the collar, squinting in the sun with his arm around Rosetta. Her left hand rests on his, and that diamond—my diamond—flashes in the Mediterranean light.

"It wasn't pneumonia," I say.

"It was not."

"Did she know she was given to you as a reward?"

"No. She didn't have to." He gathers up the photos except for the ultrasound photo, clicking the sides against the tabletop like a deck of cards, then drops them all in the folder. "That baby? It wasn't mine. I never touched her. How could I? She was a sweet girl. A nice girl, but never… never." He cuts the air with his hand. "We became friends, but not more. I swear it."

"So." I hold up the sonogram. "Whose is this?"

"A boy at St. Anselm's." He snaps it away from me and puts it on top, closes the folder, and puts it in the box as if he's too angry to talk without keeping himself occupied. "In the locker room." He grabs the gun around the outside, away from the trigger. "He took her against her will." He waves the handle of the pistol at me then drops it in the box. "Then asked *me*"—he snaps the box closed—"and her uncle for her hand, since she was ruined. The oldest trick to get a wife who doesn't want you."

I have to physically clamp my mouth closed to keep the nasty rejoinders from leaving them. He's too emotional over this to look in the mirror and compare himself to the boy who hurt my sister, and I'm too vulnerable right now to fight with the story half-finished.

"I was insulted by his stupidity. And his parents." He

slaps the box back on the shelf, still angry after all these years. "Wringing their hands that their son had to marry a whore. He was trapped, they said. But I saw them... inside their hearts... they knew their *stronzo* son would never do any better. Rosetta wouldn't stop crying. Even after I promised her she'd never marry this animal, she wept because who would have her? Who?"

I'm frozen in shock and sorrow, nearly crying as he asks who would have my beautiful sister.

"I said 'me.' I would have her. And not because her father had already given her to me. I never had to tell her that." He rubs his eyes, shielding himself from the sight of me. "I would have taken care of her and her baby and never touched her. I swear it."

"But she died."

When he takes his fingers away, his eyes are rubbed red. There's a weight on him I've never seen before. It's regret, but also deeply-buried grief, pushing up through years of false control. For a moment, I'm not the only person who lost Rosetta. He lost her too.

I'm not alone. I'm truly with him, and I can't help but put my hand over his, because we're together in this. The same pain. The same loss.

"To this day, I don't know if the doctor didn't see what you could, or if someone threatened him. Or paid him to not know. I still don't know if she could have been treated. But it was a mistake and I am sorry for it."

My questions can wait. Unable to stand another second of vulnerability, I rush to him, arms open to hold him as he shakes.

## 11

## VIOLETTA

It's one thing to know he didn't choose Rosetta first, didn't take her to bed, didn't love her more.

It's another thing to know how much he did love her, did protect her, did choose her.

Now instead of loving him in spite of my better judgment and hating myself for it, I love him and I have to say, my judgment is doing pretty great.

I feel complete and finished. Adult. Polished to a flashing shine. It's all going to be all right. I let myself relax, thinking the conversation in the basement changed my husband's mind about Damiano's offer for Gia and he'll remove his approval of the wedding.

I live in a dream where my husband's land is peaceful and all is right with the world. We eat. We swim. He fucks me with fierce tenderness and sweet violence. I cook with Celia, and when she's not in the kitchen, she creates the garden and cares for the dirt beds, choosing seedlings of cucumbers, peppers, and of course, tomatoes.

I call Gia every day. We talk nonsense five times. I keep my ears open for word of a big dinner or event, but she says nothing. I slide into complacency.

This is the first of many mistakes.

One morning, in reaching for a new toothbrush, I knock over a box of sanitary napkins. As I slide them all back, I wonder how long it's been since I used one, and in the rush to the calendar, I know damn well already how the numbers are going to add up.

---

MY PERIODS HAVE ALWAYS BEEN inconsistent, which is why I didn't think to count the days since my last until it was late in the game. Stress, poor diet, the flu—I've missed a cycle for all kinds of reasons. Sometimes I've missed it for no reason at all, but it never mattered before. It added up to a bunch of saved pads and reduced aggravation.

Now, it's different. Though it could be my body reacting to travel through international time zones, for the first time, I could actually be pregnant.

It's too soon to go to the doctor for a test, and I have another couple of days before I can even consider myself so late that I'm an idiot not to get a drugstore test.

Santino's in his office. Through the closed doors, I hear him talking to his guys.

I won't interrupt.

Before I can walk away, I hear Damiano's name in the muddle of lilting Italian murmuring, and I'm slapped out of my complacency. I lean into the door to make sense of the conversation. What I piece together is that Damiano's made reservations at a restaurant. Two tables.

Could be nothing, but it's something. It's the end of Gia. Short of breath, blind with shock, I run to my room and lock myself behind the bathroom door.

Before I freak out, I have to know the facts, and that means maintaining Santino's complacency. My late period will distract him. If he thinks he might be a father, there's no telling how he'll react. He could get even more protective. Good chance he'll hide any news that might upset me, and he knows Gia getting sold off would put me right over the edge.

After my shower, I'm so sure my period could come any minute, I stick a pad onto my underpants as a preventative measure.

---

Santino's already at the table when I come downstairs. He glances over the top of his paper and returns right back to it. "Good morning, Violetta."

"Good morning." I sit and let Celia pour me coffee. "How did you sleep?"

He lowers the news and takes another look at me. A real one, this time. I keep a neutral expression, stirring my coffee as if my period came on the dot and there's not a damn thing on my mind.

*Deep, steady breaths, Violetta. Just find out first.*

"Like the dead," he finally says and folds his paper neatly. "You look beautiful this morning."

"Thank you." I choose a pastry. "Must be a glow from last night."

He smirks, and I do too, because last night was pretty glow-worthy.

He folds his paper neatly and sets his phone on top of it, straightens his cuffs, and reclines in his chair. His hands rest lightly on the arms in a way that's so regal, I feel an urge to fall between his knees and beg to be used like a toy.

I am a badly broken woman.

Santino's eyes follow every move I make as I sweeten my coffee.

"Maybe tomorrow morning you'll set the house on fire," he says, implying tonight could leave me hot as well as glowing.

"The fire extinguisher's under the sink." I smile around my *sfogliatella*, which is when I notice he's looking at me as if I'm about to announce news that could disrupt our lives.

"Any fire that little thing can put out isn't worth setting." He moves his phone off his paper as if he's going to read it again, but something tugs on the corners of his mouth and his hand slides back onto the arm of the chair. He taps the end with a fingernail, watching me break my pastry into a hundred little flakes.

"I want to see Gia today," I say, cracking like a *sfogliatella* under the pressure of his attention.

"She's working." He goes for his paper again.

"I'll come to the café for a coffee then."

Santino snaps open the news and reads again. What

did it take, I wonder, to acquire such control? Is it from the years that separate our births?

"I gave you your phone." He scans the articles, but I don't think he's reading it. "Call her."

"I don't want to call." Petulance laces through my tone. This is not how territory is marked. "I want to see my cousin."

"What for?"

I cannot out-play Santino. Only the truth will get through. "To make sure she knows."

"Knows what?"

This asshole knows exactly what I'm talking about, but he's going to make me say it. I'm not sure if he's being cruel or thorough.

"Do you remember what happened after you stole me away?" I ask.

"You figured it out."

"Do you want Gia to be as miserable as I was?"

Santino folds his paper down and regards me silently, maybe mulling over what I've said, maybe figuring out how to shut me up. But it isn't an immediate no, which is definitely better than expected.

Finally, his mouth opens, and my chest tightens, waiting for him to tell me he doesn't care.

"You were the exception." He flicks his hand in my direction. "Most of the brides know what and when."

Why wasn't I told? Why was it piled on me all at once?

"If it hadn't been for the guy who raped her, would you have told Rosetta?"

"Eventually."

"Before you married her?"

"I don't know."

I'd like to strangle him, but there's a deep vulnerability in his answer. It's not just *I don't know*. It's also, *I never got the chance to find out*.

"Damiano's not going to tell Gia he's buying her," I say. "Her own father wants her to be blindsided so he doesn't have to deal with her being afraid or begging or whatever she'll do."

"She won't be afraid."

"How do you know? She's full of these silly ideas about love."

"So she won't see a wedding as a bad thing."

Having held back since I eavesdropped through the office doors, I didn't feel the slowly bubbling rage until I'm near the boiling point. "She should have a choice!"

Santino responds with a raised eyebrow. "You are not the one to give that to her."

"She's just like me." I have to stop myself from pounding the table. "And you know that wasn't right."

I can't tell what's happening to his face. Is he softening?

He is. This moment can't go to waste.

I slide off my chair and kneel at his feet, looking up imploringly. The supplication is completely sincere, and it's the least I'll do.

"Please," I say with one hand on my heart and the other on his knee. "Let me tell her."

"No."

"She needs a way out if she wants it."

"You cannot change these things." He puts his hand on mine and bends at the waist, speaking tenderly—as if to a child who doesn't know how the world works.

"Be careful you do not ruin something for her because of your own experience."

Was my experience so uncommon? If I'd known it was coming but still had no choice, would the wedding and the following weeks have been better or worse? And what's the difference? Knowledge is valuable, even if it hurts, but I can't explain basic human respect to a man who'd let his cousin pay a debt.

"I heard you say you wanted to tell her." I run my hand up his leg. His body is reacting to seeing me on my knees. "Let me do it. Let me give you what you want, then blame it on me."

He grabs my wrist before I reach his erection. "This is our way, Violetta." He stands and looks down at me as I collapse onto the floor. "It's our fathers' way, and their fathers, and their fathers' father before them."

"What about your mothers?"

He takes his phone off the table and leaves me on my knees, petitioning to an empty throne.

---

**—YOUR HUSBAND IS SOOOOO HOOOOOTTTTTT!!!!!**
—

I'VE LEFT Scarlett's notification up, even though I answered it. I miss the life I had when she was in it, but I'm so divorced from this kind of talk, it seems like a curious language I understand but don't speak.

In the drugstore, Armando stands a respectful distance away, pretending he's shopping for cold medicine as I browse the feminine products. I swipe

Scarlett's message away without deleting it and call Gia.

"Violetta!" Gia squeals, picking up after half a ring. "I wanted to call, but it's been so busy at home!"

"Busy how?" I try to make myself sound as cheerful as possible. "Tell me everything!"

"Oh, you know, Mama and Papa coming in from Italy just like that." She snaps her fingers, then drops to a whisper. "Mama must be going through the change, because she's been extra irritable. And Tavie? I think he has a girlfriend because he's out all the time and when he's here, he's growling at everything."

My stomach sours. Paola's upset because she knows her husband is selling off her baby, and the baby herself doesn't even know.

"Men are stupid."

The pregnancy tests are behind a locked glass door. Shit. Down one end of the aisle, Armando keeps vigil. Down the other... nothing. I walk toward nothing.

"Remember Damiano?" Gia says. "He was at the dinner last Sunday?"

"We weren't introduced." I swallow the hard mass in my throat. "But I remember him."

"Of course you do! Well, he asked my father if he could take me out," Gia gushes. "And papa said yes!"

My throat feels both dry and sticky at the same time. My tongue's too heavy to move.

Behind the pharmacy counter, a woman in a bright blue jacket with a nametag pinned on the breast pocket talks on the phone and taps into a computer. She can open the case and get me a test.

"It's tonight," Gia squeals. "What should I wear? Do

you think a dress? Or shorts and a cute top? No, that's too casual, right?"

Her parents aren't telling her what is about to happen to her because her father is emotionally lazy and Damiano is emotionally sadistic. Zio and Zia did the same, though I remain conveniently convinced it was to protect me because they thought they could wiggle out of it.

The results are the same. Our families are so entrenched in these customs that they can't even see what they're doing to their own children. The knot in my stomach turns to stone. I'm no better than any of them, because I've already decided not to tell her immediately. She wants to see him. She wants a wedding and a romantic honeymoon. Telling her might get her to my side, or coupled with the excitement she's already feeling, it might entrench her. She may accept this is for the best and think that she'd want it anyway.

For now, I have to be a voice of reason. I have to be the big sister.

"Pants," I say, waving to the woman in the bright blue jacket to let her know she can take her time. "You don't want a strong wind to give him an eyeful, you know?"

"Right!" She claps. "I don't want him to think I'm whoring it out."

Of course. Men can wave their hand and transform decent women into sluts, much like Santino was reputed to do. Gia wouldn't want a skirt to turn her into Loretta.

Who is protected.

And cherished.

And frankly? Respectable, but only because Santino says she is.

"Exactly," I say to Gia as Bright Blue Jacket hangs up and heads toward me. "Don't let him think it's more than a date. You know these Italian men."

"I woulda dropped off a prescription if you needed," Armando says, suddenly at my side.

"Can I help you?" Blue Jacket smiles.

"He's been here longer than me," Gia natters. "Since he was nineteen, maybe?"

The phone behind the counter rings. Blue Jacket pretends to ignore it.

Armando. "Or I can come get it later for you."

Blue Jacket glances at him.

The key that opens the cabinet with the pregnancy tests dangles from her waist.

Then she looks at me.

Gia. "He's practically American."

I put my hand over the bottom of my phone.

"I need a—" *pregnancy test.*

Armando sniffs.

Gia goes on and on.

The drugstore phone rings.

"I need…" Armando hasn't backed up and won't. "Birthday candles."

"Aisle seven." Blue Jacket picks up her phone.

---

"Answer," I tell Santino on the second ring.

I'm in the back seat of a parked car. Armando's in the front, patient as a saint, waiting for me to tell him to pull out so I have the impression I make the decisions around here.

"*Forzetta*," he purrs when he answers.

"Gia says she and Damiano have a date tonight."

"Yes?"

"What's going to happen?"

"Nothing. They have chaperones."

"No, I mean… is he going to take her away?"

There's a long, wordless gap that's filled with clinking cups and one man's breathing. Santino doesn't want to say. Her life could end after a dinner just as mine did, and he knows I could have Armando drive this car over there before it happens.

He also knows he can tell Armando to take me home.

"Santino." I mean to growl, but I can barely whisper.

"I'm here."

"Tell me." The force builds in my tone. "Is he forcing her into a car and driving her to a church?"

"No."

"Do you swear it?"

"What is this about?"

Oh, no, he will not change the subject or redirect the inquiry to try to calm me down. I know what has to be done.

"Swear it!"

Armando pretends he's not looking at me in the rearview. I can make another stop and run. Take the bus to Gia if I have to. Maybe Armando will catch me, but he won't hurt me.

"Violetta!"

"Swear on your mother he's not going to do it tonight!"

"I swear it." He pauses and gathers the control I know him for. "On my mother, it's not tonight as far as I know."

"Do you rule this shit town or not?"

"What is that supposed to mean?"

"Find out for sure!"

I cut the line and throw the phone on the seat. I'm not letting the days get by me like this again. I'm putting Gia in my sights and keeping her there.

Armando's phone dings. He looks at it and starts the car.

Our eyes meet in the rearview.

"Go, if he says you have to," I say. "I don't want you to get into trouble."

He waves to me. When I wave back, I'm shaking.

---

CELIA AND I PREPARE DINNER, then I send her home with a wink. I put on lipstick and give my hair a quick pass with the curling iron. I wear jeans and a blouse. Generic. Not distracting. I barely have time to get dinner on the table before I hear the front door beep, then the sound of his keys hitting the front table.

"Santino," I say.

"*Forzetta*," he says as he comes in. We stand on opposite sides of the foyer.

"Well? Did you find out?" I ask.

"I did."

"And?"

"It is just a date. Like I said."

I close my eyes to hold back tears of relief.

I still have time to break the chain.

My eyes are still closed when I feel his lips on my cheek, then my mouth.

"Thank you," I say. He takes me by the chin and I open my eyes.

"Are you feeling all right?" He's inspecting me, and I wonder if he can see the contents of my body better than any pregnancy test. I step toward the kitchen before he can tell me the truth of what I am too frightened to know.

"I'm fine."

"Armando says you went to the store today?" he asks in the kitchen, rolling his sleeves over his tight, olive-skinned forearms. On the counter in front of him are the 2 and 0 candles I got at the drugstore.

"I did." I take the chicken from the oven.

"You went to the drugstore for birthday candles?"

"Yes," I reply, chipper as a bird.

While I get dinner on the table, he changes clothes and washes his face. When he comes downstairs, he smells of soap and fresh cologne.

"If you want wine, I put the white in the fridge," I say. When he nods and brings it back opened, long fingers grasping two glasses by the base, I realize my mistake.

"Say when," he says as he fills the second glass.

I want that wine. The sticky sweet on my tongue, the warmth in my chest, the dry tang after.

"When."

He stops the pour and pushes the glass to me, then sits.

"How was your day?" I ask as if the last time I saw him in that chair, I hadn't been on my knees.

"Good." He eats, going along with my pretense that everything's fine. "Yours?"

Mine. Sure. It was great. I realized I had a missed period and went to the drugstore for a pregnancy test, but I didn't want to get it in front of Armando because he'd report right back to his employer and Gia was going on about the guy who bought her, so instead I asked about the first thing that popped into my head.

"Fine."

"Birthday candles." One eyebrow raised, he eats his chicken.

"It's coming up. Mine." As if the 2 and the 0 aren't enough of a clue.

But maybe they aren't, because he stiffens and puts on his bossman face. Why... I don't know. Maybe he has a big surprise planned? Or maybe he forgot it completely. It's possible he doesn't even know the date.

"What would you like? For a gift?"

It's fair to say he doesn't know me well enough to know what I want. That must be the source of his discomfort.

"I thought just a cake." I swirl the wine, try to read his thoughts, fail, and go on. "Maybe people? Some family? Might as well, right?"

"It is a Monday." He seems to be chewing the inside of his cheek like he's gnawing on a thought.

"We can do it the night before. Regular Sunday dinnertime. It'll be fun!"

"It will be fun." He doesn't sound convinced.

"Unless Gia's getting married that weekend."

"Definitely no." He eats, shaking his head.

He's confirmed for me, and when the tension leaves my chest, it feels as if I've been restrained for so long, I forgot what it felt like to have my hands free.

"This call to me today? About Gia?" He seems suddenly unconcerned about whatever was bothering him about my birthday.

"Yeah, I'm sorry about that."

"This panic you had… it's not necessary. There's a process."

"There is? I was somehow dragged through it blindfolded."

He stops mid chew, then starts again. "I regret that."

"I'm just saying, the process can't be such a big deal if you decided to do it differently."

"You were different," he says, still eating. "There was no debt to secure."

"Tell me." I lean on my elbows with the glass swirling between my fingertips. "Come on. Tell me the fun I missed."

"It's not that fun." Santino sits back and takes stock of me. I'm trying to keep it light, but he's a wild creature, and I know he sees through me. I assume he'll cut off the conversation, but I'm wrong. "First, as an act of good faith, Damiano will put the debt money into escrow, then send flowers. When her father confirms the escrow, he'll give the flowers to the Virgin."

"I'm sorry? The virgin is Gia?"

"No." His impatience doesn't seem directed at me, but himself. "The Virgin in the shrine."

I nod, assuming it's the Virgin Mary in the church's chapel. Putting flowers at her feet requires a big donation.

"Then Damiano will offer a ring. The father accepts it. The debt is paid. The matter is closed. She is his, and he may walk with her when he chooses." His lips purse as if he's trying not to say something. "The wedding's a formality between him and God." What is understood, but remains unsaid, is that the woman isn't part of the contract with God, just the deal between the men. "They have to turn four corners together or she will not bear children."

The night I was taken away, Santino and I walked around the block with two women following. It was romantic date and ancient superstition all wrapped into one, horrifying night.

"You didn't miss that one," I say.

He shrugs, but concedes. "When it comes to children, I won't tempt fate."

So he wants a family and will perform foolish rituals to increase his odds. All I can think is that the *nonnas* kissing chalices and fingering rosary beads must be on to something, because if I'm pregnant and my math is right, our first time was the charm.

"When will all this happen with them?" I ask.

"Why?"

"She's excited. I can't talk her—or you or anyone—out of anything. But I want her to have the things I missed."

"Not to go against her father's wishes or try to talk her into running from what she can't avoid?"

"Like I said. I want it to be better for her. I want to

talk about weddings. Dresses. Flowers. Let her get excited that maybe it'll be fun and we can plan the thing." I pick up the dishes. "That's the deal. I don't want her to miss what I missed."

I bring the plates to the kitchen sink. He joins me there without a single glass or fork in his hand.

"You cannot make this go away, Violetta."

"So you said," I singsong to make the comment less cutting.

As I move to pass him, he grabs my arm and pulls me close.

"I remember those first days here, in my house. I wanted to kill the man who made you weep like that. Rip his guts out of him. Throw his body in the ditch where I left the boy who made Rosetta cry."

When he admits to murder, a gallon of blood leaves my heart and flows to the surface of my skin. I'm hot everywhere, and his face is so close he must be able to feel the heat radiate.

"But," he continues, locking our eyes, "the guts were mine, and suicide is a sin I'm too much of a coward to commit. So I let you cry, and I swore I'd never make you cry again. But the only thing worse than hearing you cry behind that door was when you held it all inside your silence." He leans away from me a few inches—no more—and releases my arm. "I am sorry for what I stole from you. If I could give it back, I would."

"Why would you let it happen to Gia?"

"There are things you don't know."

"What don't I know?"

He opens his mouth to answer, then shuts it and takes two steps back.

"*Così stanno le cose!*" he cries instead. It is what it is. Maybe he's right, but it's bullshit.

"Then what are you worried about?"

"That you'll try, and I won't be able to protect you. Violetta, my blood violet, you do not..." He puts his hands on my shoulders and meets my gaze. "You cannot understand what will happen if I stop this marriage for any reason."

He's right. I don't understand anything except the raw panic and truth in his eyes.

"What if I told you"—I lay my hands on his arms—"I don't want her to cry. Not like I did. And I know you want her to know she's a debt bride."

"That's her father's choice."

"Damiano saw me in the hall. He knows I was listening. And I'm just a woman. A mouthy fishwife. If I see Gia tomorrow morning, and I slip and tell her... who'd be surprised?"

His features are utterly still. I can smell the wood burning. I might get this if I'm careful.

"I want Gia better prepared than I was," I say. "Maybe she'll like him. Maybe she'll be thrilled."

His nod is so slight it would be easily missed if he wasn't so motionless otherwise. "Do you swear you won't try to stop the marriage?"

The funny thing is, if you put a gun to my head, I'd say he knows damn well that I intend to throw my entire being into stopping Gia's wedding to Damiano. His desire to believe me runs hotter than his actual belief.

"Santino," I say, letting my hands drift to his chest,

"how could I even try to pull a stunt like that without your blessing?"

His smile is just short of a laugh. "You want a blessing?"

"I'll take one if you're offering."

"I bless this effort." He anoints each of my palms with a kiss. "To help my cousin tomorrow. To be a friend to her always." He presses my hands together. "This morning, you offered your mouth in exchange for a favor."

"I did." I move closer to him. He cups my cheek.

"You offered me what is already mine." His hand slides back and tightens into a fist at the back of my head.

He and I have learned to speak each other's language, so I know what's coming when he yanks me to my knees on the hard marble floor. I have no words. My brain can't make them. My body, however, is clear about what it needs. It's in the heat of his gaze, the taut restraint in his arms, and the hunger curling his lips.

"This mouth belongs to my cock." He uses his free hand to open his pants. "Show me what it does when you see it."

When his dick is out, fisted in all its thick, hard glory, I open my mouth for him. He holds onto my head with terrifying strength and guides his erection along my tongue and back as far as I allow. He pulls halfway out. I breathe, close my lips, and suck on the sweet violence of his cock.

"My cock owns your throat," he growls, yanking me off. My chin is wet with spit, and when he maneuvers my head by the hair, I am made of firing nerves and boiling blood. "Open up, so I can fuck it."

He pushes back in. I am unmoving, open lips, tongue down, throat ready to receive as he pushes deeper with each stroke. Holding back a gag, I take all of him until his cock is buried in my face with my nose pressed against him. I can't breathe, choking even as my clit throbs with want. My vision sparks to black. It's only then he lets me breathe.

"Whose mouth is this?" He presses it open like he did at our wedding.

"Yours."

"Don't ever forget it."

He takes my throat again and stays there. I am utterly powerless. Completely thoughtless. Lost to his command. Nothing but a vessel, an orifice, for his regal dick to receive pleasure.

He lets me breathe again, and I look up at him in surrender and open my mouth—his mouth—for his indulgence, forgetting everything I intend to do with or without his permission.

"That's my good wife." Santino fucks my face in quick thrusts.

His grunts and moans fill the room. I squeeze my eyes tight and focus on flattening my tongue so I can be open for him. A vessel of warm, wet skin.

"Take what I give you. I will paint the back of your throat and you will swallow every drop."

I take the hammer of his dick and the sticky warmth of his orgasm. My clit engorges so fast it hurts, and he comes inside me. I accept every bit of him. When he pulls out, a line of come drips out from my lips. With his thumb, he brushes it back in, and I suck his thumb while looking up at him from my knees.

"Let the date happen tonight." He pulls back and puts his dick away. "Go tomorrow. Talk to Gia like a woman, exactly as you say. No more."

"This is strictly girl stuff."

He meets my gaze, holds it, and finally puts his hand out to help me up. "Leave Armando home then."

From his pocket, he produces a ring of keys. He unwinds a black fob with the Mercedes logo and tosses it onto the table. It bounces and stops at the edge as if it would never think to defy him by landing on the floor.

Did I just win?

Is this a false victory?

It has to be, but I dig myself deeper anyway.

"*Grazie*," I say, then add the last lie of the conversation. "I won't let you down."

"*Bene. Allora.*" He kisses my cheeks. "I will take a swim, and after that, if you're naked, I'll paint your cunt the same color as your throat."

Together, we laugh at his silly analogy, then he kisses my lips quickly. Without another word, he goes out back, leaving me alone to slide the fob from the table, wondering why he gave me the car now for a drive tomorrow.

He must trust me.

Poor guy.

## 12

## VIOLETTA

I haven't driven a car in ages, but the smooth satisfaction of controlling such a powerful object is a fast reminder of how it felt to be free.

Not free enough to stop for a pregnancy test. Or not sneaky enough. Maybe I'm just not brave enough.

There's nothing to beat myself up about. My period's late from stress. By the time I get the test, the sheets will be a mess.

"With your parents here, Zio Angelo's house is too crowded," I say to myself in the rearview mirror, testing out a cheerful tone for the duration of a red light. "And Santino's house is too empty with just the two of us."

At every intersection, I change it up, testing casual distressed, and with a conspiratorial wink. They all sound like baloney, so I give up and figure I'll let it come to me as it comes. I'll go with the flow, the way I used to do in nursing school.

I pull up to the house as the sun is getting low in the

sky, but the Virgin Mary grotto in Angelo and Anette's front yard is lit as if it's the dead of night. At her feet sits a vase of two dozen white roses.

*First, Damiano will put the debt money into escrow as an act of good faith, then send flowers. When her father confirms the escrow, he'll give them to the Virgin.*

Shit. This is the Virgin getting white flowers. Not the church. The front yard grotto.

The money is in escrow.

Am I too late? Has the date begun? Does it matter? Once the money is moved, dinner's just to grease the wheels of the system before it's time to crush someone.

The minutes that ticked away with Santino's dick in my mouth could have been used to save Gia. My fingers tighten around the wheel. I push the brake pedal hard at the thought that he did it on purpose—as if I'm within my rights to betray his trust by coming here when I'm not supposed to, but he can't do the same for his own purposes.

But he could have held on to the car keys.

He could have kept me home by fucking me for hours.

No, Santino did not keep me home an extra ten minutes to sabotage me, but idling in front of the house is self-sabotage at its finest.

Parking the car across the street, I firm my resolve.

I couldn't protect Rosetta. I won't lose Gia.

Breathing in a little more courage and out a little more fear, I approach the gate, stopping at the shrine to the Virgin for a word.

"I'm getting you out," I say, then hop up the stoop to

knock with confidence and determination, as if the glue that keeps my insides together isn't failing.

"Violetta!" Gia throws open the door and smushes herself onto me. We double-kiss cheeks and she beams like one of the Virgin's new flowers, unaware that she's getting creamed in a game of bullshitball. "What a great surprise!"

She lets me in and closes the door. Though she's in heather gray lounge pants and a matching hoodie with a bubblegum pink crown on the left breast, her face is made and her hair has recently experienced the attention of a curling iron.

"I needed to make sure you're perfect for your date."

I wrangle the most genuine smile I can fake. "And Santino was like…" I mimic his voice and accent, pantomiming him flipping me the keys. "'Take the car to her, eh?'"

She laughs.

"Tell me!" I demand. "Where are you going? What are you wearing?"

"Come!" She grabs my hand and pulls me past the kitchen.

I wave to Paola and Anette, peek into Tavie's room to see he's not there, and let her take me up the narrow, carpeted stairway.

The word QUEEN is stamped across her butt cheeks in pink rhinestones.

"I know you said pants," she says as we enter her room, which appears to have been a cyclone's second stop after H&M, "but isn't this so cute?"

The bed is piled with outfits on hangers. She plucks up a white cotton knee-length dress with an elastic neck that can be pushed over the shoulders and puts it against herself.

"Where are you going to eat?"

"Aldo's." She snaps up a yellow bolero jacket and places it on top, twirling in front of the closet mirror.

"What can you eat there that won't make a mess on white?"

She looks at me, dead serious. "I can handle my sauce."

I make a doubtful *hm* and pick up a blue maxi skirt. Maybe she can handle her sauce and maybe skirts are better than pants, but I don't care what she wears.

"This date," I say, handing her the skirt and a white jacket so she knows I trust her with tomato sauce, "happened pretty quick. I mean, did he ask you out today for tonight?"

"We've been talking all week." She poses with the maxi and jacket, then tosses the skirt and picks a pink minidress from inside her closet.

"Really?" Not good. If she's decided she likes him, she's going to get sucked in no matter what the terms of her father's deal are.

"He had to talk to my mom and dad before he asked me." The white jacket gets flung onto the bed, leaving the pink dress alone. "Make sure there were chaperones and… you know how it is."

"I do know how it is." I sift through the hangers, using them to divert my attention from my panic, and her attention from my intentions.

She rushes into the half-bathroom with the pink dress and strips with the door open.

"So you like him?" I say, putting things back into the closet.

"He's so nice. He said I was beautiful, like, a hundred times. And smart. And he speaks to me in, like, this way… like he appreciates me even talking to him. He sent me the most beautiful flowers."

"The ones out front?"

"Aren't they gorgeous? And not just one dozen, but two!" She comes out barefooted, wearing pink, and turns to look at her backside in the mirror. "This needs to be, like, two inches shorter."

"I think if you dress it up with accessories and something over your shoulders, it'll be good."

"You're right!" She rushes back into the bathroom. "You have such good taste!"

She's about to dive into shark-infested waters. I couldn't care less what bathing suit she wears when she does it.

Giving up on rehanging everything, I stand in the bathroom doorway as she slides chunky bracelets around her wrist. "Gia, listen, he's not what you think."

In the mirror, I see her get immediately defensive. "What are you trying to say?"

"I'm sure he likes you, because who wouldn't?" I try to soften the blow. "But… remember me? My situation?"

"That worked out okay."

This sucks. I am absolutely, horribly, terrible at subtlety. I have to spit the toad, as Santino would say.

"I overheard something on Sunday."

She spins to face me, eyes wide. "Was it that he's Cosimo Orolio's son?" Before I can deny that's what I heard, but confirm the truth of it, she spins back to the mirror and continues. "They're not speaking, and Dami's so, so sad about it. He wants to get back in his father's graces and I'm like… can you imagine it, Violetta?" She fluffs her hair and puckers to herself. "If it works out and he gets to be boss of his father's business, I'll be just like you!"

"Don't you remember what it was like for me?"

"I do! But it happened so fast for you. We'll take our time. Have a real… aahh…" Her face goes blank as she looks for the word. "What's the word for *corteggiamento?*"

"Courtship."

"Right. We'll go to the other side and get all the things we need for the wedding, like people do and…" Her face goes sympathetic. "Oh, I know what this is about." She faces me and takes my hands. "I know you didn't get a real *corteggiamento*, Violetta. Or the wedding, or the shopping. Please don't feel jealous. I'd die if you resented me."

I can't help but be a little resentful that she thinks I'm jealous. "It's just a date."

She looks as if I slapped her. I'm not supposed to be pushing her into a corner. I'm supposed to be getting her out of the room she's trapped in, and I'm about to backtrack and say it could be something. Anything. If she wants the wedding, she should have it…but if she doesn't?

"Violetta!" Paola stands in the doorway wearing a dress that could have come out of my closet the day after my wedding.

"Mammà!" Gia cries. "Do you like it?" She indicates

her outfit, but Paola's already pecking each of my cheeks.

"Where did you go on Sunday?" she asks. "You didn't stay for cards."

"I'm sorry, I didn't feel great."

She takes a quick glance down—at my belly—and I freeze. Does she see something? Am I carrying Santino's baby?

*Stop it.*

Anette, the woman of the house, greets me as family even though we've only met once, then she rushes downstairs to put on a pot of water. We all follow.

"So, feeling better?" Paola asks in the stairwell, managing to look at my face, not at my midsection even though she's a few steps below me. I decide her last meaningful glance wasn't meaningful at all.

"I think it's the vacation-itis. Now that I'm back in that big house, it gets a little lonely sometimes. You know Santino… always so busy."

"He's a workaholic," Gia commiserates kindly. "You should come over more."

"I might come over here and kidnap you to keep me company," I say when we're all in the kitchen.

Paola stiffens at the word kidnap. Our eyes meet. She must know how it went for me, and I can only attribute her reaction to concern for her own daughter.

"He's good to you though?" Paola asks.

The wrong answer will have repercussions. If it's great with him, then Gia will take that as a sign that forced marriage turns out okay. If it's terrible, I'll insult my husband and become the object of pity and possibly scorn for my inability to manage being his wife.

I don't want to screw this up with a badly-told lie either. I don't want to ruin anyone's day and I don't want anyone to steal Gia's life. It's a delicate line I'm not sure I can properly straddle, but dammit, if Santino can make all these people eat out of his hands and I can make him do what I want, then surely I have some competence.

The teapot whistles like an alarm. Time's up. Answer now or change the subject. Anette shuts the heat and gets out a box of Lipton and cups.

"It was hard at first, no lie." I check to see who's paying attention and who isn't. Anette's a casual observer. Gia—who was there to see how hard it was for me—retrieves the sugar with half an eye on me. Paola, though, is hanging on my every word. It's her daughter who's being traded. "I'm still not sure what I'm doing, kind of. Am I going back to school? Do I want to? And getting used to living with someone… a man. Well, that has its own… demands."

Paola nods with grave understanding.

"But it's Santi!" Gia chimes in, talking about him as if he's a puppy.

"Is he nice with you?" Paola adds. She can be an ally in this, if I can give her enough of a reason.

"I got lucky with him." I match her gravity, but I'm not sure I'm as lucky as I claim. "I don't think everyone gets to marry a Santino DiLustro."

"He's lucky he ended up with someone so beautiful and smart like you," Gia pipes in, glancing at the clock, then dropping teabags in cups of steaming water before she looks at the clock again. "So many women see the cars and the suits and his handsome face and just want his money. It's so nice to see him with someone who understands him, not someone who uses him."

*I never had a choice,* I want to say, but don't.
*I had to learn to stop hating him.*
The thoughts rain down.
*Sometimes I think about what I lost.*
*It's terrifying.*
*No one should count on being as lucky as I am.*
*You are in terrible, terrible danger.*
"Tavie!" Gia calls.

I follow her eyes to a blur in a lightweight leather jacket crossing the doorway. He shoves one of the wireless headphones away from his ear.

Jesus. I should be dating guys like him, but he seems too young to even be my friend.

"Violetta is here," Gia adds, indicating me expectantly.

"Hey," he says with a quick wave, studying me carefully, and I remember that he's against the idea of his sister being sold into marriage.

He must think I'm trying to be an example of why it's okay.

This guy's in for a big surprise.

He stalks off, and Paola shakes her head and sighs, "Boys," making eye contact with Anette.

"Boys are nice," Gia chirps, then checks the clock.

"He's not coming half an hour early just because you're ready," her mother says.

"Which you shouldn't be," Anette adds.

"Oh, what's the harm?" Gia kisses her aunt's cheek.

She's so happy, staring expectantly at the tight bud of her life just before it blooms.

The doorbell rings and Gia gasps, bouncing up to go get it.

Paola grabs her arm. "You do not answer the door for him."

"Especially if he's early," Anette adds, then calls back as she heads for the front door. "Get upstairs."

Gia rolls her eyes and obeys, leaving Paola and I alone.

"I'm going to kill him," Paola murmurs, using the threat the way you'd use it for an intimate—half-joking, while keeping the other half undefined. This is how I know she's talking about her husband, Marco, before she gets to the next sentence. "He could let me tell her, but he cuts me at the knees." *Cuts* has a particular venom and is accompanied by a hand slicing the air.

"Santino!" a man cries from the front door.

Shit. I have no time for this. Not another second. But I don't know what else I expected him to do. I should have left a note that I was going to the drugstore for a pregnancy test. Checking every one in a ten-mile radius would have kept him occupied for a long time.

Gia is a pink streak across the doorframe as she rushes for the foyer, crying my husband's name.

"Are you letting Armando sit in the car?!" she adds before the screen door creaks. "Mando! Come on in!"

Elbow on the counter, I lean over my teacup to get closer to Gia's mother.

"Trust me," I whisper, "I'm working on it."

"Violetta didn't tell me you were coming!" Gia's voice gets closer.

"I trust none of you," Paola hisses, then pastes on a smile as Anette returns.

Now that we have two more guests, I can't sit and remain respectful, so I refill the teapot and turn on the burner. Anette gets cups. Paola pulls down a cookie dish.

"*Ciao.*" Santino enters the kitchen, kissing aunts between compliments like a mayor up for reelection. I catch his eye and he shrugs slightly while he pecks Anette's cheeks.

"Surprise?" It's all I can think to say when my husband caresses me from behind and kisses my face in greeting.

"Is it?" he asks, knowing the answer. Something you should have seen coming is never a surprise.

Armando accepts the cookies from Paola and puts them at the table as he sits. Everyone's in the kitchen like good little Italians, waiting for a suitor to arrive.

"Please, sit, sit!" Gia pulls out a chair for Santino, but he doesn't sit. "Is tea okay or can I get you an espresso?" She's slipped into caregiver mode, playing the fledgling attentive bride and hostess—the future woman of the house.

"What about me, eh?" Armando complains, waving his biscotti.

"Santino is first," Gia scolds, grabbing the espresso pot before her aunt can. "Sambuca?"

"How about we skip the espresso then?" Armando suggests.

"Mando, you are my favorite," Gia coos at him in

Italian and dances her way to the china cabinet for the right cups.

Santino takes a soft *pinole* cookie and leans against the counter, as if it's not peculiar that he showed up, fully at ease and completely commanding with everything in his purview—except me, obviously.

With the chatter in the kitchen rising, I have a moment to talk to Santino without leaving the room. "I thought you were taking a swim."

"I did." He bites the cookie. The crumbs leap into his mouth rather than drop onto his shirt.

"Awfully fast swim, that was."

"How long should it take to get wet, *Forzetta?*"

My husband holds up the cookie. He wants to feed me.

My first instinct is that I'm perfectly capable of eating my own cookie, and if I wanted one, I'd be getting crumbs on my shirt already. But I fall victim to his intense gaze and obediently open my mouth. It's milky and sweet and utter perfection. His thumb lingers under my chin for just a moment and everything inside me catches fire.

"I want to be exactly like you guys when I get married someday!" Gia gushes, fanning herself—which is utterly embarrassing. "It's so romantic, watching you two together. What a beautiful life you have! A handsome, doting husband and a gorgeous, loving wife. You guys are such a pair. Like a power couple."

Santino winks at her, then at me. I shove another piece of anisette toast into my mouth to cork the truth before it gets out. A power couple consists of two equal partners at the top of their respective profession.

That's not what we have, but it's what Gia deserves. She's not a piece of real estate. Period.

Then she says something that—coming from her mouth—sends me right over the edge.

"I can't wait to be married!"

My resting heart rate doubles. My skin emits heat as blood flows to the surface.

"No need to rush," Paola says.

"I know." Gia's mouth puckers into a perfect pout. "But married life is perfect for me. I can cook for my husband. Take care of him. And when he's at work, my girlfriends can come swim in the pool, or we can go shopping, we can see the movies. I know how busy the men get in their work. Isn't that right, Violetta?"

Wrong. It's all wrong. She won't see her friends. She won't go shopping. She won't see another movie. The people in this room know exactly what she's in for and they refuse to acknowledge the horror behind it. My heart bangs against my rib cage.

"Yes," Santino hints. "Isn't that right, Violetta?"

Besides Scarlett—who I may never see again—I can't remember the last time I saw my own friends. My return to school isn't guaranteed, and shopping isn't a substitute for freedom.

Maybe it's my innocence I miss. The possibilities. Life was a wide open road, spooling endlessly into the future. Someone stole the steering wheel and hauled me over the median, and now I'm going in the other direction.

I have to let her know. I have to save her. I have to spare her.

"Violetta..." Santino warns me from a million miles away.

"It's not—"

"Time to go," Santino neatly cuts me off. "Thank you for entertaining my wife, Zia Paola."

He kisses his aunt, then his other aunt, and finally Gia, who's tucked away her pout as she kisses the two men.

"I'll see you around, Gia," Armando says as he pushes past the screen door. "Call me if you need anything, all right?"

"I'm so glad you came by," she calls, waving.

"Gia, I—"

"*Vai*," Santino commands, and I ignore him to grab Gia one last time before he drags me out.

"You should come stay with us." I'm speed-talking. All the emotion is drained out of the words because I'm saying them so fast. "It's such a big house for the two of us, so if it's ever too crowded here, you come. Or if you want to keep me company, you can just call me. Okay?"

"Sure." She looks concerned.

But Santino pulls me through the house, and when the door closes behind the three of us, I feel Gia slipping through my fingers.

## 13

## VIOLETTA

The barefooted Virgin Mary stands in her little half-clamshell with her palms up at the vase of flowers as if to say, "Can you do something about these?"

She was forced into marriage after God gave her a gift she didn't ask for.

*Così stanno le cose.*

It is what it is.

It's always been this way.

Even God plays by the rules the king protects.

The sky and trees are painted with a rage as helpless as it is righteous. Streaks of it curl through the sidewalk, cracking them in a serpentine grip. Streetlights buzz in agony. Even the breeze whistles through the leaves at the pitch of nails on a chalkboard. My entire body is on fire.

"Violetta..."

Santino's voice is almost drowned out by the white noise in my ears. I feel his hand on my arm. The path's bricks press up against my feet, my knees, pushing my head on the hard sky until I have to crouch as he pulls me toward the front gate or I'll be squashed by the world, compressed into a base, prenatal state.

I was a healthy woman when I was stolen and dragged into this fever dream. Rosetta was the victim of a different man, but the same diseased system. Gia can be liberated, but not by safe increments.

*A mali estremi, estremi rimedi.*

Extreme sickness calls for an extreme remedy.

"Violetta." Santino pulls at me, but I appear to have stopped moving in this red hell. "Let's go."

Another command. I'm tired of commands. I am not a dog.

I pull my arm away. Behind Santino, Armando gets into the Alfa Romeo and drives down the block and out of sight. It'll be the devil and me alone in the Mercedes. Him driving. I'm just a passenger again.

"Violetta." Another warning. He grasps me again, but gently. As if I'm a dangerous animal he's trying to lure into a cage with food.

"She thinks it's cute, Santino."

"She's young."

"She thinks she's living in a TV show."

"Come on," he says, still trying to pull me, but I'm not moving. "She won't have to work. She'll always have what she needs. Won't have to worry about anything. Who doesn't like someone taking care of them?"

"Who doesn't *like*? Are you fucking kidding me right now? Have you always had that disgusting silver spoon in your mouth? Someone always around to wipe your ass so you cannot see how deeply,

deeply fucking flawed and awful this is? No? No, you had nothing? No, you were powerless? No, you busted a hundred asses to get what you have and now you're going to fuck over your own cousin to keep it? *Eh?*"

He says nothing to my tantrum. He says nothing because the neighbors sticking their noses through their beaded curtains can hear. He says nothing about the cruel injustices that nearly crippled me and now threaten someone he cares about. He says nothing.

So I say nothing.

Through the rage-induced hazy tint of crimson, I spot the little plaster shrine to the Virgin Mary and the vase of roses.

*Put the debt money into escrow, then send flowers...*
*And not just one dozen, but...*
*He'll give them to the Virgin...*

The traditions are so thick they stick to your ribs, but Mary passively holds out her hands.

*Can you do something about...*

Before my brain catches up, my body catches Santino in a split moment of inattention, and I wrest myself away, take the vase of roses, and throw them over the gate. The vase smashes on the sidewalk with a *pop*. Water streaks the concrete like a drawing of a comet.

"Santi," a man's voice comes from the stoop in a whisper. It's the daughter-seller.

"Go inside, Marco. You too, Angelo. I have this."

Santino has nothing, because I rush past him and through the gate to step on the flowers, squashing the hard buds underfoot and scattering the petals. None should remain to prove Marco ever left them for the virgin.

"Violetta." Santino's voice is now firm and calm and deep. It ripples down my spine, settles into the rage in my belly, and I wake up from a dream.

We're both on the street, white petals sprayed around like targeted snowfall.

"It's okay," he says softly, one hand out to me.

I don't care if he's angry. I don't care if he threatens me or commands me to stop. I'm ready for that. I'm primed to fight him every step of the way. But there's no way to combat this gentle, compassionate thing he's doing. He's pulling open the valve and deflating the very thing that's keeping me upright.

And suddenly, I don't have the strength to do it anymore. I throw myself against him and let his arms tighten around me. I won't be stopped. I can't be stopped. I must nullify this union and I must save my friend and cousin, and I must undo the traditions and I must, I must, I must…

"We can't let this happen." I choke on the words, unable to stop sobbing.

I collapse and Santino holds me up, trying to get me to walk. Slowly, I follow while he tells me it's going to be all right, it's going to be fine, and I don't resist. I hear his words in their spirit. He's not promising me anything past the next few minutes, which I'll get through and live to fight another day.

Before I know it, I'm in the Mercedes I drove here in, except now I'm a passenger again.

Santino starts the car, pauses, and leans into me, but not for a kiss. To look out my window. I follow his gaze. A car is double-parked in front of the house. Damiano's on the sidewalk, his arms out and his palms up, wider than the Virgin's. He's saying *what the fuck?* Marco runs down the stoop to explain or apologize.

I need to see if this is just a messy sidewalk or an insult Damiano cannot forgive, but the car jerks under me, and we take off down the block.

---

SANTINO PULLS UP to the front door and puts the car into park.

"What did I do?" I ask numbly.

"Maybe nothing." He shrugs, dismissing the seriousness of it all. "Maybe a war."

That snaps me out of it. "Over what? Gia? She's just a girl."

"She's my cousin."

"Now you realize this?"

"I don't want to tell you ugly things. I want to protect you. But you're hurting yourself, and this, I cannot stand." He shuts the engine but doesn't get out. Instead, he seems to settle deeper into his seat. "Do you remember when we were on the other side? And I broke the little *stronzo*'s hand that touched you?"

By the orange stand, a guy on a moped had grabbed my ass. Santino brought him down like a cat pulling a bird from the sky.

"I do."

"What else do you remember?" he asks.

I'm pretty sure he's not asking me to enumerate all

the ways I was turned on. "You smashed his hand under your heel. Then you let him go."

He nods to me to continue, so I rummage through the loose emotional trash I've accumulated in the last half an hour to find the scene in the smell of fruit and engine exhaust, the light of the Mediterranean, and the sound of a moped gunning away.

"There was a guy you gave money. For holding him down. And you said some blah blah blah—when you speak Italian that fast, I lose stuff. Something about a job. And a guy everyone knows."

He nods, satisfied. "Cosimo Orolio."

"Right!" I snap my fingers when the name rings a bell.

"I committed an act of vengeance on his territory. This is a crime."

"You're not in trouble for that, are you?"

"No." He *tsks*. "I would have been if I hadn't sent word back with a tribute. The man I gave the money to? He understood that."

"How do you know he delivered it?"

"We left Napoli with our lives."

At first, I can't tell why he's smiling, then I realize I have a questioning, shocked expression.

"I'm Re Santino," he says. "Right? You think that means I have all the power in the world. All I have to do is say the word and whatever I want, it happens like that." He snaps his fingers and shakes his head. "But my territory doesn't go beyond Secondo Vasto. It's a tiny speck, surrounded by a land with people who don't obey me. They don't respect my authority. And why should they? I give these people—our people—a way of life. What good do I bring those outside this town? They don't believe I can give them the way of life they want, so I have no power over them."

"And if you can't give the people here their traditions, they'll take your power?"

"Yes."

"Is that why you won't stop these debt marriages?"

"Let me ask you." He turns in his seat to face me as much as is possible. "If I do that, what do you think will happen when a man like, say Angelo, gets in over his head?"

"Don't try to convince me you're a man of the people."

"If I do not allow fathers to pay debts with daughters, someone will see a weakness. They'll come here and take this territory by force. That man? It's Damiano's father. Cosimo Orolio. I do not have enough men…" He throws up his hand. "There are not enough men in all of Secondo Vasto to fight him."

I cross my arms and face forward. "I don't want to hear about blood in the streets. These are excuses to do nothing."

"This town is between the mountains and a river. Cut off that bridge, and in a day, there will be no one left here but women and children."

"This is America."

My protest is whispered to no one, because that's who cares about the United States and its laws around here. If they did, I wouldn't have been forced to marry Santino. Gia would be going on a harmless date. Rosetta wouldn't have been sent to Italy to marry the man she was promised to because she was pregnant with her rapist's baby. If Santino says this Cosimo guy can cut us off and take over, then he's probably right.

"Damiano wants his father to respect him," Santino says. "He thinks if he can get close to me, he'll be able to take something from me."

"What is that?"

"And if I don't allow the marriage," Santino continues without answering me, "Damiano will tell everyone in the four corners of the earth who has this thing. Then a war with Cosimo Orolio will look like a game of cards."

"What do you have?" I demand.

"I have nothing." He holds out his empty palms. "You have it."

## 14

## SANTINO

There's no going back now. Once I tell her that she's the target, the value, and the center of the universe, I can't leave her in ignorance.

"What do I have?" she asks. "And it better not be a dumb metaphor for your love or a sweet pussy or something."

I laugh, because that was my one way out before I spilled everything I've been trying to keep in my control. "We should go inside."

"No." She crosses her arms. "It's been a terrible night, and now things are happening with Gia—like, I want to go back right now and make sure she's not getting sold—and you're saying this is happening to her in the first place because of something with me. And inside the house is one step farther from her. So I'm staying in this car. If you tell me something that means I need to get to her, either you're driving me or I'm going to murder you and push your dead body onto the driveway."

"Are you serious?"

"Of course I'm not serious, but I expect you to take me seriously."

I nod and settle in. Over the front door, the motion sensor lights flick off, and when we're in complete darkness, I tell her everything about how Emilio promised her sister to me in the hospital. Then I tell her about the first and only time I was in the presence of her inheritance.

---

I WAS BORN decades after the *partisanos* hanged the fascist *Il Duce* upside down in Milano, but Italy had still not been restored. Churches and museums had been looted and burned. World War Two shredded Italy of its history and culture. Artifacts were stolen, missing, never to be recovered, and smaller, regional wars went on and on.

There were few prospects on the other side. A boy could be a merchant, a scholar, or a soldier. If he chose soldier, he chose to fight for Italy or the *camorra.*

Like the father I never met, I was born a soldier. He fought for Italy, so when I was fourteen, I vowed to fight with the Cavallos. But like my father, I took up arms in the middle of a war I didn't understand. All I knew was that it started soon after Altieri Cavallo gave his daughter, Camilla, to Emilio Moretti. Half of Naples seemed to be at the wedding. Damiano and I were sneaking amaretto behind the Venetian table, and the world was woozy.

Soon after that, maybe a week, I was woken by

gunshots. A scream. Sirens. A symphony that played a few times a week and seemed a universe away until Dami and I started running packages for Emilio. I had to stand and wait as a man was beaten into chopped meat. I was threatened with a serrated knife. I saw a man's throat cut under the chin so Damiano's dad, Cosimo, could pull his tongue from the slash. I heard the man choke to death. I felt the floor bump when he writhed. Cosimo looked at his watch and asked me what the fuck I was looking at.

Then Altieri Cavallo was tortured and killed, and our boss became *the* boss.

"Did you hear what Nazario said?" Damiano whispered, dropping a bag of plastic bottles into the trash.

"I'm not here to listen."

We were barely old enough to have hair under our arms, but we'd been trucked out to the warehouse in Vicaria the same as everyone else who worked for the Cavallos. Forty hours later, I was tired from running food and water to the guys pulling crates off the shelves and tearing them open. I didn't know who owned the warehouse or what they were looking for. All I knew was that it was buried pretty deep in tons and tons of boxed-up shit, and I wasn't there to listen to gossip.

Emilio should have been out fighting Cosimo to be capo, but instead he'd brought us all to the warehouse of the devil.

"He said it's the Iron Crown of Lombardy," Damiano said.

"Bullshit."

The crown Napoleon had put on his head to make

himself emperor was behind alarmed glass in a cathedral in the north. Everyone knew that. *La Corona Ferrea* was made of nails taken from the One True Cross and was the size of an armband. Sections had gone missing and the circle reset to be smaller soon after the death of Constantine.

"Altieri passed it to Emilio through Camilla—"

"It's up by Milano," I cut off my friend. "Unless the Northerners are lying, which is possible."

"No, *stupido*." He takes a handful of plastic bottles out of the ice bin and puts them in a sack slung over his shoulder. "The missing pieces of it. The ones with the Holy Nail."

That got my attention, because it was both plausible and sacrilegious.

"Get the flies out of your mouth!" I said.

"Nazario said it. *Corona Ferrea*. He said it was so close he could smell it. And he had his hands out like this." Dami put his palms up and out. "He said it was warm, and when he walked away, I did this too and the air *was* warmer."

"Your hands are just cold from the water."

"Go." He bends his entire body to get the shoulder bag off then drops it over me. I almost fall under the weight of it. "Aisle 445. They're all there. Come on! You'll see."

I wanted to see, because it couldn't be true. Anyone who possessed a single piece of that crown would have more power than anyone could ever imagine. And Altieri had died. If he'd had the Iron Crown, he would have been protected.

But I had to see for myself.

So with the sack of water bottles banging on my hip, I followed Dami to Aisle 445, leaping over pallets, under forklifts, pushing past the bodies that had gravitated to that corner of the building and were standing still for the first time in two days. My friend was too big to quickly get through the tightly packed men, but I barely had to slow down on my way to the front, where a circle had formed around a wooden box. Emilio and Camilla were murmuring to each other. The lawyer, Nazario, held a crowbar.

The guy above me, an old-timer who kept making the sign of the cross like a fucking *nonna*, said to the young guy next to him, "They need to bring in a priest."

Younger muttered agreement.

I put out my hands.

The air was not warmer from that direction. It was more active. More alive. Hot like water running out of an electrical socket.

Emilio snatched the crowbar from Nazario. Next to me, the old-timer gasped. Camilla issued a few words I couldn't make out, but together with her sharp stare, they sounded like a warning.

Nodding to her, Emilio pried open the top of the box with a crack and flipped it off. The sides of the box collapsed as if held together by the lid, revealing a metal box covered in an ancient green-and-brown patina. When Emilio opened it, the creak was so loud, I thought the windows would shatter. The hinges stopped moving halfway.

Nazario stepped back while Emilio put his shoulder into it, and though I realized I was holding my breath, I didn't exhale. Not when the top flipped open. Not when Emilio smiled and clapped his hands before clenching them into fists. Not when he reached inside.

Only when he held up his hands, cradling just a glint of metal, did I breathe, because my legs bent under me as if knocked out by an unseen force. I kneeled, bowing my head like every other man in the vast warehouse.

When I dared to glance up, even Emilio was on his knees with his hands raised and fingers obscuring the artifact. Only Camilla was already standing.

---

"That's it?" Violetta asks, many years later and many miles away.

"What do you mean, 'that's it'? That's everything. *Tutto*. It's the lost pieces of the Iron Crown of Lombardy."

"And you all kneeling proves what?"

How can she not understand? I've painted a perfect picture.

"I felt it. I had to kneel in its presence. I had no choice. None of us did." My voice gets thin with a sort of desperation I don't recognize. I have to make her understand. "Nails from the One True Cross are melted in it. The Holy Blood."

"You were exhausted and dehydrated. You were open to suggestion. That's Psych 101."

I'm the older of us. The more experienced. I am a man of the world, willing to teach her the things she needs to know to survive, but she's looking at me as if

I'm some kind of *cretino* who has never opened a book in his life.

I've opened a few. Very few, and not since I was thirteen and my literature teacher took me aside to give me extra assignments in epic poems that I resented, but did anyway. Nothing I can quote from *The Iliad* will prove my point to Violetta though. The *Inferno* had something about powerful things inspiring fear, but I'm flailing in a soup of quotes I can't put together, feeling stupider and more confused with every second I don't respond.

"These men?" I finally say in frustration. "Dozens of us in that one room? Saints. Soldiers. Men and boys. We do not drop to our knees like whores like that—all at once—unless compelled by God."

"Have you ever heard of mass hysteria?" She's trying to be kind with her tone, but that makes it worse.

That night in the warehouse wasn't *isteria collettiva*. There was no madness. No violence. We knelt in peace before the glory of heaven.

Unless I don't know what the term really means, which I can't say or she'll know I'm an idiot. She'll never believe what I know is true.

"It was the crown," I insist. "I was there."

She taps her thumbs together, gazing at my hand. The crown ring. My own inheritance from her father.

"That's why you protected Rosetta?" she asks. "And why you married me?"

"It's why your father put you and your sister under my protection. Someone strong needs to handle the crown."

"Fuck." She faces front and looks out the window. "I can't believe this crap."

"Believe in it."

"All this trouble, for a thing in an old box that you didn't really see?"

"It's the lost pieces of *Corona Ferrea*. The Iron Crown of Lombardy. Napoleon put it on his head to declare himself emperor, but even then, the pieces were missing."

"He was an asshole. And short."

"And he ruled all of Europe!"

"He died young!"

"It is made with nails from Christ's Cross." I repeat the facts as if using different words will get the seriousness through to her. "How can it not be powerful enough to bend our knees?"

"This is ridiculous." She shakes her head and stares into the darkness, unable or unwilling to define what part of this is ridiculous. Then she gives up and looks at me. "You're saying my father stole it."

"Found what Altieri lost, then he ruled with it."

"It didn't keep him from getting assassinated."

"Killing him took a few tries, but no, it does not cure death."

"Maybe it caused him to die. Ever think of that? Maybe it gives you power, then kills you?"

Does she believe?

"If that were the case, he wouldn't have passed it to you and your sister."

"No," she scoffs. "He passed it to *you*. Rosetta and I were just a delivery method. And it doesn't matter. The talisman of power and death is an idea in books. *Fantasy* books I stopped reading when I was thirteen."

She pulls the door handle. It's locked.

"Let me go." Her voice is drained of emotion. She's making a statement, not a command or request.

I unlock it, and she's out.

## 15

## VIOLETTA

The story exhausts me. Hearing it and believing the parts of it grounded in reality, newly aware that it's affected every part of my life. Not because of its supernatural powers, but because so many people made choices about my life because *they* believed.

Now the pain of having my choices stripped from me is that much sharper. That much more exquisite for knowing the forces behind it. The anesthesia's worn off. Now I get to feel it all, and unless I get my period in the next couple of days, I'll be bringing a baby into it, and she'll inherit more than a culture of servitude.

Out of the car, I make my way to the front door, but Santino grabs me and presses me against the rough stucco of the house, between two trellises tangled with rose vines.

"I won't let anything happen to you," he says.

"Jesus Christ on the One True fucking Cross. How can you miss the entire point?" I push him away, lose my footing, and grab onto a trellis of thorns. "Fuck!"

I'm bleeding, but as much as I've wanted to see blood in the last few days, it's just my hand. Not deep enough. I want to bleed myself clean from the inside.

Santino takes my palm and puts his handkerchief in it before closing my fingers into a fist. I hiss from the pain and his tenderness. They're both unwelcome.

"Calm down," he says.

"No."

"Yes."

I don't have to dare him. His mouth presses firmly against mine, prying it open. I want to bite him, but he's too strong and I'm too weak.

The world goes quiet for just a second. Eventually, I'll hate myself for yielding, but not yet. The mental voice screaming for me to stop and grab Gia, run for the border grows silent the more Santino reins in his kisses from firm to soft, from commanding to offering.

My knees are weak and I'm so close to being a boat adrift. He can't just kiss me and make this disappear. It won't fix things. It won't undo this obscenity of a life.

And yet, like a guy looking at a stolen artifact, I want to believe.

"This is how I make you calm down." He leans past me and punches a code into the door's keypad, then he pushes it open with his foot. He's calmed me with a kiss, and now he's going to bring a sweet, docile wife into his house.

"Fuck you."

"That mouth." His voice rumbles and breaks like a wave. "Why can't you just be quiet sometimes?"

"You can't make this go away by kissing me."

He smirks, then steps just outside the door, holding his hand toward the entrance to our home.

I am suddenly hyper aware of every sound in the front yard. The night birds singing in the trees. Fountain water trickling into the pond. The whisper of the breeze in the leaves. It all adds up to a song of outside. Not just outdoors, but my existence outside the boundaries that have been set for me without me even knowing. My potential won't fit inside his house. Inside, I'll be a step closer to the captivity of his kisses, and one step further from freedom.

He waits as if he understands the importance of what I'm considering.

My thorn-bitten palm throbs when I tighten it around his handkerchief.

This story about my father is cute. The crown, the promise, the danger. It's all a tidy dressing on a gaping wound. The missing pieces of an ancient crown are an excuse to take away what's rightfully mine—my self-determination—not a reason.

I'm still committed to rescuing Gia and every girl like her, but once I walk through that door, I have to find a way to do it with him, or not at all.

"I know you're still mad," he says. "You can fight me inside, or maybe you'd like another round with the rosebushes?" He glances at my bleeding hand, then the tangle of flowers and thorns. "You'll never change their mind though. They will always have thorns."

He's thinking of changing his mind? About what exactly? And is this a tease? Will he promise to help Gia, but never guarantee it?

Or does it simply mean there's a chance?

A wave of confidence surges through my bloodstream, and I go through the doorway, into our house.

It's us together or not at all.

---

IN THE HALF bath around the corner from the kitchen, Santino won't let the nursing student with first aid training take charge of her own lacerations, and only by pulling rank and using medical terms am I able to talk him out of using of an entire roll of gauze.

"It's fine," I say, holding up my hand, where a bandage covers the wound. "It's already stopped bleeding."

"I don't like it when you're hurt." He kisses the inside of my wrist and down the elbow. "In your hand or your heart."

His lips brush my bicep, then my collarbone as his hands trail down my waist, reaching under my skirt to move down my bare thighs.

"We need to talk then."

"We will."

Then he does something I never thought I'd ever see him do, and it's so erotic, my world goes from a monochrome that seemed normal my whole life, to an explosion of color and light.

He kneels before me.

I gasp at the sight of him looking up at me like a supplicant. He runs his hands up my thighs, and I'm not so foolish to misunderstand the context. He's not begging or setting himself beneath me. He's sliding off my underwear, and yet, just the sight of his vulnerability is breathtaking. His closed eyes as he kisses the insides of my legs, working upward with upper and lower lashes pressed together in a thick black line, mouth open, one hand putting a knee over his shoulder. His tongue darts out, and when I lose sight of it between my legs, I gain the sensation of it running along the ridge of my clit.

Bit by bit, he works me with his tongue, holding me against the wall as I lose the ability to keep myself upright. I try to focus, because I shouldn't be intimate with him until I'm sure he won't let Gia be sold off, but like a train riding off into a cartoon sunset, my reality slowly shrinks.

"Santino," I groan. "This is not talking."

"Yes, it is," he whispers before sucking on my nub so gently, then so forcefully I dig my fingers in his hair as my hips rise to slide toward his waiting mouth.

By now, Santino has a map of my body and gently flicks his tongue while his fingers stroke my tenderest flesh.

The voice that scolds me for giving him my body before getting an agreement to free Gia has quieted but not disappeared. Yet I cannot fathom, in a million years, ever telling this man to stop, because the sight of him, a man of granite and power, on his knees before me, kissing my pussy, sends waves of electricity straight from my brain to his tongue. I ride his face harder and he licks me from top to bottom in broad, clean strokes, then he bites a little, just enough to remind me who has the power here.

The lump in my throat unworks itself enough to let out a moan.

"You are delicious." He runs a finger against my slit and it's so perfect I could cry. "You like this? You want to come for me now?"

Even beneath me, he's in charge, easily taking control of my body with a question I can't answer in words. He slides his finger inside me so slowly, it feels as if it's petitioning for an invitation. My hips tip against him in response.

"You." I can barely manage the tiny word.

His finger finds the precious space deep within me and another finger quickly joins it as he massages me from the inside out and blows gently on my clit without touching it. If I wasn't all but tethered to him, I'd take off in flight.

"*Fammi sentire come godi,*" he asks to hear me come, then buries his face between my legs.

Heat pulses through my body and settles in my core with the utterance of his command.

Electricity rips over my skin and heat thumps through my veins. I can't see, can't breathe, can't feel anything but the sweet heaven between my legs. It's when my stoic man moans into me that I'm finally pushed to the edge. It builds to a roaring crescendo and hurls me into the horizon of pleasure. I cry his name from there, then I crumple over him, panting as if I've just been saved from drowning.

"*Brava, Forzetta.*" Santino rises and snaps a tissue from the box.

I collapse into him as the tides of euphoria roll back out to sea. After wiping his mouth, he delicately cleans my folds and lets my skirt fall back over my legs.

When he kisses me, I drink up my taste from his

lips and tongue. He kisses my forehead and rests his hand against my throat, his thumb stroking the soft divot between my collarbones.

There's so much I need from him, and the only thing I want is for this moment to never end.

"You're dirty," he says, taking both my hands. "Come. I will get you clean."

---

I LIE ALONE, flaccid-limbed and soaking. Steam clouds my eyes, and for the first time since the sun set, it's not coming from me. The bathroom's air is heavy and dense with vapor from water so hot, my skin is red and tingly. A mountain of bubbles rises in the center of the tub between my breasts and my knees. My wounded hand rests on the ledge to keep dry.

When my stomach grumbled, Santino left fully clothed, and now he returns in low-hanging drawstring bottoms and a bare chest, carrying a bowl of grapes.

"You didn't cook for me?" I joke, well aware he wasn't even going to boil water for tea.

"A husband does not do the cooking." He says it solemnly, with the hearty cynicism of unpleasant but unchangeable truth.

"Mario Batali is married."

"He does not cook for his wife." He sits on the edge of the tub with his bowl and twists a grape off the stem.

"How do you know?"

"Cooking is his job. I don't bring my work home." He holds up a grape and I open my mouth so he can feed it to me. "I do not mow my own grass. I do not clean my own pool. I do not cook my own food."

"Lucky for you I enjoy being in the kitchen," I tease. Santino is an attentive husband in ways that give him power and pleasure, so it's rare for him to cater to me on my terms. I know it's all a game, but playing means pretending it's real.

"I ordered your zia to train you to enjoy it from a young age."

"You did not." I roll my eyes at him. "*Stronzo.*"

He laughs, full and rich. Parts of my heart sell themselves to him, and he buys in bulk. I think back to that afternoon when I was twelve and captivated by him. What would I tell that girl if I could? "One day, he'll be yours, but only in title"? Or something more frightening? "He will take possession of you like a piece of real estate and you will hate him before you love him"?

That young Violetta in my head turns into a young Gia, and I freeze with guilt. If I avoid tough conversations because Santino drew me a bath and fed me grapes, I'll be complicit in whatever happens to her.

Someone—a visitor or a neighbor who didn't know any better—once said to Zia, "Kids are different when they're your own flesh and blood." She almost lost her mind over it. Rosetta and I were not hers, maybe, she said, but she would do anything and everything for us.

I believed her, and she was complicit too.

"Open," Santino says, grape between two fingers. His hair is mussed slightly, but he still looks impeccable.

It's okay to feel loved and cared for. I don't have to

be angry every second. I don't have to ignore my own life. I can have this.

It's almost like we're back in Amalfi, where everything was beautiful and felt *right*. Being his wife wasn't a curse, it was a joy. I haven't felt this way since before we were ambushed by Siena Orolio and her bad news. I close my eyes and convince myself it's okay to be happy for five seconds.

Swallowing, I close my eyes and hum a tune I remember from my childhood, then I feel the cool velvet of a grape skin on my lips and take the fruit. Santino picks up the tune, soft and low, wordlessly singing the quiet, classic melody in a series of vowels until the chorus when I belt it out with him, our voices booming off the white marble. He continues the verse, and I'm captivated. He has a voice—deep, rich, and soulful. Exactly how I imagined it would be.

When he's done, I open my eyes and can't help but clap. "That was beautiful."

"My aunt sang to me when she bathed me." Santino's smile fills his voice. "It was an old favorite. Her mother sang it to her and her mother before her sang to her and the one before her." He rolls his hand at the wrist, meaning *on and on*.

"A century of DiLustros singing?"

"And Morettis," he says. "We sang it with your father in the car whenever we were going someplace…" He pauses to choose his words. "Someplace bad."

"You knew my father better than I did," I say, and he looks a little guilty about it. "Tell me more."

"This ring?" He holds up the hand with the diamond

crown ring. "He left it to me when he died. He always said I was like a son he never had."

Looking down over me, Santino's expression is pure yearning for something he fears he'll never have, because he's powerless to grab it for himself.

"I'm not ready for children." It's one of the most honest things I've said to him, even when it papers over the secret truth that ready or not, a child may be coming.

"Are you unhappy, my violet?" He snaps off another grape. "Should I feed you?"

I open my mouth for it, chew. He thinks feeding me will make me happy, or maybe he thinks it'll shut me up. There's no discontent in silence.

I want this man to love me. Despite everything, I want this relationship to mean something. I want it to be the thing that drives him to be a better man, and me to be a stronger woman, but it's clear we are very different people and view the world through vastly different lenses. He protects a status quo where everyone smiles because their lives depend on it.

That is not the happiness I want, and I can't help but think that if he could see the desperation and fear of the people living with the traditions he so cherishes, he'd destroy what he's worked so hard to protect.

"What you told me," I say after I swallow. "It doesn't change anything. Gia's still going to be sold, and she doesn't even know it."

"What if she's happy?"

"With Damiano? The guy trying to get close to you so he can steal an antique?"

Santino pushes the bowl aside and bends at the

waist, hands folded in front of him. "Gia wants to be married. But even more, she wants to be American. Damiano will stay here. Their marriage gives her what she wants twice over."

This level of cold calculation never left Gia's lips. This is one hundred percent Santino.

"He can try to," Santino says. "But he'll never get what he wants out of it."

"He'll never love her either."

"You can see into his heart like a surgeon?"

"I can see into yours. You want to feel good about the way things are."

"Maybe." Santino's voice warms up and drops an octave lower. He looks away from me. The admission hurts him. "If you'd known I was coming for you, what would you have done?"

I lean back, letting the water slosh around me.

What would I have done if Zia and Zio had told me? I would have been incredulous, but I would have had no choice but to believe it. If I'd been informed at an early enough age, I might have gotten used to the idea. But they couldn't have told me until after Rosetta died. By that time, the news would have been shocking.

"I would have run away," I say.

"You would have been found. By me or someone else. I tried to convince your zio to be brutally honest with you, but their choice was the right one. Telling you would have made it all worse for you."

"I'm starting to think they're all cowards."

"They love you, Violetta," Santino rumbles. "And there are times love has to lie to survive."

With the bath bubbles flattened and the water

cooled, I'm falling into the trap of thinking of myself as a commodity to be bought, sold, and traded, not a full human making my own choices.

"You had all the information you needed," I sulk.

"Knowing everything didn't give me any choice."

"Wait." I straighten, launching myself into a crouch as if I'm ready to pounce on the moment. "You're talking about it as if you're the one who was sold into a situation you wouldn't have wanted. Right? Doesn't it feel shitty?"

"This is how things have always been, and how they will always be. It is our way."

"But it can be different." I cling to his hand, relieved to know that for one minute, he can imagine what it's like to have your life stolen. I can use that knowledge. "It has to be different. *I'm* different!"

"You are different, *Forzetta*," Santino says softly, touching the parts of my face as if memorizing them. "You are different because you are special. You are different because I want you. You are different because I love you."

He loves me.

It's crazy, because of the way we started and who he is. But it's also completely sane, because the way we started is the only way I could have broken down who I wanted to be and found out who I really am.

I collapse into his embrace, because he's broken the dam, and I know I love him too.

Santino helps me out of the tub and dries me off. He leads me to the bedroom in a flurry of kisses and caresses.

I let him lay me down. I let him kiss me. I let his

hands cover my body. I let him roll me on top of him and his waiting cock, and I straddle him, on top, in control. And I know, right then, that either I will follow him to the ends of the earth, or I will pull him to the limits of his world... but wherever we go, we go together.

# 16

## VIOLETTA

My body is sore where Santino used it, and in the half-sleep of morning, I'm aware of the pleasures of every ache. Yet my dream is focused on my hand. Though the stuck stiffness of the bandage is there, it's Santino—standing in front of me, in a light blue jacket and white shirt with his palms up and elbows bent slightly—who's bleeding from both palms.

*Apply pressure.*
*Remove rings and bracelets that may compress nerves.*
*Clean.*
*Disinfect.*
*Ice.*
*Elevate.*

My feet are stuck. I can't reach him. I tell him to come to me, but he looks back at me in distress, bleeding as if there are arteries in his hands. I'm frustrated, but the dream reveals that his feet are stuck in a mound of dried plaster. Then that he's trapped inside a connected plaster grotto surrounded with pots of red roses, and then, I am as well.

Church bells ring. His olive skin goes pale as paint. I reach for him, but he's too far for the length of my arms, and his are frozen in place.

"Mrs. DiLustro?" he says, and in my dream, it's Italian for *do not come*.

If I'd stayed in school, kept on my path to nursing, I'd live in a smaller house with fewer nice things, but I'd know what to do. My clothes would have no value, but my knowledge would be priceless, and I could stop the flow of this river of blood.

The church bells in my dream are the only thing left as I wake, turning into the doorbell chiming over and over, with a pang of regret—not because Santino's not in bed with me, but because by obeying him, I'm unable to save him.

"Mrs. DiLustro?" Armando's voice comes from the other side of the door, followed by a light rap I can barely hear over the frantic doorbell dings.

Sun cuts through the windows, turning the view behind my eyelids bright orange.

"Yes?" I say, hoping he's here to ask a yes or no question. I want to go back to my dream and take control of the situation, get out of my plaster grotto and save Santino.

"Gia's here."

My bloodstream floods with cortisol and I bolt upright, remembering what I'd promised myself I'd do and who I'd do it for.

The bell keeps ringing.

"Did you let her in?" I hop off the bed, now really

annoyed by the chiming. She must be trying to wear out the button. With all the security, I've never heard anyone actually ring it.

"Yes, but she won't come inside until you're down, and just to say… she is upset."

"Tell her I'll be right down." I slap open a dresser drawer.

"Thank you."

I jam my legs through a pair of sweatpants, throw on a tank, then a hoodie over it, and run downstairs without even peeing.

Framed by the open front door, Gia pokes the doorbell repeatedly. Her cheeks are striped with mascara and her lips are wet and puffy, lines of spit connecting them.

"I'm here!" I shout and run to her with bare feet and open arms.

She stops jabbing the button and lets me hold her in the space between inside and outside for a few seconds before I drag her in. Armando closes the door. I mouth the word "coffee" and he nods, heading for the kitchen. To my new cousin, I whisper comforts and avoid asking what happened until she can breathe, then I take her hands.

"What happened, Gia? What can I do?"

She opens her mouth to speak, but her face betrays her. Her mouth twists and sadness just pours out of her like a broken dam. I have never seen someone so red with distress.

I reach to hold her, but she slaps me. The sting on my cheek is nothing compared to the burn of her rejection.

"Gia?" I ask, my hand to my face.

"Whu-whu-why did you do it?" Gia huffs. "Papa is so mad at-at me and I... I... I... why?" The words catch between her tears and vanish. "Why did you ruin everything?"

She rushes into me and I'm too naïve to flinch in fear of another slap. Even with my skin burning where she hit me, I'm operating as the Violetta of ten seconds ago, so when she collapses into me, I hold her.

"We'll figure it out." I put my arm around her shoulder, stroking her hair. "Don't worry. It'll all be fine."

Gia presses her forehead against my neck and sobs as I lead her inside, passing the couches and walking her to the kitchen—where comfort resides. Celia's setting up coffee and a cookie tray. I nod to her. She nods back silently as I sit Gia down on one of the kitchen chairs.

"Now." I take a seat, turning toward her so I can smooth the hair around her forehead.

It's nice to feel needed. I haven't had a friend in a long time or felt useful in even longer. I hand her a paper napkin from the dispenser and she squishes it up and pushes the ball into her eyes one at a time.

I'm ready to wage war against her father, Damiano, Tavie, and even Santino if I have to. I don't know what caused this beautiful girl to break like this, but I will end them.

"Oh, no, look at your face," Gia says when she finally gets a look at me. "I'm so sorry."

"It's okay."

"But I'm still mad." Her face scrunches up to stop

the next onslaught of tears. "Papa is too. So mad he says he's sending me back."

Celia slides the cookies and two cappuccinos onto the table. I thank her with a glance, and she leaves.

"Here." I lift the plate. "Biscotti makes everything better."

"I don't think I can eat." Gia looks pained to even say it. "I-I'm so sorry, I just... why did you break the flowers? I don't understand it."

If I tell her, it'll all be over. I won't be putting the lube back in the tube.

"Why is your father so mad?" I ask.

"An insult. He said it's an insult and he can't show his face."

"Is it though?" I say. Gia looks confused. "They're just flowers. You were ready for the date. Damiano showed up. All anyone had to do was lie about them falling or, you know, make a joke about how you wanted to see how far you could throw them, then you could drive over to Aldo's."

Her puzzlement turns inward, as though she's playing over last night's scene in her head and can't figure it out. "Dami said, 'You backing out?' and I thought he was talking to me, but my father answered him and said, 'no, no, no,' like *he* was the one who had to reassure him. It was weird."

"Yeah."

"Then Damiano left really mad, and I ran out to the street to get him, but Tavie caught me at the gate. He said I was acting like a whore." Retelling her brother's insult makes her chin quiver. "But I just wanted to tell him it wasn't me who broke it." A fresh teardrop falls, then another. "Then they said it was you, but they won't say why. Were you just mad at Santi?"

"Well, yes… but—"

"Can you tell everyone?"

"Listen, Gia, those flowers…" Am I doing this? I should talk to Santino before I do. "They weren't just flowers."

She's hungry for answers, and there are plenty I could give her, but there's only one truth.

"They were a message from Damiano." I'm doing this. The train has left the station. "To your father."

"What?"

"That he closed his end of the deal."

"What deal?"

She's a product of this culture. I won't have to explain that much. I want to look away, but that wouldn't be fair.

"You. You are the deal."

The vulnerability of her face melts on contact with the truth. "I don't understand." False. She's lying to herself. Stalling acceptance. "Papa said his debts were paid. That's how they had the money to come here."

"Damiano Orolio is paying them."

If I'd been told this before it happened, and if I'd believed it the way she has to, I would have turned the house upside down. Thrown any object that wouldn't break against every object that would. But Gia's not me. She's no stranger to the idea of having her body being used to pay for a man's foolishness.

"I threw the flowers," I say. "I was upset."

"Because it happened to you."

"Yes."

She nods, looking at her hands in her lap.

"I thought he liked me," she whispers, as if that's the most important aspect of this entire mess.

"I bet he does." I thumb a tear from her cheek. "Does your family know where you are?"

She shakes her head, looking through the glass doors to the backyard with her mouth tight in an expression of impending trouble.

"You don't have to call them," I say. "I can tell them you're here."

"Don't. They'll ask you questions, then come here to get me and… I can't right now."

"Then Santino will tell them."

Her face lights up. "Can he? They won't come if he says it."

"Absolutely." The word isn't out of my mouth before I'm already texting him.

—*Can you tell Angelo/Marco/Paola that Gia's at the house with me and she's fine*—

—**Why is she there?**—

He won't let me ask questions, but when I make the slightest request, he gets suspicious. I could tell him she just showed up and I had nothing to do with it, but he's going to call Armando anyway. Let the man earn his salary.

"Done." I put down my phone.

"Thank you." She takes an oval cookie crusted with almond shavings.

"If you give me the keys"—I hold out my hand—"I'll have Armando pull your car out of the driveway."

She shakes her head and dismisses the idea with a flick of her wrist. "I always park on Foothill. There's a secret spot." She dunks the cookie in the coffee, bites, sips, smiles. "It's good." Her eyes dart around the immaculate kitchen. "I can't believe you have a whole person just to cook and make coffee."

"Celia and I work together."

"Only for you and Santino."

Of course, having such a person is a ridiculous indulgence. Since I'm not at school, I could do what she's paid to do. Celia would have nowhere to go, but explaining the situation would just be defensive and betray Celia's confidence.

"Yes." I drink my coffee. "Just for the two of us. I guess more, if we had a party or something." I shrug. "I don't know who I'd invite. All my friends… they wouldn't get it, and I don't think the family actually likes me."

"What?" Gia gently rubs her eyes with the pads of two fingers. They're dry now, but still swollen. "But you're so… *you*."

I'm two people actually. One is a student at the nursing college across the river, and the other was small and silent until Santino dragged her out of the darkness.

"Oh, God, I'm rubbing my eyes. They're going to get even more puffy."

"I have a cucumber I can slice up." I try to sound casual. No pressure. But I'm desperate for her to stay. "That'll help with the swelling."

I quickly chop a cucumber into cool, wet coins and place them on a plate.

"You're so thoughtful, Violetta."

"No, I'm so selfish. I'm so sorry I wrecked your flowers and your date."

"You were upset I didn't know. And now I do."

She's half right, but I don't correct the other half.

Gia and I walk upstairs and down the hall, arm in arm. She pauses outside of my old room and touches the doorjamb. "Do you remember your first nights here?"

"I do."

"You were pretty upset."

I have several choices to make here. I'm not sure which one is the least painful for this young beauty illuminated by sunlight, red-cheeked from grief, and I decide that though the whole truth would be cruel, a lie would be worse.

"It was scary." I go into the room first and put the plate of cucumber slices on the night table. "I hadn't been away from home before. Not even to stay in the dorms at school."

Focusing on my boring history of sleeping arrangements is the most innocuous angle I can think of.

"I've been away from home for a long time." The way Gia says it—the coldness that settles over her—worries me. Before I can lead her on and change the subject, she sits on the bed facing the windows that overlook the pool. The sunlight on the water glints up at us.

"Here." I pat the bed. "Lie down."

She does and closes her eyes, folding her hands

across her chest. Her next words come out as a whisper. "I won't be scared."

*You should be, Gia. You should be terrified.*

"Of what?" I feign ignorance and put the cucumber slices over her eyes.

"Our first night. Because Dami's nice, Violetta. He really is. And he has a house halfway up the hill with a view. And a Cadillac. And he said his businesses are doing really well, but he didn't want to brag. And somehow it's all ruined." She sucks her lips between her teeth. "I don't know what happens to me now."

Downstairs, the security sensor on the front door beeps, then keys clack on the front table.

The man of the house is home early.

"We'll figure it out." I throw a blanket over her. "Just rest here for now and we'll talk in an hour."

Santino's footsteps cross the living room, probably on his way to the kitchen to look for me.

"Thank you," she whispers.

"My pleasure."

Quiet as a secret, I tiptoe from the room and close the door. On my way downstairs, Santino's deep voice crawls in from the backyard. He's on a phone call, pacing the circumference of the pool.

I open the sliding glass door just enough to slip out, then gently close it. Santino stands on the other side of the pool, legs apart, large and imposing, a statue under the high point of the sun. He looks like an angel. An angel of death, perhaps, but an angel nonetheless. He's speaking in rapid Italian, the kind my inexpert ears can only pick up every few words of—like *debt* and *escrow* and *flowers*, and names like Damiano and Marco are especially clear.

But his gaze tells me more than words in any language.

He's not happy with me.

"*Si. Ciao.*" Santino drops his phone in his jacket pocket, looking at me across the water.

"You're home early," I say.

"Where's Gia?" He crosses his arms.

"In my room."

He looks up at the windows I've often stood behind to watch him swim.

"She's taking a nap," I add. "She's very upset."

"Of course she is. You smashed her flowers."

"So?"

"You fucked up her life."

"Fucked—what? No, no, no." I stomp around the pool to his side, ready to throw him in if I have to. "Totally unfair. I'm trying to save her and you know it."

"My sweet little American wife, these symbols have meaning. And actions have repercussions."

"So the deal is off?"

He sighs the way you might before explaining the function of the circulatory system to someone who should already know how a heart works, then he gets behind a patio chair, shifting it into the shade. "Sit."

I sit, and he moves a matching seat across from me. Pauses, leans forward with his fingertips tapping between his knees. I feel like a student about to be reprimanded by a very hot teacher.

"Marco lives inside Cosimo Orolio's territory," he says. "Dami is in mine. They received a blessing from both of us. This is not just some kind of permission. It's a promise of protection."

"I thought Damiano and his father weren't speaking." I'm proud of this nugget of knowledge.

"We're all speaking when it's business."

"Of course. Gia's life is just business."

"You broke the flowers, and you are mine. So I broke them. I cut off the deal, and now I have to stop Damiano from going back to his father and inciting a war over it."

"A war? Over this?" That doesn't make any sense. A single arranged marriage shouldn't be the difference between peace and war. "Does this have anything to do with what you told me last night? About the crown?"

"It has everything to do with it."

At this point, I could say none of this is my fault because I didn't know then what I know now. If he'd been more forthright, maybe I would have behaved differently. Maybe. But what's the difference?

"What's going to happen to Gia?" I ask.

"That's up to her father." He shrugs and leans back. "The man raised me. I know his way. He'll punish whoever has the least power."

"How?" I whisper, as if the most powerless person—who's in my bed with cucumbers over her eyes—might hear me.

"By sending her home, where he'll find someone else."

"Has he considered not gambling?"

Santino ignores me, because to him and every other man in this town, Marco isn't the problem as long as Gia's the solution.

"She'll get used to being home again," he says. "Don't expect her to come back."

He lets those words fall heavy into my lap.

*Shit. Shit-shit-shit.*

"This is the way it is," he continues. "You cannot change it. Even if I let you. You *cannot*."

I caused this. I destroyed those flowers because I was pissed off, because I was trying to change a system that nearly ruined me, and in the process, I may have ruined Gia.

"I wasn't… I didn't know! I thought I was helping."

"I need you to promise me something," he says with a cartoonishly fake layer of patience.

"What?" I won't agree to anything until I've thought about it, but I need to shut up to hear.

"You need to stop trying to fix the world."

"I can't—"

"And." He holds up his hand to stop me, so I clap my mouth shut until he finishes, because once he does, he's getting a piece of my mind. "And I'm going to trust you. I'm going to trust your nose is out of everyone's business, and you're going to leave things alone and prove to me you won't make another mess like this."

My arms are crossed so tightly, my forearms hurt. My jaw aches from clenching it shut. I have a twitch in my left eye that squeezes the sunlit corner of my vision, making Santino's face go from dark to light and back again in a rhythm.

I start to answer, but he presses his fingers to my lips. "Don't. Don't tell me my trust will be betrayed, because it won't be. You will do the right thing. You. Will."

As soon as he removes them, he stands, and I look up at features obscured in shadow, blocking the light of the sun.

"What about the war?" I ask.

"If I can't stop it, I know how to fight it. But it'll happen fast."

"How fast?"

"It may have started already, so…" He takes me by the chin. "I'm going to trust you." He drops his hand. "Don't surprise me."

He walks away, touching my shoulder as he goes, trusting me so much he doesn't even look over his shoulder to make sure I won't stab him in the back.

## 17

## SANTINO

My wife's temper tantrum in my uncle's front yard may get her exactly what she wants—an end to Damiano's *'mbasciata* with Marco.

Gia will be sent home and Violetta will miss her. Gia will live. My wife might not be so lucky.

I've been playing a game of chicken with death my entire life. Staring it down in the face, telling it to play by my rules. It's a game people lose by having something to tether them to life. No one rested in the rooms of my heart, so I feared nothing and no one.

Violetta turned the tables, and even still... I love her more than I fear her.

*Santino DiLustro, you are a fucking sucker. A babbeo. You've sold your heart to this woman.*

I was destined to spend my days looking Death in the face, and I was always destined to love Violetta.

When weighed against love, death is light as a feather.

The Mercedes slides to a slow, comfortable stop

outside the nightclub. Gennaro's been here for a couple of hours already, making sure it's safe. He opens my door and damp night air floods in.

"Santino," he says. "All good."

"*Grazie.*" I give him the keys to park it.

A line of kids my wife's age line up against the wall, faces changing color with the flashing neon sign above. *!!Laser-Topia!!* To prove the point, lines of laser lights dance around it. I find the crowds, the noise, and the lights vulgar, but the kids love it, it's safe, and it's more neutral than *Mille Luci*.

I fix my cuffs, nod to the bouncer who removes the velvet rope, and walk inside with nothing more than a raised hand of recognition from the woman behind the plexiglass and another security guard.

It's not like the nightclub in Vasto where Emilio's crew did his business after dark. *Éternité* was an old-world oasis in the middle of a city that seemed to be forgetting the past. Big bands, slicked-back hair, three-piece suits. Our way of life was preserved there. The tourists who found it thought it was quaint, and we let them believe it, because it gave us a cover for a business that was not quaint at all.

"Santino." A familiar voice comes from behind me as I'm about to enter the loudest part of the club. The woman it came from wears a dress that could be red or white—it's hard to tell with the color of the lights—with a crossover at the neck that hides what it's legally required to hide and no more.

"Loretta." I kiss her cheek, and she doesn't encourage me to linger like she used to or look at me with an unspoken offer on her face. There was a time

I would have pushed her through the first door I could find and fucked her like an animal behind it, but no more. I never had to tell her that was over when I married Violetta, and she never had to confirm.

"Tommy's waiting for you." She's the manager here. I got her the job as a way to keep her occupied when I wasn't fucking her, and it turned into a passion. A woman needs something to do before she marries and has children.

"Good." I wait for her to take me to him, but she doesn't.

Her brows knit. I know this expression. It's worry, but not the kind for the future consequences of today's hardship. No. This is immediate concern that something will happen on today's clock. "What's going on, Santi?"

She never got into my business and doesn't expect a detailed answer. Not from me. I can't speak for what Damiano tells her.

"*Cosa?*" I ask.

"Everyone's carrying."

"So?" There's nothing strange about that. The only thing strange is her worry that anyone's going to shoot up the place.

"Re Santino finally rolled his ass in here!" Tommy, the club's owner and Loretta's boss, interrupts in a white suit and black shirt. "They was going to start without you."

"No, they weren't." I smile and put a heavy hand on his shoulder. The man has irritated me for most of my adult life, but he knows where his bread is buttered, the customers love him, and he's terrified of me, so I haven't bought the club from under him.

"Loretta," Tommy says, "Mikey needs rolls of quarters. I'll take care of the *capo di capo* here."

She nods to him, then once to me, and I read her like the newspaper. She's telling me to be careful.

I will be.

Past the doors, the space stinks of sweat and alcohol. The air's cut with the promised lasers, and the music isn't more than a beat and a warble. At a back table, Damiano jabs a cigar between his teeth. A woman in a green dress leans over his shoulder and lights it. When she stands, I recognize her as his niece, Theresa Rubino, from Green Springs. The girl whose cunt stink was on Roman's tongue before I replaced it with the taste of blood.

She waves to me timidly and goes back to the bar with her friends.

"Sit, sit." Tommy indicates my chair. "You having the usual?"

"Sure."

Two men stand in the corners with their hands folded above their dicks. Gennaro is one, but the other… I don't know. Damiano's guy apparently.

He shouldn't need protection here. Not from me.

Damiano and I shake hands, and I sit.

"You going to introduce me to your friend."

"Oh, sure." He waves the man over, speaking Italian. "Lucio, this is Santino, the *capo* of this shithole town."

I shake the man's hand and hold him long enough to look him in the face.

"You're from the other side," I say in English.

He just smiles.

"I saw you peeking out of the closet when I was fucking your mother in the ass," I add.

Lucio keeps smiling, then glances at Damiano.

"You're a fucking dick," Damiano says to me. I let the man's hand go. "He's one of my dad's guys. On loan."

I have to reassess this entire situation. Cosimo sent a guy for his son, who he's barely on speaking terms with. For what? To protect him? To spy on him? Both?

Or to start planning the coming war?

"Sit down, would you?" Damiano says to me, then switches to Italian for Lucio. "Back it up."

The man moves back to his dark corner. As a young woman offers me a cigar, and I refuse, Damiano leans back and makes a show of checking out her ass, and with a shake of his hand, declares it gorgeous.

"How old are you?" I ask him.

"Old enough to tap that." He watches her leave as if he's some kind of ravenous animal. I don't know this cigar girl and I don't care, but who is this guy trying to marry my cousin?

"You'll have more respect for Gia."

"That your way of getting to the point?"

"I'm not interested in hanging around"—I indicate the club, the noise, the flashing lights—"this."

"You're such an old man." He rolls his cigar on the edge of the ashtray. "All right. So fine. Get to the point. The flowers."

Damiano leans back and crosses his arms, cigar between two fingers, with the face of a guy who's been wronged and insulted over and over. He reminds me of a shark. If you don't provoke a shark, they don't bite. But if you do, and the shark thinks they can get away with it, you'll bleed into the sea.

"You think I want to talk about *flowers?*" I ask as if I don't know what he means.

"You got something to say to me, Santino? You think I'm not good enough to marry into your family? Just say it."

"So Lucio over here can go back to Cosimo and tell him?"

"No, so I can send a fucking carrier pigeon. If I wanted my father to know, I'd pick up this thing here. It's called a phone. What the fuck is going on with your wife? I thought she was mouthy, but knocking shit over?"

I know when I'm being provoked, even slightly, and talking about my wife like this is incitement. He wants me to lose my temper so he has the upper hand… not tonight, but tomorrow and the next day, when he tells everyone I'm too weak to think before I act.

"As far as you're concerned, it was the wind," I say. "And if you back out, you've insulted me, my uncle, and my cousin."

"My money's where it belongs." He jabs his finger against the table so hard the knuckle bends. "I already bought a ring. A new one."

He knows how my wedding went and that Violetta's ring was Rosetta's first. Another thing I regret.

"So there's a deal. Unless you want out. Do you want out, Dami? I could get in your way if you do, but I won't."

For my wife's sake, I hope he wants out. I'll protect

that decision from his own father and Gia's. He taps his cigar, curls his mouth, looks around as if the answer's written in lasers.

"What's your problem?" I ask.

"Violetta was supposed to be mine."

The possibility of this doesn't scare me. She was never his. She was born to be mine.

"You were too slow, and Emilio meant for me to marry a daughter first. You were there."

"You shoulda come to me," he says.

"And if you had a problem, you should have brought it to *Il Blocco*."

"No one knows where the fuck Corragio is!" He slams his hand on the table, breaking his cigar. "I was going through the channels the right way, and you…" He flings the cigar pieces into the ashtray. "You just dropped in like a fucking ghost and took her."

"She's mine. This is the end of it. She knocks down a vase of roses, kicks it, flings it into the sky, it's my business."

"I could tell them," he says in a low growl. "All of them. One word that she's inheriting the crown and every gray-haired old capo and every soldier with four whiskers on his chin is coming for you."

"But you won't." I stand. This is over. "Not in front of your father." I nod toward Lucio. "He'll kill you for letting someone else in line before him."

Damiano's up like a shot. "And he'll kill you for what you did to me."

With his wide eyes and set shoulders, I can tell Damiano wants to hit me, and I wish I could let him try, but our business isn't done.

"He may end my life," I say. "But we both know he won't lift his little finger for your sake."

Before he can utter another threat, I leave. It's the greatest favor I've ever done for him.

---

My wife waits for me in the bedroom like a child on Christmas morning, kneeling in the middle of our bed, nipples hardened to dark points in the white silk nightgown.

"Where's Gia?" I ask, taking off my jacket.

"Her mother called. She went home."

"*Bene.*"

"They said you met with Damiano."

"Did they?"

"What did he say?"

"He will let go of your insult."

Her mouth drops and her eyes open wide, but she collects herself a second later. "So what's our next move?"

*Our.* Violetta wants us to be a team now. Wants to play the game now. Wants to enter into my world.

"There is no next move. That isn't *our* business." I take off my shirt and fold it neatly over the desk chair. "Our business is on that bed."

"It doesn't work like that."

"*Zitta,*" I hush her. "There's nothing in it for him anymore."

"What do you mean?"

Can she sense the half-truth? Is she nosing around

what I'm leaving out? Or does she just want enough assurance that she can relax now?

"It means pull up your nightgown and show me where to leave my come next."

Her throat ripples when she swallows, and she grabs a handful of nightgown and stops. "Are you sure about Damiano?"

If I tell her that—from what I can see—there's nothing in the marriage for him, she'll ask if that means the wedding is off or not. When I say I don't know yet, she'll push harder and something will break.

"I am sure." I unbuckle my belt and snap it from the loops. "I told you to show me your body."

Satisfied, she pulls her nightgown up to her neck and displays her gorgeous tits, her belly, her cunt. All I can do is stare and pull the gown over her head.

I slap the pillow. "Put your head here."

She obeys as the last of my clothes drop to the floor, and I jerk her legs up and apart, exposing her soft pink invitation and the tighter promise below.

She puts her hands between her legs. "What should be your reward for ending Gia's wedding?"

She's being coy and cute, but I don't like it.

"No," I say sternly and get off the bed. "This game… you do not play."

"What game?"

"You don't open your legs as a reward." I get my belt from the floor and use it to tie her wrists to the headboard. "You open them because you want to." Pushing her legs back open again, I position myself between them and slide myself along her cunt. "You still want me to fuck you?"

"Yes."

"How?"

"*Voglio che mi scopi…*" She deliberates every word of the request to fuck her, then stops, thinks, and adds a word. "*Difficile?*"

"Do you mean 'hard,' *Forzetta?*" I can't wait for confirmation, but push inside so hard she cries out. "You say it like this. *Scopami.*" I lick my thumb and press it to her clit. Her eyes flutter closed as I make circles.

"*Scopa—*" she elongates an *aah* of pleasure.

"*Scopami. Di. Brutto.* Say it."

I thrust for each word and toy with her endlessly. As soon as I see her getting close, I demand she speak again.

"Yes," she replies breathlessly.

I can go all night, watching her will drain away into desperate submission. I press harder against her nub. "What do you want?"

"To come."

"*Italiano,*" I demand. "Say it perfectly."

I want her to fuck it up as much as I want her to get it right.

"*Scopami di brutto, mio Re.*"

"Good girl," I say, and I mean it. She is good. Better than good. "You will now have the longest orgasm ever had by anyone."

Deep as I can go inside her, I circle her clit harder and faster, until the dark world locked within her bursts open. She is silent and explosive all at once. Full and glorious. When her body slowly folds in on itself and expands again, I know she's at the height of her pleasure, and I release into her, erasing every doubt I've ever had about this woman.

As I roll off her, I let myself believe the problem is solved. She'll be how she's supposed to be. She'll do what's expected of her and no more, and at the same time, I'm aware this is a lie. I have not taken her completely. I will never quiet her doubts. And I fear she will never fully turn into a wife.

## 18

## VIOLETTA

The night he gave me the longest orgasm ever in the history of the universe, I fell asleep so hard I broke my ability to open my eyes before ten in the morning. I just lie there in a state of half-dream, with the sun bursting behind my eyelids, letting the all-rightness warm me from the inside out.

He fucked me again the next morning. During the day, I speak to Gia. Her father told her things had changed, but not what.

"Do you think the *'mbasciata* is off?" Gia asks. I can't read how she feels about it one way or the other.

"What if it is?"

She pauses.

"I want to be married," she says, then breathes through another long pause. "But... no offense... not like this."

"No offense taken."

The call ends with a relieved sigh on my side.

For three more days, the sheets remain crisp and

white, and I can't avoid it anymore. Lord knows I'm going to give birth before Santino notices I haven't had my period. First, I want confirmation. I have to pee on a stick today.

As I get out of bed, the house rumbles with the echoes of Santino's voice from downstairs. There are pauses but not replies. He must be on the phone. We're going to have to put some rugs down, because sound bounces around this house like a ping-pong ball and the floors can be rough on tender young knees.

Before I say anything about the floors or putting a fence around the pool, I have to make sure there will be a baby in the house.

"Hey," I say with a kiss, joining Santino in the kitchen, freshly showered.

"*Buon pomeriggio.*" He snaps an empty cup from the row on the counter.

"It's not afternoon yet."

He pours me coffee, serving me. I try not to make a big deal of it, even when he puts in sugar so I don't have to.

Does he know my period is late?

"*Grazie,*" I say. Why is he even home? It's not Sunday, the only day he spends the morning in the house.

"Do you have plans today?"

Something's up. He can't be counting the days in my menstrual cycle, but who knows?

"Do I ever?" I ask.

"*Bene, allora.* Finish your coffee and we go."

He drives the Alfa with the windows open and I let the warm summer breeze break against my cheeks. My right hand taps on the top of the door and my left rests on the gearshift, over his. The crown ring he wears on that hand is hard against the underside of my fingers. He hasn't told me where we're going. I'm okay with that until he turns onto the bridge over the river and my curiosity gets the best of me.

"Where are you taking me?"

"It's a surprise."

The tower of St. John's creeps over the tree line, and I wonder about school. I wonder why I haven't thought about it, wished for it, or asked him about it. Maybe because I don't have to. It's summer anyway, and I'm already registered for fall. Or maybe I've been too distracted by the insanity my life has become.

And now I think about what happens to all that if I'm pregnant, and I don't have to wonder if another decision can easily be taken away from me.

"Santi," I say, squeezing his hand, "is it school? Are we going to school?"

He takes his attention from the road long enough to look at me, and something in my expression must tell him that I won't take less than a definite answer. "No."

"Good." I relax and turn back to the view of the river with fishing boats, the V of jet-skis, the diagonal hatch of piers on the shore.

The tires buzz over the textured metal plate that ends the bridge connecting Secondo Vasto to the rest of the world.

"Do you want to go to school in the fall?" he asks at a red light.

What I want could be irrelevant soon, but he asked what I wanted, not what's possible. That doesn't make the answer any easier.

"I'd be the only married person in the class."

"So? You're there to study."

"What if I get a bad grade? You going to beat up the professor?" I ask.

"What's a bad grade?"

"A B plus."

"Oh, for that?" He shrugs and turns into a residential area. "Just a black eye."

"What about a D?"

"That's failing?"

"That's passing. Barely."

"Then I will let him live. Barely."

He's joking, of course, but I pat his hand in thanks for letting this fake professor live through my unlikely near-fail. I don't need to ask about an F.

"This is a nice neighborhood," I say.

The streets curve around clean sidewalks shaded with old trees. The lawns are lush and short. The houses are painted soft colors and trimmed in white. Flowers, birds, and butterflies thrive inside a bubble of perfection.

"It's called River Heights. They say it's very safe." He strokes my pinkie with his thumb, then slows by a property with ten-foot hedges and an open driveway gate. When he pulls into it, a pale yellow two-story house is visible. He stops behind a silver Lexus SUV. The house's front door is wide open.

"So," I say, "who lives here? What's going on?"

He gets out of the car. A man with a thick moustache walks onto the porch, and Santino waves to him. I open my own door before my husband has a chance to, and get out into the beautiful, blazing sun.

"Come." Santino grabs my hand and takes me up the front steps. He's like a kid who's too old to be excited by his birthday, but young enough to be delighted with the presents. The mustachioed man on the porch wears a light gray suit that's too small around the belly and a red tie that's just a little wider than fashionable. The breeze has zero impact on his dark brown combover, and there's something vaguely familiar about him. "Bosco, this is my wife, Violetta."

The man takes one of my hands in both of his. "Such a pleasure."

"Bosco is a real estate agent."

"Ah!" The sound escapes my lips when I realize why I recognize him. "From the ads on the bus benches."

There's no FOR SALE sign on the lawn. That's my excuse for standing there thinking we're having lunch with the guy or something.

"Guilty!" Bosco opens his arms and quotes the ads. "Number One *paesano* in our *paese*!"

I can't help but laugh at his pride in the silly slogan.

"I admit," he says with some humility, "River Heights isn't my area, but I have it on good authority that this is a *primo* neighborhood. Safest you can find. The tiptop! Come!"

He steps backward, waving us through the door. Whatever fog of clueless ignorance I was floating around inside dissipates, and I look at my husband, who's beaming like a guy who just swallowed the sun.

The space is bare, leaving the hardwood floors and white walls completely exposed.

"The security system? Just updated to 'smart security,' they call it. Open plan in the living room to the kitchen and this dining room, right here, so you can talk to guests while you prepare dinner. I warn you, there's no kitchen in the basement, but if your husband wants to put one in for you, there's room next to the wine cellar."

"Santi?" I say, peering up a staircase that sweeps at a graceful curve.

"They just put in brand new appliances." Bosco opens the huge refrigerator, showing off the pristine interior like a woman turning letters on a game show. "Also 'smart,' they say."

"*Che?*" Santino replies as if he has no idea what I'd be asking about right now.

He knows. He has to know. Why else am I here?

"Six-burner stove!" Bosco delights. "Maybe only one kitchen? Be like a real American housewife. June Cleaver. No?"

He looks between us. I have no idea who Bosco is talking about, and I stopped paying close attention after Santi acted as if I knew what's going on.

But Bosco continues like a soldier someone wound up all the way. "I think I'm showing my age. But here's for the man of the house to cook… a brick barbecue in the backyard." He unlocks the sliding door to the back, which is completely paved except for a patch of manicured grass.

No. I don't want to go there yet. I put my hand on the graceful curl of staircase banister.

"Violetta?" Santino asks, tugging me, but I tug back. I want to see upstairs.

"Oh!" Bosco cries, jumping in our direction. "Let me show you the master suite!"

He hustles up the stairs ahead of us.

"What are you doing?" I ask Santino softly.

"I didn't want to spring it on you on your birthday."

"I see." What I see is a man who's sprung one too many things on me and very much wants me to think of him as changed.

"If you don't like it," he says, "we can look at another one."

"No, I…" I hadn't even thought about liking it or not liking it. "It's beautiful."

"Good."

Santino pulls me up the steps and I run past him, giggling, to a wide hall bathed in sunlight. Bosco waits in the wide doorway to what has to be the master suite, but I know it'll be gorgeous. I head for the bedroom next door.

The window seat is coated in fresh white paint, and the walls are a gender neutral butter color. It's bare as a bone, but the crib goes on the shared wall with the master suite, and the changing table is opposite. I look at the ceiling and see a small hook. There was a mobile there to occupy the baby while they were changed.

"*Forzetta*," Santino murmurs, putting his hand on my shoulder with two fingers on the bare skin of my neck. "You want to sleep in the guest room?"

"This isn't the guest room."

I open the closet. A little window on the facing end lights the walk-in space. A few wire hangers dangle from the rods on either side, and the walls are marred by strips of white paper and shards of exposed plaster. Stickers were pulled off. A cartoon character or flowers. Vestiges of the last occupant.

"It's a nursery," I say.

He shrugs. "We could need a nursery some day, no?"

I should tell him I'm late. He deserves to know. But I'd so much rather be sure.

*You can't always have what you'd rather.*

"Yes." I go to the window and look down. Just below, there's a crystalline pool for Santino to slice into. He'll push me against the edge of it and kiss me until I'm as liquid as the water. "We probably will."

I don't say when. I'm not ready to even insinuate a maybe. There's no coming back from those conversations.

I hear Bosco enter the room, but Santino holds his hand out to stop the agent from interrupting us.

"Bigger then?" my husband offers.

Another square foot won't change a thing, but I don't know what will, because I'm not sure what changes I need.

"What's wrong with the house you have?" I ask.

"I thought you'd like this one. The location." He indicates the window.

The tower seems close enough to touch. He isn't offering me a view out a closet window. He's offering school without a commute.

"This type of house," he continues. "It's better for having people around."

"It's so far from everyone though."

"There are these things called… *come si dice…*" He

snaps his fingers by his ear like a guy trying to lure a memory out of the dark. "Ah!" He points. "*Cars!* They can come in their cars."

It's hard not to smile when he reveals his sense of humor.

"Maybe," I say, looking at the school's brick tower that signaled I had to change busses. Every morning, it meant I was coming closer to where I belonged. "Maybe."

But now I belong to him.

*Tell him tell him tell him.*

And I'm still a little mad about it.

And there's still so much I don't know, but I haven't planned an escape in a long time, and I'm not sure I'm ever going to want to leave him.

*Tell him tell him tell him.*

From his pocket, his phone rings. He hesitates.

"Get it," I say. "I'll let Bosco show me around."

He kisses me and answers the phone. I leave Santino in the baby's closet so the realtor can show me the brick barbecue.

---

Santino's leaning on the car, talking on the phone when we're done with the house. He hangs up when he sees us. I should tell him to take me to the drugstore, but as we drive away from Bosco, who's waving from the front porch, and out the front gate, there's no choice to make. Santino's tight as a drum. I'm not telling him shit right now. I don't think he can handle it.

I put my hand on his, and he strokes my pinkie but doesn't loosen up. His tension radiates outward, filling every inch of the car.

"Are you all right?" I ask, assuming he'll say he's fine, and even if something is wrong, it's not my business.

He defies my expectations and hands me his phone. There's a text from Gia.

*—Dear Santino. I won't be at work today. I'm sorry. Thank you for giving me the job. It meant a lot to me. I'm going back with Mamma today—*

There's no more.

"What does she mean by 'going back'?"

"I can take you home," he says at the light before the bridge. "But it's in the opposite direction, and you won't have a chance to say good-bye."

*I'm going back with Mamma today.*

"Gia's going back to the other side?"

The light turns green.

"Decide."

"Decide what?" I ask.

"Airport or home."

There is no decision.

"Airport."

Santino swoops into a U-turn at the intersection, causing a symphony of horns, shouts, and screeching tires, gunning it to make the next light. I grip the dashboard and his hand to try to keep steady.

"Is that what you were on the phone about? She's getting sent home?"

"They're not *sending* her home," he says, slapping the shifter into a different gear. "They're *bringing* her home for two weeks. To get the right things..." He stops as if he doesn't want to say it.

But Rosetta went to Italy for the right things too.

"For the wedding?" The engine's roaring so loud I have to shout, but I would have raised my voice anyway. "You said you took care of it!"

"Did I?"

Did he? Or is that what I assumed he meant?

"You said he had nothing to gain."

He takes a turn at a yellow light, and with a gear change and a lurch, we're speeding down the highway. His full lips are thinned by the tight clench of his mouth.

"That's what this house is about," I say, then continue when I get no response from him. "You're trying to placate me. You think if you buy me, I'll let her—or anyone—get sold into marriage. All I cost is a house."

"No," is all he can get out.

"Say you're not a liar."

"I did not lie." His finger juts at me, but with his eyes on the road, the pointing loses its power. "I thought I had more time."

"Is that why you're driving to the airport at ninety miles an hour?"

"You want to say good-bye or no?"

This is him doing things for me. The house I didn't ask for, in a neighborhood he'd hate. The death-defying trip for a simple good-bye. All of it, covering the fact that he didn't do what he told me he'd do.

"You were supposed to stop it!" Both fists shake at him. I want to punch his face, but he's driving.

"She wants it." He jabs his finger at me. "I talked to her. Gia wants this marriage. She said so. What are you going to do? Tell her she can't have it because I fucked it up for you? I ruined your life, so you ruin hers? So *you* don't feel bad? Queen Violetta won't bless the deal so fuck what Gia wants?"

He's spoken to me like a child and a servant. He's been heartless and cold. But he's never spoken to me with this particular mixture of anger and respect.

"She doesn't know what she's getting into."

"Bullshit. You want her to have the choice, but you don't want her to choose."

"Fuck you." I cross my arms and sink into my seat. "She's being sold."

"And she knows it. You confuse yourself. It's her life, not yours."

"I'm not confused," I snarl. "I'm very clear about the difference between consent and force."

"Yes, I forced you. I didn't take you back to Naples to have a dress made or to get *bomboniere* from Abriana Dolce. You had no bobbin lace veil. You had no time to consent. This is what I did. I. Fucked. Up."

My body stays upright, but inside, I can no longer hold up my own weight and my heart sinks into my gut. My life. My wedding. My marriage. The things he ruined, forced, and took for granted, in that order.

"Why?" I ask. "Why did you move so fast?"

A wrist over the steering wheel and the opposite elbow on the door, he rubs his lower lip, clearly thinking.

"I'll tell you." He puts his blinker on, checks his mirrors, and exits to the airport. "On your birthday. Right now, you put on a good face for your cousin."

The airport closest to us is too small to service international flights, but we pass it right by anyway and go to the smaller, private terminal.

Small planes dot the tarmac and surround the main runway. Santino drives to a jet surrounded by a handful of cars. Men load bags into the cargo hold of the jet that took us to and from Italy.

"That's your plane," I say.

"I had to placate them too. The plane ride's cheaper than the house."

"Is there anything you can't just buy?"

"I got the plane as collateral on a loan." He makes a lap around the little jet and stops behind the last car. "Owner defaulted."

"Did he offer you his daughter first?"

"I was already spoken for." He puts the car into park.

"Jesus Christ." I shake my head. "He'd give up his daughter before his plane."

"It was the strategic choice. I can take care of her and the marriage would protect him from me."

The logic is so real and so cynical I can't refute it.

I get out so I'm not obligated to answer. Santino meets me on the passenger side, putting his hand at the base of my neck as we approach Paola. She's wearing red lipstick, big sunglasses, and a headscarf, looking ten times more glamorous than the day I met her in an old apartment in Naples. Santino kisses her, then goes to Marco, leaving us alone.

"How is she?" I ask.

"Thrilled," Paola says, without enough sarcasm to make the statement untrue. "She gets to be married to a man who can keep her comfortable and she gets to stay in the United States."

"But does she love him?"

Paola takes off her sunglasses, revealing that she's not wearing any eye makeup.

"What does that matter?" she says, looking at my ring, then back at my face, as if asking who the fuck I think I am.

"I guess it doesn't."

She puts her sunglasses back on. "You can say hello. She's in the car." Paola points at a Lincoln. "She didn't want tan lines. You know how brides are."

"Yeah. I do," I say without irony before going to the Lincoln Continental and rapping on a back window.

The door unlocks and I take a deep, calming breath. If Gia wants to be married, she'll tell me. If she doesn't and I'm tense, she won't. So I put on my happy face and get in. Gia throws her arms around my shoulders. The door clicks closed behind me.

"Hey," I say. "I had no idea you were leaving!"

"Totally last minute. Look!" Gia thrusts her left hand under my nose to show off a huge round diamond solitaire. "Damiano asked me this morning."

Fuck. She's accepted his proposal. Maybe she's not being forced like I was, but she's still being sold. She's still shackled to a man for reasons that have nothing to do with her at all.

"It is... Gia, this is so fast."

"Isn't. It. Beautiful?" She needs me to weigh in on the ring, and I need to stay focused.

I take her hand to move it out of my face, and it's shaking. Her eyes are puffy and her lips are pink and swollen. Wadded up tissues litter the seat and floor of the car. She's been crying.

"I'm going to miss your birthday," she says quickly. "I'll bring you back a present to make up for it."

"Are you all right? Gia, talk to me. Did you have a choice?"

"Please don't make a big deal about it, Violetta. The engagement's fast, yeah… I don't have time to do everything… and I'm a little—" She cuts herself off. Was she going to say leery? Angry? Sad? Scared?

"Did you have a choice?" I ask again. She's allowed to make stupid decisions for herself, but I can't walk away without knowing if this stupid decision was hers.

She shakes her head, but if it's an answer, she tries to cover it up. "It's not like what happened with you. Not the bad parts."

That's enough to tell me she didn't have a choice, but my arguments die on my lips. The bad parts are close enough to what happened with me, and the good parts she imagines are not guaranteed for her. The worst for me was the lightning-fast speed of the wedding though. Gia has time, which means I have time.

"I might have married him anyway." She shrugs. "It's just confusing. I don't know how to feel and…" She sucks in a hitched breath as if she's about to cry. "The idea of being traded bothers me, but…" She clears her throat, swallowing her tears. "I'm sure I'll be fine."

"I am too." I am sure of no such thing.

"Do you ever wonder…?" After a deep breath, she finishes her thought. "What if we could have all the things that come with being married, the house and the kids and you know… the *respect*." Her voice hammers that last upside of marriage as though it's the last nail in a coffin. "Even the big party with all your friends and family… and everyone congratulating you and being happy and proud… but without the guy?"

It's called liberation. I thought it was woven into the fabric of my life, but it was just a stain Secondo Vasto wiped away.

"I'm sorry, Gia," I offer sympathy, but her affect swings again, and she waves it away.

"It's fine! Hey, I can have it all *plus* a cute guy I have a lifetime to get to know. Right?"

I can't keep up with her shifting attitudes. I don't envy her mother or anyone she meets on the other side in the next few days, but mostly, I don't envy her. The constant changes must be painful.

"Have you set a date?" I ask, trying to sound excited and casual.

"Right when we get back!" She takes my hands. "Will you be my maid of honor, Violetta?"

Fuck no. I want nothing at all to do with this. I'd rather set the church on fire.

But my preference for arson doesn't matter.

"Of course, but…" I can't let my complicity sit there unchallenged. "When you get back, if it's still all too fast, you can stay with us. Santino will protect you. You can just wait a bit."

She looks at me, breathes through a hitch, blinks. "It

is fast. I think that's freaking me out a little, but Papa says he can't go home until the money's paid or the man he owes…" She lets out a little laugh. "He exaggerates. So much drama for a man."

"Stay with us," I whisper.

There's a shadow over our hands and I follow it, thinking Santino's trying to rush us, but it's Paola, putting on lipstick in the window's reflection.

"I've got it all set in my head." Gia touches the corner of her eye as if her mascara's bothering her. "It's going to be the most glamorous wedding you've ever seen." She sniffs. "And Damiano? He's renting the perfect place in the hills."

She's pretty and innocent, naïve even, but not stupid.

"Gia," I say firmly, and the smile melts off her face. "Come home with us."

"Are you not happy for me?"

"I want to be happy for you in ten years." I squeeze her hand. "I don't want someone to sell your tomorrows for a wedding today."

"Don't say sold. I'm not being sold. I would have married him anyway. It's just the timing that changed to help Daddy."

She's ashamed, but I don't know if she's ashamed that she was sold into marriage or that the man she's crowing over doesn't love her.

"You don't have to do this," I say. "Santino will get you out of it. I'll make him."

She turns her whole body away from me and faces front. "Did I tell you? Damiano's paying for everything. I'm going shopping from the minute I get off the plane until the minute I get back on. He says to get real confetti almonds, not these horribly fake things you get here."

"Gia," I say, intending to offer her a place to stay while we deal with Damiano, but she ignores me.

"I'm going to bring back pounds and pounds of them. And custom figurines for the cake! There's a shop on Corso Meridionale my mom wants to get them from. I'm even making a special trip to Burano Island to get lace for the gown!"

When Gia finally looks at me, her brows are knitted —pleading me to go along with it all. The confetti almonds. The lace. The cake. She wants my permission, and if I don't give it, I may lose her.

I grit my teeth, gather every bit of energy I have, and pretend to be happy for her. "Wow! I can't wait to see it all when you come back. We'll go get lunch and you can show me pictures. Whatever you don't get in Italy, I can help you do here."

"That's perfect." She sighs happily and reclines in the seat. "You just had your wedding a few months ago and know what it takes."

She was there. She knows it took nothing, because it was nothing, but she's telling herself a story about me and I'm not even an active character in it. Which is more or less how my story started.

"Americans take so long to plan a wedding, but we can do it like that." She snaps her fingers. "We could have ten huge weddings in the time it takes them to have one. Don't you think?"

"I do."

To her, this may be close enough to what she always told herself she wanted.

Am I the terrible person for rejecting it? Am I the selfish wife who can't appreciate the privileges of marriage because they're going to someone else?

Maybe. But I'll still spend the coming days trying to find a way to stop this madness. I have two weeks with Santino to put an end to this bullshit charade. It's not like Gia can't live without the guy for the duration of a real engagement.

But only a couple of months ago, Santino walked me around the four corners of the block to make me his, and I knew less of him.

*They have to turn four corners together or she will not bear children.*

Gia may return to see me prove the efficacy of that superstition.

"I think you're going to be a great wife, Gia."

"Thank you for everything." She throws her arms around my neck. "Next time, we'll have to go to Italy together while our husbands work." Her voice hitches up an octave in false excitement when she says the word *husband*.

"Seeing you safe is all I could ask for," I say honestly, and hug her tightly. "You have become a very important person to me. I wish you nothing but happiness."

"You're the sweetest." She kisses my cheek. "I know I will have the best life because you will be in it."

Santino opens the car door and leans down to see us. "Senora and senorita. It is time."

We pile out of the back seat. Gia runs to her

parents. Santino puts his hand on my shoulder at the base of my neck to slow me down.

"What did you do?" he asks in my ear.

"There's nothing I can do. She's brainwashed."

Armando stands at the base of the airstairs with his hands folded in front of him. Paola goes up, then Gia, who stops to throw her arms around him, pulling him close, on tiptoes. He pats her back, but won't show any more warmth. She belongs to another man, after all.

They separate, and she bounds up the stairs. At the top, she grasps the railing and does a perfect royal wave with a shining in her smile before disappearing into the plane.

As soon as I lose sight of her, my stomach twists like a dishcloth. It stays that tight as we get back in the car, as her plane taxis to the runway, as the quaint airport full of play toys bought with blood money disappears in the rearview mirror.

"She seems happy, no?" Santino interrupts the spiral of my thoughts.

The morning commute traffic has gotten denser, suffocating the intersections. It looks like my heart feels. "Sure. Like she got an email from a Nigerian prince."

"I don't understand." Santino changes lanes and someone behind us honks. "Which Nigerian prince?"

I stare at him, debate explaining it, but sigh instead. "Never mind."

"You're angry with me."

I shut down. I cross my arms and stare out the window, stewing. If he can't see why selling an innocent girl, or any girl, into marriage, whether she thinks she's happy about it or not, is barbaric, there's no point bringing up the obvious again.

"Violetta." He snaps his fingers in my face. "Speak."

I swat his hand away. He can't tell me to speak or what to do. I'm his wife, not his dog.

Santino jerks the steering wheel and throws the car across two lanes of traffic. I'm flung against the door, then into the dashboard as he slams on the brakes. The traffic erupts in angry horns. He grabs my face in his hands.

"You will talk to me. You are my *wife*." I try to pull away, but he holds firm. "Tell me, Violetta. Tell me the problem. She's happy. Why can't you be?"

I smack his hand until he lets go. I throw open the door, narrowly missing the concrete barrier on the side of the road, and get out.

"Violetta!"

Santino's shout is lost in the wind and the cars zipping by. Any one of them will flatten us because he didn't get what he wants.

Well, maybe because I'm not getting what I want. It's not even just about Gia. It's about *me*. I barely remember what it feels like to *not* be his wife, to *not* feel this close to danger.

"Don't you understand?" Santino grabs for me and I roll out of the way. The cars driving past ruffle and flare up the bottom of my dress and I can't muster the energy to care who sees what's underneath. "There's no problem!"

I spin around on my heel, but catch on some loose gravel and nearly slip. Santino reaches for me, but I push him away.

"Talk to me!" he shouts.

"About what? About you? Or Gia? When I first saw her, she was everything I left behind. She was everything that made me who I was. All those things about myself I had to let go of when you forced me to marry you. But now? Now I see her and I don't even know if any of who I was had value and I don't know if who I am now has value. All I want is to know someone else in the world can decide for themselves if they're worth a damn. Not a price tag. Not how big a debt they cover. But if they're worthy humans. But she'll never know and I'll never know, because you suck, and I suck, and it all sucks. I don't know where I belong and it doesn't even matter."

"What am I supposed to do?" Santino yells over the traffic. He extends his palms. "I can't unmarry you."

"Yes, you can," I yell back. The words come out so violently, they break past generations of marital tenacity. "You know it's not right. Prove it. Prove you could have me without forcing me."

I know this is asking more from him than I've ever asked before—more than asking him to pay the debt.

"Are you kidding me?" He looks at me as if I'm stark-raving insane.

"I'm not crazy!" I yell again.

"I never said you were!"

"Then quit looking at me like that!"

Angrier than ever, my whole body hurls toward him but slips on a piece of tossed trash, and my world goes sideways. It happens in slow motion, the world turning, the cars honking, the heavy stench of burnt rubber on blacktop.

Santino yanks me back to the side of the road, panting. The driver of the car that almost hit me throws us several middle fingers before peeling back off into traffic.

I could have died, all because of this stupid, awful, horrible group of men who think they can just control the world with—

"And then you go jumping into the road!?" Santino's angry Italian interrupts my own panic. "You could have been hurt! Get in the car!"

He pushes me back to the car, keeping his body firmly between the rest of the road and me. When I look at him, I see the horror in his eyes. So when he opens my door and pushes me inside, I let him.

I could have died. Again.

When he gets back in the car, I can see he's exhausted, and it's because of me. He dragged me into his life, and if you put a gun to my head, I'd bet he regrets it. Without me, he'd be muscling his way through his days according to the rules he grew up with. But here I am next to him, challenging him at every turn.

Santino earned this torture and more for what he did to me. Kidnapping me, imprisoning me, making me love him. I don't have sympathy for what he's done and I don't excuse it. But I still love him, and that's the absurdity I can't figure out.

We have to be together for a reason. There has to be a higher cause. Some greater good I can make from what I've been through. But first, Gia has to be freed.

We're about a mile from his house when I break the silence. "Can you pay Marco's debt?"

He sighs with both impatience and resignation. "Paying the debt insults both men. It says they aren't in charge of their own affairs."

"Yeah, well, Marco isn't or he wouldn't be in this problem."

"He's not in a problem if he can pay it, and he can."

"By selling his daughter."

"These are traditions."

"Change them."

"Traditions are not laws." He looks at me when he turns onto the street we live on. "A law is signed one day and changed the next. There's no congress or parliament to change tradition by signing a piece of paper, because traditions... they are an agreement. No one writes it down. No one has to. The understanding is there." He jabs his sternum. "The power I have—the power your father had—it is only given because it is *agreed*."

My glands spit adrenaline into my bloodstream. I'm mainlining rage so hot I have to clamp my jaw shut and breathe, breathe, breathe. Only when he's in the driveway can I speak sensibly.

"You're saying if you use your power to fix the traditions that give it, you lose your ability to wield it."

"Yes."

"What's power for, if you have to work so hard to keep it?"

He parks at the door and waves away Armando, who rushes up to help us out of the car. I've twisted around to face Santino, but he won't look at me.

"You're not happy," he says.

"I guess not."

It's not hard to admit that, because how can happiness be the point in a marriage arranged by fiat and entered into by force?

"We are Catholic," he says. "We don't divorce."

On his lips, the word divorce sounds like a foreign language. The jab of pain in my chest when my heart skips a beat is fleeting and replaced by a dead weight. Divorce is what people who married for love do when the thing that kept them together dies. The traditions that tie Santino and me are thriving.

"I know."

"You want an annulment then?" he asks with a calm that makes any answer seem consequence-free. It isn't. But what he's trying to tell me is that I can say yes, and whatever the consequences may be, they will not be imposed by him. He looks me right in the eye. "Yes or no?"

This is not a test. It's not a drill. It's not sarcasm or an offer he'll snatch away.

He's serious.

I can end this thing with him.

I can be free again.

All I need to do is say yes. I want an annulment. The sooner, the better. While the sheets are as clean as my conscience. Before there's a child involved.

But the dashboard clock changes and still—locked in his gaze—I say nothing, because I don't want to end this marriage. Not now, because I need to stay close to Gia, and maybe not ever, because I want, with all my heart and not a bit of my head, to stay close to him.

Santino's trap isn't the traditions or the threats anymore.

I'm living in the prison of my own feelings.

He isn't offering me an annulment. He's offering me a choice.

He's laying everything he has on a single bet, and he's going to win.

## 19

## VIOLETTA

I leave the car without telling him what I want because even though I know what I want to say, I don't want to say it. Once I do, the words can't be unspoken and the offer won't be made again. If I want to leave, I'll have to run away.

"I need to know now," he says once we're alone inside his house.

"I'm not letting it go," I reply. "If I stay, don't expect me to let what happened to me happen to anyone else. I don't want to make your life a living hell, but I might have to."

"Old sins have long shadows." He tosses his keys on the table. I've never seen him miss, but this time, they slide over the surface and clap to the floor. He doesn't pick them up. "Every day, I wish I was more for you. I forced my way in, but I can't force you to stay."

"It's not about me anymore. She's terrified, Santi."

He holds out his hands, a gold ring on each fourth finger. The crown ring is modest on the back side—

indistinguishable from the wedding band on the left. He's offering me what he has. Nothing. He can't help me because he's helpless. He has no power to do it. Both hands are tied in gold.

I lay my hands over his.

"I know." He looks down at our clasped hands. "Those first days... I couldn't see you. I couldn't let myself." He won't look at me, just at the gold bands that decorate our fingers.

"Help me end this," I whisper. "You're not a bad person."

He waits for the qualifier—the "but" before the twist of the knife. Instead, I leave the statement unarmed.

"You should be careful." He cups my face, close now, his words of caution lighter than a breath. "When the devil caresses you, he wants your soul."

"Maybe you're the one who should be careful."

His lips meet mine before my last word is finished. The soft pressure of his mouth doesn't demand a response. It doesn't even ask. The kiss is not taken from me, nor is it willingly given. When our mouths open together, nothing is exchanged, neither consent nor command, because what we create can never be owned or stolen by either of us. It is ours—woven from our in-between space, from the warmth of our bodies escaping through the cracks in our hearts.

More than our wedding, this kiss is a sacrament.

"If I release Gia," he says, "will you forgive me for not releasing you?"

"I do forgive you. But what if I didn't?"

"I'd release her anyway." With another kiss, he

presses me against the wall, the gentle vulnerability of his mouth turning hot and hungry.

"Wait." I push him away only far enough to let my lips make words. "You will?"

"I will."

"You'll pay Marco's debt?"

"No."

"What then?"

"I'll give Damiano what he really wants."

"Is it—"

He cuts me off with a kiss before answering. "It's not Gia. Not even a wedding."

The aggressive shape of his hardness pushes against my thigh, and I lift my leg to his hip to move the shape to center. He takes that leg under the knee, then the other, and I lock my ankles around him, digging my fingers in his hair as he kisses me, drawing him closer. I want to eat him alive. Crawl inside him and rest inside his skin. Consume the soul he thinks he's sold to hell, because it is desirable—a prize worthy of eternity—and mine is a devil's caress.

Everything has a price.

"What about the next woman who's sold?" I ask, pulling away only slightly. He's trying to kiss me, but I'm not having it. "Will you bless it?"

"Ask me later."

"Now," I demand, then soften it so he doesn't get defensive. "Please."

"I told you I don't like this game."

"I have one last card to play." I move his hand to my backside and give him the coy smile of an innocent. "Are you all in?"

"I have been *punto tutto* from the beginning." He grinds into my soft center. "I will end it, and I may be killed for it."

"You won't be."

With my legs wrapped around him and his hands under my bottom, he carries me up the steps to his room, where he lays me on the bed and removes my clothes piece by piece, touch by touch, kiss by kiss, until we're a combined beast of writhing limbs and grappling hands. His lips make a line from my throat to my breasts and belly before he buries his face between my legs, licking me with the full width of his fluttering tongue and sucking gently on my nub until I'm so lit up, I could set the city on fire.

"More," I breathe, clutching his hair.

He flicks and strokes my opening, then moves his mouth there, softening the edge, then moves lower and hitches my hips off the mattress to reach even lower and—

"*Oh.*"

His tongue ventures into unexpected places, startling me. I push him away, but Santino captures my hands in his own and gently runs his tongue along my asshole. It steals the air in my lungs, and two strokes of his tongue later, I'm putty in his hands. Every flick ignites something deep within me, an urge and an itch I didn't know existed. His grunts deepen and I feel his body thrust against the bed. The act of licking my ass is turning him on, and suddenly things click together.

"Santi," I whisper.

"Say yes or no now." He gets up. "This won't wait."

He presses his thumb against the tight wetness of my asshole.

"No," I say, and he removes his thumb, looking at me over the curves of my breasts. "No, I don't want an annulment."

He blinks as if he needs a moment to take in the timing and substance of the answer.

"I know your heart," I add. "I know you want to free Gia, and you'll do everything you can. I know how hard that is for you, but it makes me want to stay with you, whether you succeed or not."

He gets up on his knees and wipes his mouth with his wrist, towering between my spread legs. The heavy hardness jutting from his pelvis is both a threat and a promise. His command and dominance has muscled past whatever vulnerability he showed downstairs.

"You ask a lot of me, *Forzetta*." Lifting my legs, he takes my ass cheeks in his rough hands and spreads them. "Too much for a wife who hasn't given me everything I want."

A hot chill runs down my spine and settles where his attention pierces me.

"What do you want?" I ask. I know what he wants, but he has to say it.

Each of his thumbs rests on my asshole, spreading it, opening me to a new type of desire.

"I want to fuck this tight little hole."

"You want to hurt me," I say.

He smirks and lays his finger on my lips. I part them so he can rest it on my tongue.

"I don't need to fuck your ass to hurt you."

I close my lips and suck his finger.

"I need to own you. My wife. All of you." He leans back, removing his wet finger, then presses it against my exposed rear. "Breathe." With my inhale, he slides in to one knuckle. The sensation is so new, I buck and groan. Lightly brushing against my clit, he goes deeper. "Does this hurt?"

"It's only a finger."

He leans over me to open a night table drawer, plucks out a tube of lotion, and cracks it open with his teeth.

"It might hurt." He squeezes a line of white lubricant on his hand, then between my cheeks. "For a moment." Two fingers enter my ass with no resistance.

"Oh, my God," I cry, then I'm utterly open-mouth speechless as he twists those fingers, removes them, and pushes in again, while using his other hand on my clit. The threat of pain hovers on the other side of the sensation, and if he doesn't break down the door, I'm tempted to invite it in.

"Your ass is so fucking tight."

His fingertips slide along my folds where I'm so slick I can't tell where the pleasure in my clit begins and my stretched muscles end. I'm past shame or discomfort. I'm not worried about pain anymore. I want it.

"Take it," I say, because I'll say anything right now.

"Take what?"

"My asshole. Take my ass. Fuck it." I'm so close to breaking, I'm near tears.

"Your ass is going to worship my cock, but first I want to feel how it comes."

He flicks my clit faster. I should have come by

now, but the way his fingers stretch me hold the orgasm at bay. He's smiling. He knows exactly what he's doing.

"Please. Fuck my ass so hard. Please."

"You're the dirtiest virgin I ever met."

"God, yes." I am filthy, indecent, and I'm breaking into ecstasy, asshole pulsing around his fingers to draw them deeper, blind in a pleasure more intense and a surrender more complete than I ever imagined possible.

Twisting with his touch, I'm face down when he removes his fingers and I feel something cold and wet on my ass. More lube. He pulls my hips up.

"Knees apart," he says impatiently.

I spread them.

"Now," he says, breathlessly rubbing the head of his cock between the cheeks. "Now you are mine."

"I am yours." Sliding a hand between my legs, I feel how wet I am. My body has ceded utterly. "Take me." My whispers are heavy with want. I am so hard in love it hurts. "Take what you want."

The last word ends in a squeak as he pushes against the tight opening.

"You are mine." He is all muttering growl, lost in a prayer of possession. "You are mine."

Gently, his cock breaks me open, and I feel the split like a tear in my very core.

"Slow, my violet," he whispers, pulling out. "If we go slow, it will only hurt for a moment."

"I trust you."

"*Bene.*" He shifts me to my side, puts one of my legs over his shoulder, and straddles the one on the bed.

Now I can see him and the expression of care he intends to take, and that relaxes me.

"*Bene,*" I say, smiling.

He pushes into my ass again, and I'm split again. As gentle as he is, the act is not. It tears and expands, distends and breaks, marking and scarring a piece of my body forever.

We work into a careful rhythm, thrusting and rocking. He stops every few strokes and massages my clit so my body can catch up, then, without warning, the pain is rerouted into pleasure, and the stretching turns into submission as he drives deep and stops to close his eyes as if in prayer.

"Violetta," he whispers.

"Santino." I pant. My body begs and pleads. "Don't stop."

"Not yet, my blood violet." He bends the leg over his shoulder, exposing more of me. "We come together."

"Tell me when, *amore mio*."

My Italian cracks him. He slides one finger over my clit and uses the other to steady us as his thrusts grow harder.

"Now, *amore mio*," Santino commands.

We come together with broken shouts and tight grunts. My body stretches and contracts. I shake, I cry, I scream. Santino works my clit as we ride the waves together. As he marks me deep inside, I surrender to the man he is and the man he promised he could be.

Santino pads back from the bathroom with a warm, damp towel. He cleans me up carefully, whispering in two languages. How much he loves me. How much I am his. How much he is mine. Then he lays next to me and pulls me close, kissing me hard, his breath minty and clean. "I thought I would lose you today. It made me crazy."

"Would you have given me the annulment if I wanted it?"

He's silent for a minute, looking at me with a gaze deep into himself. Then he snaps his focus back to me.

"Yes." He frowns, brushing the hair from my face and stroking my cheek. "But there would have been consequences."

He rolls onto his back, and I scoot closer to him, tucking my head on his shoulder.

"Such as?" I figure the answer will be a few words about the consequences to me. Being chased forever. Being caught and broken over his cock like a twig. Or the consequences to him. Shattered heart? Endless sadness?

"What I gave up, other men would try to take. I would be unable to protect you unless I locked you in my basement."

I get my elbow under me and put my face between his and the ceiling. As over-the-top as the declaration of love I expected might have been, it probably wouldn't have demanded a reasonable response the way this one does.

"I'm just a nursing student who didn't marry well."

"You're a treasure worth stealing."

Our sweet love talk got very serious, very quickly,

and there seems to be something besides his subjective feelings about me at the core of his promise.

Getting my knees under me, I straddle him and put my hands on his chest as if that's the way to speak to his heart. "Like you did?"

His manner snaps from tranquil to alert like a folding magician's wand released from inside a sleeve. Our postcoital cocoon has been torn open.

"Like I did. But I'd throw the pieces of the crown away before I hurt a hair on your head. You are the precious thing, *Forzetta*. You are unique, and powerful, and beautiful. That crown puts you in danger, and it keeps you safe. That's why I want it."

"Too bad. Your lust for power is kind of a turn-on."

He laughs, cupping my jaw and stroking my cheeks with his thumbs. "What is power, my blood violet?"

"Belief," I whisper then kiss him. "It's people believing you have it. No one thinks I'm powerful."

"I do."

"If that's your final word," I coo, dropping my cheek onto his chest, "I will accept it."

"Will you?"

"*Lo voglio.*" I repeat the words he told God I used at our wedding, when a cry to be free was manipulated into *I will*, because the first way to have power of choice is to get your husband to believe you have it.

## 20

# SANTINO

Laser-Topia is more pleasant hours before it opens, when the house lights are on and the exclamation points aren't flashing. The club is far less excruciating without darkness to cover the patches in the matte black walls and the lights distracting from the stains in the floor. It's a real place.

Damiano sits on a barstool, nursing an amber liquid, spotting me in the mirror behind the bar. The bartender wipes down glasses with a dingy gray towel. He's a young, handsome guy with light brown hair and the potential for a gut in ten years.

"Robert," I say as I slide onto a stool.

"Hey, man. Loretta said to pour you something."

"San Pellegrino."

"You got it." He snaps a green bottle from the fridge and leaves to get ice.

"The little wife not like it when you drink or something?" Damiano says.

I just smile, flicking away a crumb from the bar's surface.

He knows nothing about the power of wives.

---

DAMIANO and I were like brothers. We loved each other and hated each other. We pulled each other up and dragged each other down. We both knew I was Emilio's favorite, but we were partners. When we thought he was going to die, we agreed it was too soon for us to try to fill any vacuum he left. When we were ready to have our own territory, we'd run it together.

Those were the rules until the day Emilio gave Rosetta to me.

When Damiano left the room without promising to honor our boss's wishes, I chased him to the end of the hall. He was getting into a crowded elevator. I stuck my hand in the doors and, after they bounced open, wedged myself next to him.

"Fuck you," he murmured.

A pretty nurse gave him a look. She was too young to be such a prude, but out of respect for her, I didn't tell him to go fuck himself.

In the lobby, we went right for a couch in the corner that was bordered by tall, brass ashtrays. I took out a smoke even though I didn't want it.

"He's going to live, you know," I said.

"Yeah. And he's still giving it all to you."

"He's going to be buried with the crown up his ass and you know it."

Damiano laughed. I laughed. It seemed like it was going to be all right. Nothing had to change.

"You know," he said. "The last few days? When we all thought he was gonna kick? My dad?"

"Yeah."

He didn't have to say another word. Cosimo had taken over as if the territory was his birthright, but he would have to relinquish control when Emilio was out of the hospital. He was loyal, but ambitious. A week with a power vacuum was a dangerous time.

"When he hears you basically got the crown?" Damiano shakes his head and blows smoke. "Feel sorry for your ass."

Emilio's preference for me wouldn't protect me from Cosimo, who could kill me in an instant. And if I killed him, I'd have to answer to Emilio, who'd probably kill me just to prove the preference didn't exist.

"Don't tell him," I said. "Please."

Camilla Moretti came down the long hospital hallway in a brown, ankle-length wool coat and black boots, hair flying behind her. Her strides were long and confident, as if she was the daughter of Altieri Cavallo, not the docile wife of a capo who was almost drowned.

"I won't." Damiano stamped out his cigarette. "Fuck, I'm pretty sure he'd slit my throat for being second in line."

We shook hands on it just as Emilio's wife reached us.

"Mrs. Moretti," I said with a respectful bow. "We just got out. He looks good."

"Did he give you the state bar license number yet?"

she asked me without mentioning her husband's health. "For the American lawyer?"

I wouldn't know what she's talking about for a few days, but I didn't want to admit ignorance when she seemed to know more.

"No."

She nodded and turned toward Damiano. "Your father is here."

"Cool. I was just up there, so I don't think I can go again."

She *tsk*ed. "He's in first floor recovery. Just getting out of the ER. You should check on him."

Damiano ran one way. Camilla calmly walked the other.

I finished my cigarette, thinking Emilio had put in the order to put Cosimo in the ER to tell the man who was in charge.

---

It had never occurred to me that Camilla was taking care of business while Cosimo playacted the role of boss. Not until I sit at the bar of an empty club with Damiano, watching Pellegrino bubble around fresh ice, thinking about the power of wives, did the possibility occur to me clearly enough to dismiss as nonsense.

The days to my possession of the crown are ticking away, and none of this old stuff will help me.

"What do you want?" Damiano asks, tapping his fingertips together like Venus's clamshell gnawing on the goddess.

"The Tabonas? When they tried to grab my wife on

Flora Boulevard? You came to *Mille Luci* to tell me, as a friend."

"I warned you in good faith."

"I didn't give you the appreciation you deserved."

"Damn right." He puts down his empty glass. "And now you called me here because you want something. So spit the toad."

The roar of an industrial floor-buffer starts behind us.

"Call it off with Gia," I say.

"What? Why?"

"Because I'm asking you to."

"I just overlooked the whole broken flower thing," he exclaims.

"You were going to anyway."

"Fuck you." He taps his glass and Robert pours him another finger of amaretto.

"Listen." I turn to face him, because I'm not interested in trading insults anymore. "Twice now, you asked to come back. As friends. As business partners. Like it was."

"It was good."

"It was. I've been thinking, I have no one in my organization I can use when things expand."

With a single, sharp nod, his whole demeanor changes from guarded and suspicious, to excited. "Which they will. When you get the *corona*, boom. World at your feet."

"And that's coming soon."

"So you know how to get it?"

Damiano's willing to marry a woman he doesn't know to get on my side of the veil. The admission I'm about to make proves my good faith by shifting the veil just enough for him to trust that he'll be inside my world.

"Yes," I say. "I know how to get it."

"Wow." He clicks his glass with mine. "*Salute, coglione.*"

Calling me a jackass just as he finds out I'm close to the crown is a sign he's going to be casually disrespectful when no one's looking. I drink my Pellegrino rather than correct him. There will be plenty of time for that.

"So what are you thinking?" he asks. "That school over the river, maybe? What's the play? Those kids don't carry cash, but there's plenty of receipts."

"True. It could work."

"And I have an angle on the real estate market over there."

"Good. But first..." I wedge the lime between my teeth and pull off the pith. "I'm going to end the *'mbasciata.*"

"What?" He blinks hard, eyeing me sidelong as if my stupidity can't be looked full in the face. "You're serious?"

He thinks I'm an idiot, but I'm not. I'm just a fool blindly chasing love over a cliff.

"With the *Corona Ferrea*, you can expand your territory to the four corners, but *this* crazy shit is what you want to try to do?" he asks.

"There will be no more debt brides." I jam the sucked-dry peel into the ice. "Starting with yours."

He laughs, then waves, rocking in his seat as if his body can't contain everything he wants to say.

"Man," he says, shaking his head with false regret, "I'd really like to take you up on that. But you're just not getting it. This entire thing with Gia? It's out of my hands now. That's not my money. It's a deal I brought to my father, and it was good enough for him to smile on me. That's *his* money, and if you have the choice between insulting him and walking away with your life, or insulting him and ending up in the ground? You shit on his lap. You kick his dog. You fistfuck his mistress, but you do *not* throw his money back in his face."

"We'll see about that."

He gets off the stool and slaps my shoulder. "Call me."

I'm left with a choice I never wanted to make. My wife or a war.

---

"I'm going to miss dinner," I tell Violetta on the phone as I get into the Alfa.

"Okay. I need to go to the store for the party and some woman things."

"Make Armando a list." I'm being more terse than I want, but I have bigger problems on my mind than her feminine products.

"For the party stuff, it's fine, but for the other stuff… it's the kind of thing a woman does for herself."

Especially now, with her birthday so close, I don't want her outside alone. "Celia can go with you."

"She's off tomorrow."

Flora Street taught me a lesson I don't want to learn

again. If the Tabonas had succeeded in taking her, I would either be standing in the rubble of Secondo Vasto or I'd be dead.

"You go with Armando or you don't go." I start the car. "And go to the drugstore over the river. The big one, by the school."

"Why?"

"Damnit, Violetta, just do it."

Silence. I should apologize for snapping at her, but I need her to do what she's told.

"Please," I add. "Trust me."

"Fine." She hangs up, and I'm left staring at Genovese Street out my car window.

Fucking Christ. I want to make her happy and keep her safe. That was what the house by St. John's was about, but I don't know how to do either.

If I could take her away—far away—and live with just the two of us, I would do it. We could start over. I'd run a café and she'd run her life around simple things. Our home. My cock. Eventually, children. And she'd be happy, because she'd never know of another 'mbasciata, or think it was in my power to stop them.

That's how it started.

Not with a decision. Just a desire for a life I didn't want.

All I wanted from that fantasy was for her to forget what I'd done and what I'd allowed. She said she forgave me, but she'd never forget.

## 21

## VIOLETTA

My strategy is to get the guy in the bright blue jacket to meet me at the front with a pregnancy test, and it works. I bring a basket full of birthday party junk—streamers, candles, little plastic tooters, and party hats—to the register.

Bright Blue Jacket puts the test on the counter, pushes his thick wire glasses up, and says, "This is the one you wanted?"

Yes, it is, because it's just like every other test. One line for the status quo. One line for time to change the world I live in.

Two lines for an immediate decision. Raise a child in it, or leave it.

"Violetta!"

I spin around to find Santino's zia Anette, then I turn back to the cashier who's still holding up a pregnancy test.

"That's the one," I say quickly, then I hold my arms

out to Anette for a kiss on each of her blush-heavy cheeks, while the beeping of the register goes on.

"You shouldn't come here for that," Anette says, flicking a finger toward the items being shoved into a plastic bag, and I tighten. She saw the test. Is she telling me to go to the doctor? "Lorenzo owns a party store on Fifth."

"Oh. I didn't know." I don't care either, but shame for my ignorance is a good excuse for my hot cheeks.

She takes out an old flip phone. "I have to drop by there to get something for Gia's reception."

Gia's reception? Santino said he would end it. Maybe Anette didn't get the memo?

"I'll call Lucia right now and have her tell him you're coming."

"Did someone say party?" another voice asks. It's Scarlett getting rung up at the adjacent register. I feel attacked from all sides. "That's impossible since I'm not invited!"

I hug Scarlett so tightly I'm just short of breaking a rib, and when I let go, her eyebrows are knotted with concern. We move away from the counter.

"Violetta?" She's looking me up and down as if she's never seen me before.

Scarlett's going to ask me if I'm all right and I'm not going to lie. I'll tell her straight out, right in the drugstore, and Anette will hear it.

"I thought you were in Monaco," I say.

"Ugh! Don't get me started on my father's business."

Anette comes up to us, clapping her phone closed. "Are you coming? I have to go today or the ribbon won't be here in time. Is that Armando?" She waves him over.

I never wanted or needed party supplies. The birthday dinner will be like any other except for a cake, which isn't a big deal, but why is Anette in such a rush for a wedding that may not happen?

"How long will the ribbon take?" I ask to make conversation.

"Paola's giving me agita. Now-now-now. Everything now. She called me at two this morning—from her lunch."

I'm getting the feeling the wedding isn't being called off at all. My heart pounds like a drum. I want to run to my husband and choke him first and ask questions later, but I can't. I have to breathe. I don't have the whole story.

"Do you have time for coffee?" I ask Scarlett.

"Well, duh. Yeah."

"Lorenzo closes at four," Anette says.

"Oh, I'm so rude. Aunt Anette, this is my friend Scarlett from school. Scarlett, you met Santino. This is his aunt."

They exchange greetings, and I realize the pregnancy test is at the bottom of the bag, totally visible pressing against the thin white plastic.

I have to get out of here.

"So tell Lorenzo I'd love to come by another time, okay?" I kiss Anette before she has a moment to object.

I pull Scarlett into the street, toward the Leaky Bean, sure Armando's hot on our heels, trying to look inconspicuous.

"Who's the hot guy following us?" Scarlett whispers.

"He's really nice. But no."

"Is he your bodyguard or something?"

"Kind of."

"I knew it!"

We enter the coffee shop, where a duet of acoustic guitarists strum a song with unremarkable lyrics, and I go right for the counter and order for Scarlett first.

"Green tea, and double espresso shot with lemon."

The cashier blinks once, tilts her head just enough for one red braid to slip behind her shoulder, and smiles. "We don't have lemon."

Of course they don't. I'm on the wrong side of the river to drink lemon with my espresso.

"That's fine." I catch sight of Armando at the door. "Make it two."

She gives me a number on a stick, and Scarlett and I sit at a table with the number between us.

"Don't think I didn't see it," she says. "You're knocked up?"

"If I knew, I wouldn't need the test." I put the bag on my lap and shift the box to the middle.

"Are you excited? Or… too soon?"

Normal question in the normal world. No one else will ask me that.

"Yes." I drop the bag between my feet. "And yes."

"How does that husband of yours feel about it?"

When I walked in here, my only intention was to get away from Anette before my day was sucked into a party-supply vortex where I'd have to avoid questions and meaningful looks about the pregnancy test. I never intended to tell Scarlett anything about my situation, but I've caught her at some weird moment. She's not talking about herself but leaning forward in silence, waiting for me to fill her in.

"I haven't told him," I say.

"Are you keeping it?" Another question that would only be asked on this side of the river.

"Yes."

"So why do you look like you want to throw yourself over a cliff?" Her eyes scan mine. "Is he all right with you?"

"Of course."

"Don't be mad I'm telling you this, but if you need somewhere to go and you forgot the helpline numbers, I have them. Or you can stay with me. Whatever you want."

"You're a good friend."

"So do you need help?"

Our order comes. I send the extra espresso to Armando. He waves to me when he gets it. Then I face Scarlett.

"He is good to me." I sip my coffee from the tiny paper cup. "And I love him."

"Good." She relaxes so much I realize how tense she was. "Really, that's good, because as soon as I saw that guy, I was worried."

"You didn't seem worried. You sent me a text that he was hot."

"Yeah, well, he is. But he had a gun on him, same as that bodyguard you have." She shrugs. "And all of us from school? We all know you, but honestly…" She blows on her tea. "We also know what goes on over the river."

"What goes on?"

She sips her tea with an abundance of caution. "Like, the mob and shit? And police jurisdiction stops at the bridge. Supposedly, it's like this other whole world on the other side."

"How come I didn't know you felt that way?"

"Why bring that up? So you can get hurt?" She tries to sip again and does a little better. "Not interested. You seemed okay. You never said anything. But then you obviously didn't go on your trip, and Signore Hotstuff showed up, and I thought, 'Oh, yeah, that's a thing that happens over there.' So I just filed it. Figured I'd see you in September."

My future education is a big fat question mark, but I don't tell her that. She's seen the pregnancy test. She knows it already.

"It's everything you say," I tell her, realizing—as the words come out—how silent I've been on the subject. "Everyone's in everyone's business, unless it's real business… and you're a woman. Then it's definitely not *your* business. But there's peace. Zero crime. I mean… except the stuff that's against the law."

Scarlett chuckles.

"Everyone agrees on how things should be, more or less," I add.

"Even you?"

Stalling, I finish my coffee.

"Espresso's thicker from a Moka pot." I put down the ridiculous, toy-sized mug. "And the rim should be rubbed with lemon, which you can't do with a fucking Dixie cup… but when there's a world war on and you don't have enough water? The citrus sanitizes it so you don't drink… basically sewage. And if you have to drink chicory because the fascists raised the coffee tariffs? A drop of sambuca corrects the bitterness."

"I take it you don't like the espresso." She looks at me over the rim of her green tea.

"Sambuca ruins good coffee. It's not necessary anymore. The war is *over*. And that's how I feel about a lot of what goes on where I grew up. We're correcting things that don't need it anymore. We have solutions for problems that were already solved in other ways, and now we're calling them traditions we have to live by. And all I'm saying, all I think with my whole heart, is that if you like sambuca in your coffee, drink it. But don't tell me I have to correct something that's fine already, then call it tradition and act like it's normal."

She sits back, cradling her cup at her chest, and shakes her head. "You lost me at the war being over."

"I'm sorry."

"I just want to know you're okay."

"I'm fine. But I'm not okay with the way we are. Things have to change, and if I have to be the one to change them, so be it."

"Fine." She shrugs. "But are you inviting me to your party or not?"

I laugh, but no. She can't come to this party. Nothing on this side of the river is powerful enough to change where I'm from.

She tells me about a guy she met in a fender bender with her new BMW, who she asked on a date in the ensuing road rage—right after threatening to put a tire iron through his windshield. By the end of it, I'm laughing so hard my side hurts.

And unlike the last time I saw Scarlett, I can see the

future. There's no reason not to see her again. I can go to school and have the life I want.

This time, when I hug my friend and say good-bye, I feel as if I have the power to make anything possible.

I do have the power. It makes me smile uncontrollably in the back seat of the car.

Armando looks at me in the rearview. "Happy today?"

"You could say that."

My phone dings. There's a message from Gia.

I open it, reading a series of short, textual bursts, and each one is a punch in the face.

22

## SANTINO

Engraved inside our wedding rings, where a date or a line about love would usually go, is a number—a lawyer's bar license, given to me in the days following our meeting with Emilio in the hospital.

After Rosetta died, I looked up the number so I could tell Nazario Coraggio it was all over. The deal was off. But there was no such license issued.

When I heard Damiano had designs on Violetta, I married her, then tried the license number again. Nazario protected himself—the license didn't lead me to him, but a partner in a generations-old international firm, with an office a hundred miles away, in a part of the state with high rises and a Starbucks on every corner.

The receptionist denied there was a Nazario Coraggio in the firm, then gave me a phone number to call on a certain date.

Today is the day.

I made it. Violetta won't have to read about the

numbers in my will and find the lawyer herself. It's here. The secret is safe. The crown is safe. She's safe.

Behind a locked door to the back room of *Mille Luci*, I take out a new phone and dial the number the receptionist gave me. When the lawyer picks up, I recognize the voice immediately.

"Nazario?"

Emilio Moretti's consigliere—*Il Blocco*—coughs dry and hard.

"Santino DiLustro." He says in Italian, "You made it."

"So did you. I thought they buried you in the sea."

He *tsks*. "No. I know how to stay low. But you? You're a big piece over there now."

"Big piece over a small territory."

"With a target on your back so big a child could hit it." Nazario Coraggio is a born consigliere. He never holds back advice, whether you want it or not. "Emilio said you were the patient one. The one who sees the whole…" He stops for a coughing fit. "You lost the picture when you married her so fast. No courtship, no nothing."

"I had no choice. Damiano was going to claim her."

"You could have started sooner."

Explaining that I stalled because of Rosetta is pointless. My guilt and regret mean nothing to him. "I did what I had to do."

"You did what you *wanted*."

Arguing with a man who's right will get me nowhere.

"How much longer is this lecture going to go?" I look at my watch even though he can't see the cue over the phone. "I have things to do."

"You do." He wheezes. "You have to secure your position before you get what you were promised, or it'll be taken away from you."

"By who? I ran the Tabonas out already."

"They're trash. It's the Orolios you have to worry about."

"I have Damiano under control," I say.

He sighs as if his point is a target a child could hit, and I'm missing it over and over.

"You have to play defense for a few more days. Don't make any moves." He coughs twice and swallows the rest behind a guttural groan. "Fortify your position."

"*Bene*. I will."

"You do not appreciate how precarious your situation is."

"I do."

"Cosimo's looking for a reason to hit you."

"*Cristo*, can you make your point more clear? Or would you like to come here and knock me over with a lead pipe?"

"I'm an old man. All I want is to see this thing put in safe hands. Then I can die."

"It will be safe."

"I know."

He gives me a time to be at the lawyer's office. I don't write it down.

---

"Violetta?" I call up the stairs.

She's supposed to be home, but she's not in the

kitchen or by the pool. I keep looking. She's not in her room and she's not answering when I call her name. I turn the corner around a blind hallway in my own fucking house, and I'm stopped by cold metal against my cheek.

It's a gun.

Someone shorter than me is holding it. I look without moving, but I already know who it is.

"Violetta," I say softly, with my hands up. "You're not going to shoot me."

"You're a liar."

She has my grandfather's gun with the World War Two bullets still in it, and she knows I'm telling the truth. She's not going to shoot me, but her eyes are red-rimmed and her mouth is twisted into a snarl. She thinks she might pull the trigger, and what she believes she's capable of is more important than what I think she's going to do.

"Put that down."

"You said you'd call it off!"

There's no point in pretending I don't know what she's talking about.

"I said *I will* stop the *'mbasciata*. I can't now. Not without the crown." I speak calmly, but it's not stopping the trembling that's taken her over from her face to the two hands holding the revolver. "Do you know how to use that?"

She clicks the hammer back, proving she watches television, but not that she understands how sensitive the trigger is.

"Gia says the wedding's still on. They're doing it.

What the fuck, Santino?" She takes a hard sniff, and her breath hiccups. "Why are you letting this happen?"

In the shake of her hands and the break of her voice, she's losing control of herself, and that trigger's like a virgin dick in a wet cunt. The slightest friction and it's all over.

"I can…" I don't finish the sentence on purpose, because I don't want her to react.

Instead, I grab her wrist and push it away, wrestling her down. The gun fires, leaving a long path of smoking splinters in the hardwood floor.

That could have been my brain.

If she'd killed me, what would happen to her?

How many men would come for my wife? And what would they do to her?

The thought of her being torn apart because I'm not here to protect her steals every ounce of my control. I become what I am and always was—an animal.

## 23

## VIOLETTA

The opposite of love is apathy, and there's nothing indifferent about my feelings toward my husband. I hate him for letting me love him almost as much as I hate him for loving me.

    And I don't want to shoot him. I don't even want to hurt him. But I don't know how to get through to him that what he's allowing is worse than a sin, and I don't know how to get out of the situation in the hallway without shooting him. I've gone too far.

    When he wrestles me to the floor, the gun goes off. The power of it against my palm is so great that it loosens my fingers, freeing itself—and I'm grateful to Santino for making sure the bullet landed anywhere but his skull.

    He gets off me and picks up the gun. For a moment, I'm sure he's going to give me a taste of my own medicine in the form of a bitter threat of death.

    Instead, he points the gun anywhere except at me. I'm in a crouch when he opens the cylinder and lets the bullets clatter to the floor. He swallows fire and breathes rage.

"Do you know what you almost did?" he growls, tossing the gun onto the hall table. It makes a clattering racket that echoes off the walls. I can still get to it, but it's empty.

I'm terrified and aroused at the same time, but I'm also angry enough to get my feet under me. "Killed a liar."

In one step, he has me by the throat, pressing me to the wall. I'm submissive, powerless, and immediately wet. He doesn't hold me hard enough to choke me, but he's forceful enough to pin me still with the pulse at the base of his hand throbbing against my neck. Intoxicating danger and solid protection mingle in my brain, and the blood in my veins thrums with electricity. I let him handle me, knowing he would never, ever harm me.

"You want to know what they'd do to you?" he says through his teeth. His grip tightens on my neck, but my nipples harden and an insatiable need grows between my legs.

Maybe I don't want to know, but I nod against his hand.

"Tell me," I croak. "But don't *lie* again."

Santino snarls and pushes me into my bedroom, snarling and grumbling to himself in indecipherable Italian. I land on the bed on my back with my legs akimbo, struggling to get them under me quickly. Instead of fear, the knot of desire grows bigger and tighter, pulling the threads of my humming nerves together into an ever-spinning ball of need at my core.

"You're going to let him marry Gia. For money."

"To stop a war!" His voice rumbles across my chest and I really think I might combust before he even touches me.

Santino grabs the neckline of my dress in both hands and pulls them apart, ripping the dress in two, leaving me exposed and backing away, yet ready to be ravaged.

"You're an animal," I say, flinging myself at him with no plan but to get closer without giving an inch.

He grabs me by the waist and throws me over the gold-painted dresser. The carved wood edges dig into the tender skin of my stomach. My pussy quivers at the pain and the roughness of his hands as he flings the back of my dress up and spreads my legs apart.

"You're an animal," I repeat, but this time, it's not an insult.

From behind, he shoves my thong aside to split my most sensitive lips. I gasp at his touch and he murmurs to himself in Italian. His finger runs the length of my seam, rough like the rest of his touch, and I begin my slow, glorious death.

"How are you so wet?"

"Fuck me and find out."

He smacks my ass. "That mouth." He smacks it again. Hard. "Do not speak to me like that in my own home."

"This is *our* home," I manage.

"You cook!" *Smack*. "You clean!" *Smack*.

My ass burns from his blows, and still I want more.

"You run the house." *Smack*. "You talk to the other wives about who's a whore." His hand drops to my right nipple and pinches hard. I see stars behind my eyelids and my breath catches in my throat. I'm seconds from coming and there is nothing else in life I need more, right now, than this. "But you do not get into my business."

"Gia's my business!"

"Nothing!" His fingers work my nipples so hard the pain threatens to morph into an orgasm. "You hear me? Nothing of this again!"

I summon all my strength, open my eyes, and look over my shoulder. "Make me."

He takes me under the chin and pulls my head back. He's so tall and long that his torso covers me. "I'll choke the back talk out of you, *Forzetta*, God help me, I will."

"Fucking try."

He lets go, but the pressure of his body pins me hard against the curved edges of the wood. I hear him unbuckle his belt.

"Tell me how bad I am."

"You are so fucking bad." His belt is out of the loops with a *whick*. "Why does torturing me bring you so much joy?"

"Because you're a good man."

"And you need to learn your place."

"What are you going to do about it?" I give us both a last taste of defiance before complete surrender.

He wraps the belt around my neck and holds it closed while his other hand opens his pants to release his cock. I am a fool. I underestimate his ability to take me places I don't think I want to go until I arrive.

"I'm going to stop you from talking." He yanks me back by the belt. "You like that. Eh?"

"I love it."

He pushes my legs open with his feet, holding them wide.

"Because you are a naughty fucking American girl." In one thrust, he's deep inside me, pulling me to him by the throat.

"I'm so bad."

"Just take it." Santino presses my hips down.

He doesn't want it to be easy. God help me, he wants to destroy me and I want him to. I want him to take me to the edge more than he wants to go there.

"Hurt me," I egg him on.

"I'm going to break you." He smacks my ass and the sting is pure pleasure.

"Yes."

"Stop talking."

He rides me like a jockey using a belt as a rein, hips at a gallop, then a canter, then a run, faster and deeper than any man his size should. I squeal.

"That's what your voice is for. Now take it."

This is not sex. It's punishment. It's violence. It's a drug and I'm an addict.

"You like when I talk."

"I like when you're fucking quiet!" he roars.

Then he picks me up, throws me over his shoulder and pitches me onto the bed, dropping me onto my back. Towering over me, he grabs behind my knees and pulls me to him, the back of my dress sliding against the duvet, and spreads them wide.

"Your mouth needs to talk less." He shoves four fingers inside me, tugging on the hood of my clit, sending shockwaves of bliss up my spine. "And your cunt needs to talk more."

His fingers are slick when he pulls them out.

"I want more."

He shoves them in my mouth. I taste myself, gurgling around hard knuckles.

"You don't know what you want." He heaves his massive cock into my waiting, begging cunt. He's loose and feral, angry and passionate, trying to impale my heart with every thrust.

"This is what you need." He grunts, cupping my jaw with his palm and pushing his fingers into my mouth. "To be put in your place."

The heady fumes of an orgasm build into a mindless fog. I am nothing. I do not exist outside him and the building promise of release. He owns me. I'm his toy. His American whore. His growling in Italian comes from the other side of an ocean.

"You. Stay. Out. Of. My. Business." His thrusts punctuate each word.

Euphoria finally cracks open. Everything goes rushing to my pussy as the earth opens and the heavens cry, and I scream his name the moment before he thrusts me into voiceless oblivion.

He curses, closes his eyes, and lets his fingers slide from my mouth when he comes. He stumbles back with his dick out, shiny and wet, leaving me panting on my back. I wipe the hair from my face, but my arms are overcooked noodles and flop back to the bed.

Santino takes me by the ankles, spreading them to the width of his arm span and wedges himself between my legs. Is he going to fuck me again? Right now?

"Are you hurt?" he asks with his forehead touching mine.

"I'm fine."

He doesn't seem satisfied. I pull him down to me.

"No. *Mi*..." he starts, but can't finish without swallowing. "*Mi dispiace.*"

The Italian words for an apology are "I am not pleased," and in this case, he means it literally. He's not pleased with himself. He's ashamed and regretful.

"Look at you. Look what I did. Your dress is torn. Your throat will be bruised. Inside... I hurt you."

"I'm fine," I say again.

"No!" he shouts, standing, still fully dressed with his dick out. "You want to help Gia. Where's my excuse? I wanted to *hurt* you for no higher reason. This..." He holds out his hand to indicate my body as if what he sees is illustration enough. "This is not what a man does. A man keeps his wife safe, even from himself."

When I get up on my knees, I feel the back of the torn dress draping over my calves and wrestle out of it.

"I asked you to do it." I toss the ruined dress on the floor. My thong's so stretched out it's falling off, so I roll onto my back and whip that off as well. "I begged you. I egged you on."

"That's not a reason to beat you like a dog."

"Stop, please. It's not like that."

I throw the destroyed underwear to the side, and when I do, he sees me from behind and falls in the ornate wingback chair as if he's been pushed. I get up and check the mirror. My bottom is almost fire engine red. I don't remember him spanking my ass that much, but I was distracted by my craving for more. Admittedly, it hurts—just like my sore pussy and aching shoulders. I can find plenty of other parts in pain, but Santino's posture is hunched. He's covering his face, but not his eyes, as if he has to look at me to understand the wrongness of it.

"No," I say. "What we did together is beautiful. Please don't turn something so good into a sin."

"It's not good!"

"If I said stop, would you have stopped?"

He rubs his jaw, unable to meet my gaze. "I don't know."

"Would you have wanted to stop?"

"Yes, but… I was outside myself. Violetta." He comes to me and cups my face, finally looking me in the eyes. "I lost control. This time, you liked it. What if next time you don't? What will I do then?"

"You'll stop." I reach for him, laying my hands on his cheeks. He looks confused, perplexed even. He doesn't look like the mighty ruler who defends against hardened killers and mouthy women. "You're *my* husband. Mine. I won't let you give in to inertia. It's my job to make you a good man, Santino, a great man. I'll fight an army to clear you a path between you and who you really are."

I let my hands slide away and get off the bed.

"I know you want to help Gia, and I know why you think you have to wait. But you can't. There is no time." I look away. "Because I'm worried about the baby."

I look back at him, waiting for the recognition of what I'm saying.

He whispers my name like a prayer.

"I'm worried if we're having a girl, and you don't

stop this from being okay right *now*…" My sobs rush so fast, I can barely get the next part out. Santino reaches for me, but I put my hands out to keep him away. "I'm afraid you're going to sell her."

"No." His first word of denial is laced with awe and surprise, but falls on deaf ears.

"I didn't kill you, but I will. To protect her, I will slit your throat while you sleep."

"Why are you talking like this?"

"Because I mean it. I love you, but I'm not making empty threats. My daughter will be born free."

"No child of mine—" he starts, but I put my hand over his lips.

"No child. Say it. Say no one will be born with a price tag."

Without a stern word or command, he takes control of the conversation, tenderly holding my neck and jaw in his huge hands and putting the tip of his nose to mine.

"I swear to you now, my wife, my *Forzetta*, my blood violet, that as far as my territory stretches, every daughter and son will be born free. There will be no more arranged marriage. No debt brides. No forced weddings. So help me God, I'll burn in hell for everything I've done, but not for breaking this promise to you."

I take him by the wrists and put his palms on my belly. "Your promise is to her."

"*Sì*." When he agrees in Italian, I believe him, releasing doubt and fear.

"Thank you." My voice cracks and the tension flows

out of me, because believing him is all I want right now.

He kisses the tears from my cheeks and neck, getting on his knees and wrapping his arms around me with his ear to my stomach, listening to the sound of life growing inside me.

## 24

## SANTINO

Kneeling before her while she sobs, my brain is soup being stirred. I feel the meatballs bang on the spoon. Escarole gets tangled in the handle then washes away. This and that. No and yes. Up-down-sideways. Save her and free her. Bring and take. Lock and key.

All the while, I'm being cooked, and there's no going back to who I was or what I wanted before. The times I wanted to crawl inside Violetta and live there were prayers made whole. I've taken root, and I cannot bear her misery any more than I can stand for her to be in danger.

Then today, I became the danger, and I swear two things.

One, I tell her. No one will be told who to marry.

The second thing, I swear to myself. I will not lose control with her body again. Not like I just did. She can shoot me first.

I'll be as rough as she wants, but I will not hurt her in anger. I am not a child. I am not a baby crying for milk or a frustrated toddler. I am a man, and I decide what I do and what I do not do. No matter what she does, I will keep my head about me. I cannot stop her from setting my life on fire, because I struck a match and burned hers to the ground.

I don't know why it took me until this moment to see it so clearly, or why the threat of a daughter was the only thing that could remove the scales from my eyes.

My wife's life was destroyed in a single day. She was dragged to the church. She was forced to live in my house, under my rules. I have every power over her, and though she'll be fine tomorrow or the next day, in my heart, I know that I was so angry she put a gun to my head, I could have killed her just now. I also know now that from the moment I saw her, I never chose to let her live. I've been a car speeding ahead, steering around the curves with a broken brake. Today, I would have finished what I started. I would have crashed and broken her body, but I came inside her, and once that happened, the car ran out of gas.

Violetta and I got lucky. She wasn't forced to marry a heartless man, and I didn't marry a mindless woman. But fortune is not a friend to everyone.

I have to be a man and break the world so Violetta, Gia, my daughter—none of them have to depend on luck just to live.

She kneels with me, then we lie on the floor together. Her sobbing slows to calm breaths. I rub streaks from her face. I want to give her a bath to wash my filth off her, but if I do that, I'll lose my nerve. She can bathe herself.

"We're not going to end this from the floor." I get

my feet under me and hold my hand out to her. "Let's put the gun away."

I help her up. She hands me the gun, but I don't take it. When she starts for the basement, I redirect her down the hall, past the double doors to the room reserved for business.

She was never meant to come in here, but that's all changed. I can't put closed doors between us any longer. I will have her by my side as I expand. Her counsel. Her voice. Her castle joined with mine.

With her, I will rewrite traditions into laws.

I turn on a lamp and sit behind my desk. I open the sideboard drawer.

"Put the gun here, where we can get to it."

I let her place it there, and slide it closed.

She takes a chair by the window and crosses her legs, tapping on the wooden parts of the arms with impatience and expectation. How can I still want to fuck her, now that she has a life inside her?

"I have a plan," she says.

"Okay." The engine of the gold-faced clock grinds and ticks.

"You offer any father who wants to sell his daughter a low-interest loan."

Biting back a laugh takes more strength than anything I've ever done. "I'm not the state government or a bank."

"Which means you don't have to get a committee to sign off. You just do it."

"And what if they sell their daughters anyway?"

"Why would they if you can refinance the loan?"

"And every loan shark and bookie from here to Naples would just nod?"

She shrugs. "Fuck them."

Now, I laugh, because she thinks too much of my influence, and too little of my power.

"What you're missing, my sweet *Forzetta*, is that *'mbasciate* is usually the groom's prerogative, and the father is eager to get her gone without paying a bride price."

"Jesus Christ, are you serious?"

"And the debts?" I put my elbows on my knees. There's so much to explain. "Not always the case. Sometimes the marriage is to join territories or avoid a war."

"Gia's marriage is all the above."

"Yes. And she'll be married before I have the crown."

"No, she won't be." Her gaze is far-fixed, searching for a way to undo what's been done. "What if you have to stop it? Like someone forced your hand or something?"

"Someone like my wife?"

"Maybe." Her eyes are everywhere, taking in the layout of the room and the things in it. "I never asked you about your grandfather's furniture." She rubs her thumb along the ornate curve of the chair's edge.

"What about it?"

"Why won't you get rid of it?"

"I love it."

"You know it doesn't go with the house, right?"

"I know. But when my mother was raped and the man didn't offer to make an honest woman out of her, my grandfather rejected her. Threw her out."

"Wow. Asshole. What about your grandmother?"

"Dead. My aunt Paola found her sister in an asylum in Aversa, then found me with the Sisters of the Assumption. I was born in the Montesanto Metro station. And still, my grandfather wanted nothing to do with her or with me."

"But Paola took care of you."

"Only when she got married to Marco, who I will always be this grateful to." I hold up a finger and thumb an inch apart. "But no more than this much. Paola took a job and moved my mother to Trieste, then took me in. My grandfather still wouldn't meet me. He let his daughters live in shit instead. So." I lean back and spread my arms, indicating the entire house and everything in it. "When he died, I took his things and put them in my house so every day, I sit in his chairs and eat off his tables. I won. I beat him. I own his life now."

She nods, looking around the room with fresh eyes. "You really know how to hang on to a grudge."

"It's in the blood."

"Yeah. Speaking of blood…" She stands. "Mine's low on sugar, and I can't think. Can we finish this in the kitchen?"

She's not asking for permission, and I have the choice to follow her or get left behind.

## 25

## VIOLETTA

His voice rattles the windows of my dream, which has no story or point. No lesson. It's just pink lines crisscrossing my vision. Two. Four. Ten. Bifurcated. Crisscrossing. Never curved. Always in parallel pairs like elongated equal signs. A web across my vision in every direction. I'm not panicked. I'm not trapped inside them, trying to escape. We're just in the same noplace, the pink lines and I, coexisting.

I went to bed alone, but the lines vibrate when he speaks, and somewhere between sleep and wakefulness, I know he's beside me.

"Take it," he mutters.

I think this is a warning that he's going to penetrate me. My body heeds the words and rushes liquid between my legs.

"*Prendilo e basta*," he says the same thing in Italian.

Mostly awake now, I can tell his flat affect means he's sleeping, not getting ready to fuck me. With a deep breath, I'm aware enough to see the blur of him lying on his back next to me. I put my hand on his arm.

"Santi," I say gruffly. I half hope he's dreaming about sex. I wouldn't mind a little right now.

"*Prendilo e basta.*"

*Just take it* is not the same as *take it*. I'm not rousing a horny man, which becomes even more clear when I move my hand to his chest and I can feel his heart pounding. His arm twitches.

"Hey." I get an elbow under me. "You're having a dream."

"*Mi fa schifo.* I hate it. *Non lo voglio.*" He's getting more distressed.

I hate seeing him like this. Powerless. Afraid. It makes me feel alone without him, and I'm exposed and defenseless, but there's also a voice in me that hasn't spoken since nursing school. Right now, it's given expression through that vulnerability.

It says I am useful. I am strong. I have power over him that I can use to heal.

"Santino." I shake his chest, but his agitation only grows. Fully awake now, I straddle him and cup his face, saying his name again. "You're having a dream."

His eyes open wide as saucers, and his hands grab my wrists hard enough to hurt. I don't have a moment to struggle or gasp before he's flipped me onto my back, holding my hands over my head and pinning me to the bed with his pelvis.

"I will destroy you," he growls in my face.

"Santi," I squeak, then breathe as much as I can under his weight. "Santino." My pitch drops a little.

"I will erase you from this earth."

"Santino." I'm more steady now. "Santino."

He exhales and blinks. Then shuts his eyes tight and holds them before opening up, conscious enough to finally see me.

"*Cristo.*" He lets my hands go. "Violetta."

"I'm right here." I lay my palms on his cheeks.

He says my name again, but with less shock. "Are you okay?"

"I'm fine."

"I am so sorry." He turns his head to kiss my hand, then my wrist. "You're not hurt?"

Before I can reassure him, he gets on his knees and whips back the covers so he can see me in the moonlight.

"I told you," I say. "I'm fine."

When his shoulders relax, I know he believes me, and when he kisses my face, apologizing over and over in two languages, I know he's awake.

"What were you dreaming about?" I ask.

He doesn't tell me. Instead, he says, "It starts today."

---

WE'VE BEEN PLANNING all week, and because I'm part of his thinking, I haven't made any sudden moves. Haven't stolen the car, broken a vase, or made a single phone call that would signal an end to the status quo.

Even in Italy, when I felt happy and unencumbered, I was anxious, and I don't realize this until I can ask him anything and get a full and complete answer.

He tells me the deal with the rings, and what the

numbers engraved on the inside mean. In the event of his death, he arranged for me to find out what they are.

I memorize the numbers. I memorize the address and the time of our appointment on my birthday. All this happens in between a plan built around a promise.

We can go to the lawyer any time, but we're going first thing Monday morning—the day I turn twenty. My party will be on Sunday night—the last chance to break Gia's wedding and fix her life, before all eyes are on us.

At the party, I'll force Santino's hand in front of everyone, and he'll react to keep the peace.

He doesn't think it'll work, but I have to believe we won't have to resort to the brute force of plan B.

---

CELIA and I are wrapping *braciole* when Gia calls from the other side of the world.

"Happy birthday!" she says.

"That's tomorrow."

"Oh, these time zones always confuse me." I hear the bustle of a café and the honking of car horns behind her.

"The party is today," I add. "So it *feels* like my birthday."

"I wish I was there."

Personally, I don't. I'm glad she's thousands of miles away. While she's away, I don't have to worry that she'll try to stop us, or scuttle the plan by trying to help, or blow the secret.

Somehow, planning ways to buy out her arranged

marriage right in front of her seems more offensive than doing it behind her back, but it relieves me of having to treat her like a full human with agency over her decisions—because she isn't, and I hate the practical, real world truth of that.

"When are you coming home?" I ask.

"Tomorrow night." She pauses. "Dami told me it's going to happen right off the plane."

*It* means the wedding. At least he told her himself. He's braver than I expected.

"Why so quick?"

"I don't know, Violetta," she snaps. The mood swings I observed in the back of the Lincoln are still happening, and I don't blame her.

"Are you okay?" I say.

"I guess." She doesn't sound convinced, but she's definitely trying. "He seems all right when we talk on the phone, and I remember why I liked him in the first place."

So they've been talking. That's actually good. It shows an investment on Damiano's part that'll soften the blow if I fail to stop this atrocity.

"He understands me," she adds.

"Does he?" This is not what I expected to hear at all. The women of Secondo Vasto do not strive to be understood. They bend to their husbands' needs. "Like how?"

"Like…" She stops, pausing to think about it for so long, I fear the line dropped. "We make plans together."

The wedding, of course. He dictates that it has to happen whiplash-fast—inserting himself into the family just as Santino and I get the crown—then probably agrees to all the other plans a bride makes.

"I'll be there for you," I say. "Whatever you need."

"Do you promise?"

"I do."

"That makes me feel so much better."

She tells me her departure time, and together we do the math of time zones, and I realize she'll be landing as Santino and I will be driving to the lawyer's—where we will pick up the one thing that can keep her from being sold into marriage.

I don't tell her I might be breaking my promise to her by about an hour so I can keep a promise I made to my unborn daughter. If everything goes perfectly, I can keep both.

## 26

## SANTINO

"Coming through!" Violetta chirps like a bird and slithers like a cat around the kitchen's obstacles.

She salts the water, tests the sauce, and pours another glass of prosecco in one near-fluid motion. Violetta is like the ocean's shifting waves. She is the stars dancing around the moon.

Watching my wife work the kitchen for her birthday party, knowing we planned the most important piece of it together is a joy I never could have imagined.

When Emilio promised me one of his daughters, I gave up on the idea that my family life would ever be normal. I was right. My life with her isn't normal. It's much better than that.

After everything she's been through, all the upheavals and secrets and lies, the frustrating, maddening days, Violetta is earth in the kitchen and fire in stilettos.

When Celia's out of the kitchen for a moment, I

come up behind my wife and slide my hands around her body. One sneaks under her blouse and the other strikes out for an olive like a snake. She slaps my hand, but I keep tight on the olive and feed it to her. She smells like basil and yeast, like Napoli, like home.

"I want to fuck you on this counter right now."

She reaches for the olives. "You can if you help me clean it first." She feeds an olive to me over her shoulder.

"I'm going to clean it with your bare ass." I savor the salty brine.

"We have a job to do tonight," she whispers. "Keep your mind on it."

A small herd of children stampede into the kitchen, followed by a group of her family. Violetta's six-year-old cousin, Tina, wriggles between us to grab a handful of olives. My wife swats her away, but slips Tina a smaller bowl of sweet black olives. The kids disappear to stick them on their fingers.

She kisses me once and attends to her guests. Violetta and Celia pass out jobs to our zias and nonnas, who joke about us having only one kitchen. This is my wife's first gathering as the matriarch, and she's already a master.

If we get past this, she will have many more.

She's more comfortable than I have ever seen her. She's the dream hostess every man wants in a wife, and I wonder if she'd be the same if we'd met under other circumstances.

"Re Santino." Zia Madeline, the woman who raised my wife, kisses each of my cheeks. "You look well."

"All Violetta's fault."

"And I see she did the antipasto herself." She points toward the tray where the black olives have been carefully placed hole-side-up so the children can stick their fingers in more easily.

"She is the woman of the house."

Behind her, Violetta rushes to her zia, who scoops my wife into a big hug. They chatter as I answer the door for Angelo and Anette, who arrive with Lucia, Tavie, and his girlfriend, Diana. As soon as I greet them, Anette asks me where Violetta is.

"Why does everyone ask me for my wife?" I spread my arms wide. "Am I no longer good enough?"

"Don't feel bad, Santi. Only your family knows you."

"May you choke on an olive."

Anette pops one in her mouth and heads for the kitchen, catching Violetta as she's bringing out fresh wine.

Marco comes in after his wife's family, patting down his combover. He looks lost without Paola and Gia, but holds his head high as if he has a place in the pecking order—ten kilos of pride in an eight-kilo suit. He nods to me like an equal, and I make a conscious decision to shake his hand instead of punch his face.

All this trouble is because of his betting habit.

"Congratulations," I say. "I hear Gia's going to be married when she gets back from the other side."

"No need to waste time," he replies with a shrug. "Like you did. Just go." He raises his hand to indicate Violetta, who is perfect and mesmerizing despite rushing around. "My sister-in-law told me your wife was buying a pregnancy test."

"So she was." I offer nothing more than a satisfied

smile.

"Good," Marco says, taking that for a yes. "It all turns out in the end."

"It can turn to shit in the end too," I say, looking down at him. "And if you're not careful, you'll step in it."

"What does that mean?"

It means that with his neglect and disdain, he turned me into shit, and it's only a matter of hours before I mess up his fucking shoes.

"My wife says I shouldn't write fortune cookies." I hold up my glass. "*Salute.*"

We clink and he takes his leave to poke his pinkie into the hole of a black olive, eating it off like a child. What a joke of a man.

Violetta charms Tavie and his girlfriend with a story about an afternoon we had on the beach in Italy. Our eyes meet and her cheeks warm in the most beautiful way, as I remember the way her naked body looked under the blazing Napoli sun. I wonder how much of that story she disclosed. Angelo charms her in return with a story about a fish. Zio Guglielmo and Zia Madeline laugh with her over the children trying to steal bread with their olive-tipped fingers. My second cousin, Oriana, passes her baby to Violetta, who rocks and coos with her.

I didn't know my mother, so I don't miss her, but in that moment, I feel the empty place where she should have been.

Beside me, Marco is replaced by Violetta's zio Guglielmo.

"She looks happy," he finally says.

"She is."

We are quiet once more, as I doubt whether I have the right to speak for her.

"Thank you for raising her so beautifully." I raise my glass in toast to him.

"Anything is possible in America." He raises his own glass, and we toast the country where dreams meet reality.

Violetta clinks her glass of prosecco to announce dinner is ready.

---

THE LIGHTS ARE OUT and the little fires flicker over the red script of *Happy Birthday Violetta*. My wife glows, then during the last stanza of the song, she looks at me and smirks.

It's now, and she's ready.

"Make a wish!" Elettra cries, eyes big with her own wishes. Her mother brought the cake and Violetta gave them the 2 and 0 candles for the top.

Violetta blows out her candles, and I know she has no wish. She has a demand that has turned into a plan. Everyone applauds and the lights go on.

I stand and raise my glass. "To my beautiful wife, Violetta," I say in Italian. "Who has made me the happiest man in the world."

Everyone *aww*s. It's like a fucking movie.

"*Salute!*" I toast.

"*Salute!*" everyone toasts back.

We all sit and Anette starts to cuts the cake, when my Violetta stands and taps her glass with a spoon.

"I have an announcement to make," she says in Italian when she gets every last bit of attention.

She gets a gasp and an uncomfortable titter from my left. It could be that she's speaking Italian when so much has been said in front of her with the assumption she didn't. Or it could be that a newly married woman usually has only one kind of announcement to make.

"My husband, Santino." She raises her glass to me, and I nod as if I suspect she's going to surprise them with a pregnancy announcement, and approve by raising my own glass to her. "The man you men all call the king—while we girls pretend we don't know why…" She looks around and the women giggle. "Is going to pay Marco's debt so Gia can choose who she wants to marry."

Tavie leaps from his seat, shouting, "Yes!"

The room falls as silent as death. No one will look at me. Outside, even the birds don't dare to chirp. My house could burn down from the heat of their shock and awe. And in the middle, surrounded by blurred faces of confusion and horror, is my smiling wife, who lifted my world up with a beautiful party in a role she so masterfully played and then destroyed it with two sentences in Italian.

I sit there as if I'm ignorant, as if I'm almost—almost—impressed by how she manipulated this situation. As if I wish she'd done it to someone else, instead of turning her genius against me.

So I laugh. I laugh loudly and hard. I laugh so forcefully the others have no choice but to laugh with me lest they show their disloyalty.

Even Marco—especially Marco—laughs as he's

supposed to. The hardness in his eyes, however, says this will require some smoothing over. I don't like the way he's staring at my wife or the glances he casts my way. Marco may have raised me, but once I became a man, it is for my zia Paola I show him respect, and now I will have to lean into that all the more.

I straighten my sleeves, clear my throat, and make a show of taking a sip of prosecco. Everyone follows, and little by little, order is restored.

Violetta says nothing as she serves the cake, but she stares at me with a sultry look, challenging me like a beautiful tyrant in stilettos.

I follow her into the kitchen as the women clear the tables. Children weave between us, sneaking pastries and chasing Armando, who shoots me a few cryptic glances. I grab Violetta's arm and pull her by the pantry.

She tries to play coy and runs a finger down my chest. "I know you're feeling frisky right now, but there's an entire house full of people who want to play cards."

I grab her hand and pin it above her on the wall. "You are so fucking sexy."

"Make him an offer, Santino." The smirk leaves her face and is replaced by something fierce and earnest. "Go be a king *and* a saint."

"And I'll bring the devil to bed tonight."

Before I can kiss her, she slips past me, back out into the kitchen. Tavie runs in, breathless.

"Is it true?" he asks, pushing through the women to get to me.

Violetta returns to the dirty dishes as if nothing has

happened. She's ruthless.

"Say it's true!" Tavie shakes me from my brief stupor.

"Tavie," I warn, pulling him into a quieter corner.

"It has to be true, because I'll kill him if he touches my sister. I swear it on my mother's life."

"*Ma smettila!*" I shush him. "Never, ever swear like that unless you intend to kill your mother."

"I swear it." The boy points his chin up and scowls. The quiet cousin, who long kept to himself and never made waves, grows before my eyes into the man we joked he wasn't. "On my mother's life, I swear it."

"Go sit down, Tavie." I lay a heavy hand on his shoulder. This is not his fight. "Go."

"Zio?" My niece, Lucia, stands behind me with her cousin's baby on her hip, too young to know when she should be silent. "Is it true, Santi? Are you going to do it?"

All the women stare at me expectantly. No one hushes the girl or scolds her for asking such questions. They want to know. This affects them, and it's their business.

"These are matters for the men," I say, then leave out the back before I can see their reaction. As I slide the glass closed behind me, muffled sounds of kitchen life resume.

Outside, the men gather for a quick smoke before the cards are dealt. Time to act as though I'm putting out a fire my wife started without me.

As soon as I arrive, every man nods in respect before he puts out his smoke and silently goes back inside in a great exodus.

Every man, that is, except Marco.

He squares off and stares at me, blowing a line of cigar-reek from the side of his mouth, away from my face. I pull a single cigarette from the pack in my pocket and pack it along the box. Nothing is said as I reach for the steel Zippo in my breast pocket, or when it clacks as I open it and we breathe the smack of fresh kerosene. Not a word is said until it's all back home inside my jacket and I exhale.

"You may speak," I say the second time I inhale.

"You understand," he says with just enough respect to counter his own insult at being bailed out like a child, "I cannot go home with this hanging over my head." He rolls his cigar between wet lips, then puffs. "The contracts are signed. The business is done. Cosimo's blessed it. Damiano wants the marriage and he is paying the debts. There's no need for you to stick your nose in it. All due respect, of course."

"Stick my nose in it?" I shrug as if that's an interesting way to put it that doesn't deserve a more violent response.

"With all due respect."

"When you sent Gia—your daughter—to America, you asked me to watch over her. You put her well-being in my care. And I took that seriously. I've kept her away from dishonorable men and risky activities. I gave her a job to keep an eye on her for you. Here, in America, she is my responsibility because you asked for her to be. So don't you come here now and tell me it's not my business."

"After all I've done for you," he sneers. "This is how you treat me?"

I snap his fucking cigar out of his mouth and point the hot side at his face. "All you did was ignore me. You treated me like shit on your shoe because I didn't come out of your balls. You called me the little bastard of the house and wouldn't give me three euro for a fucking train to visit my mother. And I still would have paid your debt from the beginning."

"I don't want your money," he says from the bottom of his guts. "I'm just going to pay the way I want. It's my prerogative."

Marco's got a little laugh to his tone that makes me want to break every bone in his body. It's a chuckle of *we're all men here*, and a wink of, *così stanno le cose*—it is what it is. What are you going to do?

I stamp out his cigar.

"My wife misspoke," I repeat the agreed-upon lie. "But I'm not going to turn her into a liar. I will pay your debt, and in return, you will not sell Gia into marriage."

"You know your chickens," he says without seeming to have a single reservation. "Look at how you came to marry your own wife?"

Calmly, I wedge my cigarette between my lips as the skin under my collar runs hot, and my blood carries instructions to my body faster than a thought. In less than the blink of an eye, my fingers grip his throat.

"I came to marry her out of duty, Marco."

Marco gags, gripping my sleeve. I didn't realize how many years I've wanted to choke him, because it feels better than anything I've ever done.

"Do you understand?" I squeeze tighter, sucking on my cigarette and exhaling out my nose.

He nods against my fingers.

"Liar." I squeeze until his knees buckle. "You don't understand duty."

My uncle's face is bright red. He's choking out something that could be apology or curse, and I let him go to hear which it is. He drops back, hand to his throat, landing on the patio couch.

Behind me, someone coughs. All of the men are outside, staring at Marco gasping for air. No one runs to his aid.

*Bene.* They need to see this.

I turn to address the men gathered behind me. "Any of you. When I speak, I speak one time. You do not question me. And when my wife says I'm paying this *cavolo*'s debt, you assume it's the truth."

I start back inside, where the women have set up the table for cards and the TV for the children. I can hear their chatter and coins clinking as if everything is back to normal. Violetta waves me in. I want to be on the other side of that glass with her more than anything.

"Santino," Marco calls timidly, so I stop and look back. "When my daughter returns…"

The last part of his sentence falls into silence, but I know it ends with him telling me what I already know. That the wedding is happening as soon as Gia gets back, and if I want to change the arrangement, I have to tell Damiano and Cosimo Orolio. They can—and will—refuse.

"Do not ask me another thing. Your job isn't questions. It's obedience. You'll know when you know."

I go inside to play cards, and the men follow.

## 27

## VIOLETTA

"It was a lovely evening." Zia kisses my cheeks and cups my chin. "You make me so proud, Violetta."

My cheeks flush red—in part because I have missed the connection with my zia in person, in part because her compliments always make me wonder what my mother would say, but mostly because I took a risk today and it paid off. That threshold between adolescence and adulthood was not only crossed but eviscerated, and my family got to witness it firsthand.

Violetta Moretti is not a plaything. Violetta Moretti is not a toy. Violetta Moretti is a dangerous bitch who will move mountains to save people she loves.

Violetta Moretti is going to be a good mother.

"Thank you for coming. I have missed you so much." I squeeze her in a tight hug.

Zio comes from behind Zia and the three of us stand there for a moment, savoring this. I don't know when I'll be able to see them again, not after what I just did. I changed the rules.

I would do it again in a heartbeat. The power I felt commanding that room, laying the groundwork for a plan I concocted? Intoxicating. And there was never a better cause. I swear on my life. These bastards aren't going to steal another girl over money or territory or a few chunks of old metal ever again.

"It was lovely tonight, Santino." Zia nods politely to him.

"You'll come again," he says.

We stand outside, Santino and me, arms around each other, as these last guests climb into their Buick and drive away. I have so many memories of my aunt and uncle, but now I don't feel grief when I think about them. Maybe I really have finally grown up.

Their tail lights clear the driveway, leaving me alone with my husband.

"Did you make the offer?" I ask.

"I did." He nods and goes inside.

"And?"

"I told you he wouldn't accept."

I sigh and follow him. No words need to be spoken. We have to move to the second part of the plan.

"Upstairs," Santino says when we're inside the house and the door is locked.

I hesitate. Is he angry that we have to go to plan B? Or just surprised?

"Now," he barks.

He's so big when he yells, and all my defiance melts away, and I run upstairs. He catches me in the hall before I have to decide which room to run to, picks me up and carries me to his room, throwing me on the bed.

"Undress," he orders.

My breath catches in my throat. I study his face. There's something else there, something besides the desire to peel me open and devour the soft, sweet flesh inside. It curls darkly under his skin like blood set free of veins.

"Undress," Santino commands again, but in Italian as if that has more force. "*Spogliati.*"

It does.

My fingers fumble with my straps. Maybe there's a different name for the power I cannot define.

I'm naked in front of him when I see it clearly.

It's fear. He's afraid of the partnership he's offered me, and he's afraid of what I'll do with it. Or he's afraid I'll die. He's afraid he can't protect me.

I can't parse any of it, but it all leads to one conclusion. Santino is human. He thinks he's showing me his power, but he's lonely and desperate and afraid, just like me. I, Violetta DiLustro, am not just a wife to service him, but a companion and a mate who needs and who is needed.

"Santino—" I start.

"*Basta.*" His pants and underwear drop to the floor. He steps out of them neatly, revealing his powerful cock—more magnificent than ever. He grabs my hand and puts it on the glorious beast, and it hardens even more. "*Succhiami il cazzo.*"

*Suck my dick.* I flush warm and drop to my knees, opening my mouth obediently. All insolence is gone. I just want him to use me. I want him to show me I fucking matter. Never do I feel that more than when his cock is in me and his hands are on my shoulders, as his powerful frame comes with ragged breaths.

I take a deep breath to steady myself, so I don't come before he can touch me. Mixed with the fear from only twenty minutes earlier, I want nothing more than to have my entire world obliterated in dark pleasure.

"Tomorrow morning," he says from above. "Tell me what you do first."

He pulls out his cock. I breathe. "Call Anette. Tell her I want to go with them to pick up Gia."

Santino takes my cheeks and squeezes, pressing my mouth open. He isn't gentle. He's forceful. He's scared. He's mine. His length threatens to choke me in one thrust, sending hot electricity through my veins.

"You beg them," he says. "You cry. You tell them I want you to live over the river and you don't want to leave." He twists my hair in his hands and pulls just enough, and I respond with gasp and a groan. "You don't want to be alone in another house with only one kitchen, so far away."

I rule this man's cock. I build into a quick rhythm, sucking and licking his length with each stroke from my lips, then he pushes me away.

"I just can't be alone right now," I say, spit dripping down my chin. "I don't assume Anette told him about seeing me at the drugstore. With the test… because he told you that, not me. But if he mentions it, I say I'm pregnant and I want to tell Gia right away."

"I don't believe you." Santino drops onto a high-backed leather chair, legs apart, elbows resting on the tufted arms. The fear is gone; the power is not. "Come here."

I stand between his legs and he turns me. In the mirror, my naked body blocks him. He puts his hands on my waist and guides me down, impaling me on him. We are slick and smooth against each other, root to root without friction or resistance.

"Oh," I gasp.

"And then what?" he asks, spreading my legs open.

I can't see him. Just the edges of the chair and the place we're connected.

"On the drive there." I move up and down on him. "I tell them you've been thinking… and you decided to set up Gia and Damiano over the river. And you want to show him a big surprise before Gia gets home."

"Do you want Gia to marry?" His hand snakes between my legs and fondles my clit.

"Yes, I've…" I stop, unable to finish. He slaps lightly, bringing me back to my senses. "I've come around. Our babies can play together but… Santino… I'm so close."

"Finish." He taps, then rubs my clit as I speak.

"Not so far away over the river." My hands work with his, touching my clit, his wet shaft, his fingers twining with mine. "I'll be so happy to see Gia. I'll tell her it's okay she's getting married today. I'll be at the church. Right beside her."

"Then I pick you up to come home."

"To get ready." I'm so close to orgasm I can barely think. "But we don't. We go to the lawyer. And when we come back… we have… can I come now?"

"And when they find Damiano in the basement?"

"The next day. Oh, God, I can't hold it. I'll act

shocked. You act shocked. Bosco says, he…" My breath comes in sharp gasps. "Didn't know the cellar locked automatically. But we have the crown and… keep going. I feel you everywhere."

He thrusts his hips up and deep into me, then again, fucking faster, our hands tangling between our legs until I can't hold it. I fall back against him and come with the back of my head against his shoulder.

"That's right," he murmurs, then groans in an exhale, exploding inside me. After he settles, he pulls me into him. "And we'll have the crown before the sun sets. By the time Damiano's out of the basement to claim Gia, there will be no more forced marriage where I wear the crown."

"Thank you," I whisper. "Thank you."

The clock Santino hangs on the wall to spite his grandfather erupts in thick chimes.

We both look at it.

It's midnight.

At the last chime, my husband looks at me and says, "Happy birthday."

## 28

## SANTINO

When I first contacted Bosco about this house, I thought I was trying to make my wife happy. It's close to the school and away from the eyes and ears of Secondo Vasto. I thought I was keeping her safe, because once the crown is in my hands, I'll be a bigger target than before.

I fooled myself. I wasn't trying to make her happy. This house was meant to placate her.

I'd tried to buy her silence, but she wouldn't sell.

In the early morning hour, the concrete walls of the foundation keep the cellar chilly, as they should. Hammers bang on the outsides of the windows. Drills whirr. A man installs a new lock at the top of the stairs. The basement will be sealed tight in no time.

This will be a fine *cucina* for Gia—I run through the lie I'm going to tell Damiano—it's safe, and near enough to St. John's University that Violetta can take her to the American coffee shops easily. His new wife will be happy here.

I call him. He picks up on the fifth ring.

"Dami," I say. "I have something for you and Gia. A blessing."

"I heard you tried to buy Marco out. That ain't a blessing."

"My wife had ideas. I was covering for her. But she's been corrected." The last word carries the weight of definite threats and possible violence. It seems to satisfy him.

"Can it wait until Gia gets in? We're getting hitched today."

"I have an appointment."

He pauses. I don't break the silence.

"It's her birthday today, isn't it?" he finally says. He's aware of the importance of the day and not afraid to mention it. Now I can either tell him I'll keep my promise that he can join my business, or I can prove it.

"You want to come to the lawyer's? See the crown's pieces again before we reveal them?"

He'd have to put his wedding on hold, and doing so would be a proof of trust. Nothing would change about the plan though.

I'm not surprised by his quick reply.

"Nah. I'll see it when you get back. Where's this blessing you got for us?"

I give him the address and he estimates he'll be at the house in an hour. Probably less.

My phone rings. It's Vito—a man more trustworthy than his brother Roman, who I am sure told Theresa Rubino that I was engraving numbers inside wedding rings.

"Pronto," I say.

"The lawyer's office is secure as I can make it with what we got," he says. "But..."

"Spit the toad, Vito."

"We got Carmine on the roof across the street, but we got holes on the other side of Gateway Ave."

Having to bolt the windows in the River Heights house has stretched my men thin, but this has to be done, and though no one knows where the lawyer is, it has to be secure, and Violetta can't be left alone.

"How many do you need?" I ask, walking outside.

"Four, but we can make it with three."

I have five men locking down the basement, but only three work for me. The other two install locks and window bars for a living.

"I'll call you back." I cut the call and walk around the house.

Gennaro's no carpenter, but he's nailing a window shut before it's barred. Two more of my guys are clearing the cellar of anything that can be used to tie, break, or cut. I approach a man in a red sweatshirt who's crouching at the base of the house.

"How long?" I ask him.

He flips up his welding mask and checks his watch. "Fifteen minutes?"

That means twenty or more.

"Ten," I say, figuring I'll get fifteen. "And it's an extra thousand for you."

He looks as though I'm asking him to jump over Vesuvius for a million, but he really wants the money. "I'll try," he says, then flips down his welder's helmet.

I have one man left. Armando, and he's at the house with Violetta.

I start to call him, but instead, I call her.

"My beautiful wife," I say.

"Hey," she says smoothly, and I think of how much more I want to fuck her than I want to be here playing with the locks and windows.

"Did you call Anette?" I ask.

"They're coming to get me on the way. I didn't have to beg too hard."

"Everyone has to hear you say it," I say, looking at my watch again and finding no surprises. I pace back into the house. "Do it for me."

She playacts her story, complete with teary gasps and hiccups. "Santino? Hey, it's me. Can you meet me at home? Then I pause like I'm listening." She pauses. "In the bathroom, I was gushing. Bleeding so much. It was terrible. Please come home. Please."

She can pull this off. I have no doubt. But the minutes between now and when she's picked up are critical. A loud grind and a hard smack come from the other side of the house. I go to it. The man putting the lock on the basement door curses and drops something heavy.

"When are they getting there?" I ask.

"Should be five minutes?"

It's eight o'clock. The lawyer is an hour away, and our appointment is at ten. Damiano will be here in half an hour. The airport is forty minutes away from my house. I calculate everyone's placement on the map and how long it will take to put all of them into place.

The locksmith heads for the front door.

"Where are you going?" I ask him.

"I need a different size. I think I have one in the truck."

"You think?"

He shrugs, and I can keep him there to yell at him or let him go check, so I turn my back on him.

"Everything okay?" Violetta asks.

"Is Armando there?" I ask.

"Yeah, hang on." She gives him the phone.

"Boss."

"The minute they pick her up, I want you to get over to Vito, in the city."

The locksmith is standing in the back of his truck, still empty-handed, so I may have to keep my guys here to nail the fucking door shut behind Damiano, but yeah, everything is fucking fine.

"Leave the house alone?" Armando asks.

"You there to protect the furniture?"

"They're here!" Violetta's voice comes past Armando's agreement that no, he's not there to protect the furniture.

"Verify it's them, then do what I asked."

"Got it." He hands the phone back to my wife.

The locksmith is in the back of the truck, checking another compartment.

"*Forzetta.*"

"My king."

"Today will be tricky," I say. "Things might go wrong. If you asked me a month ago if I could trust a woman—even my wife—to do what we plan today, I would have laughed."

"You would have been an asshole for it."

The locksmith jumps off the truck bed with a box in

his hand, and my body can barely contain the relief.

"Please be careful today," I say. "If one hair on your head is hurt, I'll use the fire of hell to burn down heaven."

"Can you stop with the drama? I'll be fine."

"You're everything to me."

"I love you too," she says. "I have to go."

"*Bene.*"

"*Bene* yourself." She makes a kissing sound into the phone, and I think this is over, but she continues. "Hang on. Armando wants you."

The phone gets handed over.

"Boss." His volume drops and I can hear the floor creak as he walks to the other side of the room. "It's just Marco."

Violetta's safe enough in the car with my uncle. He's not a soldier or a killer. He doesn't know how to hurt her. But I expected something different, and I don't like surprises.

"He says Tavie came along, so with Gia and Paola, Violetta makes six. There's no room in one car on the way back."

"She stays home," I say. "Go get her."

I hear him doing as I say, saying, "Santino says she can't go" as a car door opens. My wife grabs the phone and the gravel crunches under her feet as she walks away.

"What the fuck?" she hisses.

"Do not get in that car."

"Why not?"

The locksmith comes back in, smiling. "Boom!" He holds up the box.

I give him a thumbs-up and leave the room.

"Because I don't like it and I don't trust it," I whisper to Violetta.

"That's it?"

"What else do you need?"

"Common sense? Reality? Or is this intuition from the same part of your brain that believes some ancient artifact has, like, real power?"

"Do not mock me."

"Okay, okay… look, I have an idea."

"No ideas." I don't know how to be more clear. She needs to stay home with Armando. Vito will have to do without him. If she leaves with Marco, something bad will happen, and I can't explain how I know because yes, the knowledge doesn't come from my mind, but from knees that bent unwillingly and a heart frozen with dread. "I don't want to hear them."

"I'll be alone with him," she pitches the idea anyway. "I can talk to him. Apologize for last night. Try some diplomacy."

"No."

"He's going to leave without me," she says in a panic.

"You stay. Put Armando on."

"This is you being controlling and bossy."

"This is me protecting the only thing I love in this world," I snarl, holding back a hurricane of rage.

She takes a deep breath, and I wait for her to argue again. This constant resistance is going to get her killed, and if that happens, starting the war I'm trying to avoid won't fill a fraction of the hole in my heart.

"Fine," she says in the growl of a woman agreeing with a clenched jaw.

"Listen," I say, "you lose sometimes. When we get back, they'll be married and we'll fix it. I promise."

"Stay there and meet him," she says. "It works without me. I was just there to distract them. My job was to make them think it wasn't you getting in the way. It's messier, but all we need to do is make sure they're not married before you get back with that stupid fucking thing."

She's right. Her job was to keep the unwilling bride distracted while I trapped the groom long enough to change everything.

"All right," I say. "Tell Armando to stay with you."

"Thank you!" She makes a kissing noise into the phone and hangs up.

This should be a victory. I should see the road clearing in front of me, but something is wrong.

It's not that Damiano didn't ask me about last night's conversation with Marco or Violetta's announcement. Word must have gotten to him. I have a song and dance ready to go, but he only texted back that he'd come.

He's getting married today, and he thinks he's coming here for a renewed blessing. A gift. A smooth path.

He can't know what we're planning. Armando doesn't even know.

And yet… something is wrong.

Something is very, very wrong.

Ten minutes later, a text from the airport terminal comes in. It's a bill they always send when a flight plan is complete, and in this case, the plane carrying Gia and Paola landed half an hour ago.

## 29

## VIOLETTA

I hang up with Santino and shake my head. They say women are the dramatic ones.

Not that the day's activities aren't exciting and theatrical, with high stakes and the prospect of victory for me, someone I care about, and an entire community of people. All that's true, but the execution on my side's pretty simple. All I have to do is say stuff. And all Santino has to do is close a door. All we have to do is get to the lawyer's office in time to get some artifact that's going to save the world because Santino believes it will.

Then it'll be okay. But in the meantime, Gia needs me. She's going to get off that plane terrified and it's my job to make sure she knows I'm on her side.

Armando approaches, and I wave.

"Santino says to let me go. He says you know what you have to do?"

He nods. "I got it."

Armando opens the passenger side door of Marco and Anette's Buick.

"Hey!" I say to Marco, who's driving alone. "I hear it's just us?"

"Just us." Armando closes the door, and Marco heads for the open gate off the property. "Tavie has his aunt Anette."

The gate clacks closed behind us, and I look back with a string of doubt that maybe I should have listened to Santino.

Too late now.

Marco and I chat about the weather, the traffic, the innocuous events of my party the night before, but the person I'm pretending to be has something on her mind.

"I just wanted to say…" I stop and clear my throat. "I'm really sorry about what I said last night. I didn't know it was insulting to you, but Santino said it put both of you in a bad position."

"It's okay."

"I know you can make decisions for Gia and I'm sorry I questioned that. I think she'll be really happy, and I've decided I'm going to help her."

"Don't you think you'll be a little busy?" He glances at me, then back at the road. "Someone put a flea in my ear"—he winks—"that there are two people sitting next to me?"

My giggle is only half fake. "Well, it's early, but… yes!"

"A wedding and a baby! We are truly blessed."

"Yep." It's really easy to sound chipper and excited as long as I focus on my baby and not Gia's wedding.

This whole thing's going to be a piece of cake. "So she brought a lot of things back?"

Marco blows his cheeks and exhales, flipping his hand up. "I'll tell you one thing. She's already got spending her husband's money down to a science."

Good for her.

We're at the light before we turn onto the bridge when Marco curses. "*Cazzo!*"

"What?"

"You don't happen to have the brooch my wife gave to you?"

"It's home."

"Gia was very clear. She said she wanted you to bring it for her 'something borrowed,' and I forgot. *Che stupido.*"

"We can grab it on the way back."

"Yes. Good." He seems to wave it off, then reconsiders. "I don't know. She's been so emotional. Paola says so. Crying over everything like it's the end of the world. And she said clearly to bring it, but… nah. She has to toughen up."

Even though I know the marriage will be out the window by tomorrow, I don't want Gia to accept things she doesn't want, ever. I also don't want her to be upset or distracted while I do my song and dance.

"Let's go get it," I say. "We have five minutes to spare."

---

WHEN WE GET to the gate and it doesn't open right away, I remember Armando is gone. I can either lean over Santino's uncle and punch the keys, or I can tell him the code.

"Keep it running." I'm out of the car before he even says a word. "It'll take a half a second!"

I run around the front and punch in the numbers. The gate opens. As I run down the driveway, the sound of the Buick gets quiet in the distance. If he even puts it into park, I don't hear it in the time it takes me to put in the door code and run into the house, up the stairs, and into the room I keep as my own, even as I sleep in Santino's. I open the top drawer of the ugly dresser that was owned by an ugly man, and I dig around for the brooch, then remember I left it in the bathroom.

I slap open the jewelry box in the bathroom. Find the brooch face down against the green velvet lining the drawer.

Wouldn't it be nice if she saw it on me? And I offered it before she asked? No matter what happens after that, we'll have a moment where we both wanted the same thing and I gave it to her before she asked.

I swing open the gold latch behind the pin, and before I have a chance to lift my head, a voice comes from behind me.

"Happy birthday." When I look in the mirror, I'm face to face with Damiano Orolio. "If I were you, I wouldn't move."

But he's not me, and he's not supposed to be here. He's supposed to be at the River Heights house, so I turn to him. I don't make it all the way around before he has me painfully by the hair, driving me to my knees.

"I told you," he says.

"Let me go!" I drop the brooch and clutch for the place where my scalp feels as if it's being torn off, but he's shaking me so hard I can't get a grip.

"Sure."

I'm launched into the bedroom. Sliding over the slippery floor, my lower back smacks into the corner of a bed leg. The pain is a wake-up call. I need to be faster, stronger, and more afraid.

"I'll let you go." I start to get up, but he throws me down, pressing his knee to my back. "When I have what I want, I'll let you go to the bottom of the fucking river."

He tugs at my left elbow, and for a second, I can't figure out what he's doing. Then I realize my arm is under me, and his weight on my back is keeping it there.

"What. You. Want?" Every word is a breath I can barely get out.

"Your ring." He grunts, but won't relieve the pressure.

I don't give a shit about the ring. It means nothing to me. But Santino said not to let it leave my finger before he even told me why. Understanding the reason is one thing. Now I understand the threat.

"Fuck off." I wiggle, making it harder for Damiano to take his knee off without losing me.

He gets off me to pull my arm, but though he's strong, I'm quick enough to get out from under him. I back into the window. There's nowhere to go, and I have to keep my hands behind me so he can't get at the ring.

"Why?" I ask.

"You don't know?" He seems incredulous, simultaneously mocking both my witlessness and the impossibility of my ignorance. I'm a stupid woman who can't possibly be this stupid.

"The stone. It's big but—"

"Fuck the rock. He never told you what was engraved inside it?"

I gain nothing by telling him Santino told me everything about the engraving. If Damiano knows, he knows. "No."

"It's a license number for a lawyer." He steps forward. "The one with the appointment you're going to miss today. And when I get it, I'm going to know where to go and get your inheritance. The one that was promised to *me*."

As far as I'm concerned, he can have the ring.

He can have the stupid crown.

But there's a piece missing to all this.

He can't just walk into the lawyer's office and pick up what my father left to me.

Maybe if I was dead, or I was married to him, and neither of those things will happen as long as Santino DiLustro is breathing.

I gasp when I think of it.

Damiano knows where Santino is, but Santino's waiting for Damiano to show up to a house on the other side of the river. My husband's a sitting duck.

"I'll give you the ring," I say.

One of his eyes narrows. He doesn't believe me.

I hold my left fist to my chest. "But you call Santino right now. Tell him you're here. By the time he gets here, you'll be gone."

"When he gets here, he'll be dead."

Damiano grabs my hand, but I hold the fist tight. We wrestle. I twist and fight. He spins and throws me some direction that could be up, or left, or both and neither. I crash into the dresser. Heavy things fall. The ornate clock. A brass lamp.

He punches me in the face. I see every star in the sky.

"We can do this easy," he says from the other side of consciousness. "Or we can do it fun."

The stars fade. I'm leaning on the dresser. I grab a fallen plaster statue of a half-naked woman by the throat and swing wildly, hitting his bicep.

The blow sends him rightward by half an inch, but doesn't slow his advance.

"Fun then," he says, slapping me this time, but so hard I'm thrown against the wall.

Swinging wildly, waiting to get hit again, I stumble back into the bathroom. I aim the naked woman for his head, but he sees me coming a mile away. He grabs the statue by the base, yanks it from me, and throws it over his shoulder. A gurgle of nausea pushes up my throat.

"I'm going to get that ring whether I hit you again or not."

I don't want to get hit again. I really don't, but I can't just hand over the ring. Not now that I know why Santino told me not to.

"Come get it."

The ease of getting me face down on the floor proves I never had a chance. He was playing with me from the beginning. This time, my left arm isn't under me. The ring's stone is inside my fist.

"Open it," he demands.

On the floor in front of me, three Furies dance on a carved seashell.

"No."

"I'll cut your fucking hand off." He digs his fingertips into the seam between the heel of my hand and my knuckles, peeling open my fist.

It doesn't hurt, but I scream from the effort it takes to fight him.

"Fuck, you're a fucking bitch." He tries to get the ring off, but I won't uncurl the knuckles.

"You wanted the fun way." I'm all growls now, watching the Furies frozen in time, knowing I'm going to lose.

"So do you," he says, bending the entire finger back.

The pain sends a shock from my hand to my heart. My scream goes from effort to agony, and thinking he's won, Damiano shifts. I snatch the Furies with my right hand, twist, and ram the pin deep into the first exposed body part I find—his wrist.

His eyes go wide. He leans back, the shell and gold oval flapping in the hinge. "Bitch."

He's more mad than in pain, and I'm fucked. I pull out the brooch before he has a chance to do it, and without wasting a second or holding back the force of my entire body, I jam the entire pin into his eye. He screams with the cameo covering his impaled eye, half his gaze covered by the fury of women.

I run out of the room and slam the door closed, snapping the deadbolt Santino used to trap me in that room a million years ago. I'm safe, but I press my back against the opposite wall and slide along it, afraid to turn my back on him.

With a loud *pop*, the door cracks at the seam. He's shot out the lock. The deadbolt holds, but the wood around it is shattered. I run and almost make it down the hall, accompanied by the sound of cracking wood behind me. Right before the stairs, my feet are yanked out from under me, and I land on my hands and chest.

"Where you going, little girl?"

I'm dragged back by the ankles. My shirt crawls over my bra as I try to grab for the hall table and miss. My hand drags over the long, splintered bullet hole I shot into the floor. Twisting, I look behind me at my assailant. Damiano's facing forward, pulling my legs like a plow horse.

"Stop," I say weakly. I don't expect him to obey me, but I have to object. "Stop!"

He ignores me and pulls me into my room. I grab the doorjamb just for the sake of resisting. He pulls me hard, but I hold.

"You're cute," he says, dropping my ankles.

Whatever he's about to do next is lost in the sharp beep of the front door opening.

I scrabble up. Damiano grabs me by the back of the neck and pushes me against the wall next to the doorframe.

"Violetta!" Santino calls. The keys slap on the front table.

"Scream," Damiano hisses, pointing his gun at the place Santino will appear when he follows the sound of my voice. "Do it."

"You," I snarl, fighting his entire weight. I can't see

much now, and I realize the eye that isn't being pushed against the wall is swollen shut.

"*Forzetta*," Santino calls from the kitchen casually, as if he expects me to be at the airport, but he's checking anyway.

"Oh, that's cute," Damiano says. "Now, let him know his wife's waiting for him in the bedroom."

"He knows you're here." I strain against him.

"No, he doesn't."

"Your fucking car is in the driveway."

He *tsks*. "Don't you know about Foothill Street?"

I do, but everything's a jumble, and I don't know how.

Damiano growls in my ear so close I feel his spit. "Let him know you're here before I make you scream."

The second Santino knows where I am, he'll come up here, and screaming that there's danger will only get him here quicker. There's not a chance that Damiano's bullet will miss Santino's head as soon as it appears.

There's no force I can apply to get away. He's too strong. And there's no risk I can take that won't risk the baby inside me.

Somewhere, my phone rings.

"What do you want?" I croak.

"I want what I was promised." The pressure against me lessens. "Emilio Moretti's second daughter."

"What?"

Damiano pushes off me. I turn. He's taken half a step back into the room. The brooch left his eye bleeding and swollen. He may lose it, and he may not care, because it barely slows him down.

My phone's still ringing.

He grabs me by the elbow and drags me toward the window. I won't help him do whatever he's trying, so I let my legs go limp under me, and he flings me against the wall of windows. The glass rattles and shudders as my body hits it, arms up to soften the impact on my face.

Damiano pushes me against the window. Below me, Santino stands at the edge of the sparkling pool, looking up. His phone is between his hand and the patio tile, stopped midair in a time loop—falling, falling, falling as he reaches inside his jacket for his gun.

It's out, cold and black in his fists, the diamonds of his crown ring glinting in the sun.

My phone stops ringing.

Santino aims for the window.

He's not going to shoot me.

He can't hit Damiano from there.

He won't fire. He'll come up fast, thinking he's saving me and cornering Damiano.

He'll know he's at a disadvantage, but he won't win.

He has to know this.

"Come on up, *stronzo*," Damiano growls. "Come and get her."

Santino lowers his gun, looks ahead, and is about to start forward, into the kitchen, up the stairs, and to his death.

I don't know how to help him. I don't know how to stop it.

Santino stops.

Good.

Damiano chuckles as if he knows something I can't see.

Santino's right hand drops. His grip loosens. The gun falls. He takes half a step back, to the edge of the pool, with his palms out in front of him. He says something I can't hear.

"That's right, baby," Damiano murmurs in my ear. "Get close."

A woman appears from the kitchen with a gun held forward in both hands, and it takes me a second to recognize her wavy brown hair and yellow sundress.

"Gia?" I croak. Then I shout, pounding on the glass. "Gia!"

Santino looks up at me, and our eyes meet just when the gun cracks. His limbs shake and his chest goes concave where the bullet hits him. His legs are thrown from under him and the force of the shot sends him backward, into the placid surface of his pool.

"No!" I scream.

The water gathers around Santino's lifeless body.

She hit him in the chest.

Did it miss his heart?

Just a lung?

Damiano lets me go. I tear myself away from the sight of my husband, my lover, my king sinking. I know how to do this.

*Surface.*

*Flip.*

*Swim.*

I have to get down there. See the wound. Stop the blood. Call 9-1-1. I turn and face the man obstructing my path out. Three thin red lines dry on his cheeks as if he's been crying blood. He's between the door and me, legs wide and arms out from his body, elbows bent, ready to grab at anything he can reach.

"Please," is the only word I have.

He licks his lips.

*Please.*

*Secure area.*

*Check breathing.*

*Check pulse.*

*She shot him in his heart.*

"Let me by," I say, trying to get around Damiano on his blind side, but he blocks me.

*Administer CPR.*

*Beg him to live.*

"I can save him!" I scream.

"I know," is all he says before he pulls his fist back and hits my face so hard the world goes black.

TO BE CONTINUED IN MAFIA QUEEN

## ACKNOWLEDGMENTS

1. About the word *'mbasciata*. You may be the sort who's going to look it up, or you may speak Italian and think I've lost my mind, because it literally means embassy. It also means an arranged marriage, but that's a specific local dialect, so you'll find it, but you're going to have to look hard.
2. The orphanage and institution in Aversa and Trieste are made up. Kind of. They existed in those places, but not in the time span suggested.
3. Bar license number length and alphanumeric format varies by state. I'm not getting into which state these books are located in because this story is a love letter to a place that doesn't exist. So, to my lawyer and lawyer-adjacent readers, I appreciate you noticing. You're my people.

# ALSO BY CD REISS

### The Edge Series

*Rough. Dark. Sexy enough to melt your device.*

*He's her husband but he's rougher and more dominant than the man she married.*

*Rough Edge*
*On The Edge*
*Broken Edge*
*Over the Edge*

### The Submission Series

*The USA Today bestselling Series*

*Monica insists she's not submissive. Jonathan Drazen is going to prove otherwise, but he might fall in love doing it.*

*One Night With Him*
*One Year With Him*
*One Life With Him*

### The Games Duet

*The New York Times bestsellers.*

*He'll give her the divorce she wants on one condition. Spend 30 days in a remote cottage with him, doing everything he commands.*

*Marriage Games*

*Separation Games*

### The DiLustro Arrangement

*Twisted. Dark. Gritty. Will knock you off your feet story.*

*An epic mafia romance trilogy that sets a new bar for just how dark a hero can get.*

*Mafia Bride*

*Mafia King*

*Mafia Queen*

## PAIGE PRESS

*Paige Press isn't just Laurelin Paige anymore...*

Laurelin Paige has expanded her publishing company to bring readers even more hot romances.

**Sign up for our newsletter to get the latest news about our releases and receive a free book from one of our amazing authors:**

Stella Gray
CD Reiss
Jenna Scott
Raven Jayne
JD Hawkins
Poppy Dunne

# ABOUT THE AUTHOR

CD Reiss is a Brooklyn native and has the accent to prove it. She earned a master's degree in cinematic writing from USC. She ultimately failed to have one line of dialog put on film, but stayed in Los Angeles out of spite.

Since screenwriting was going nowhere, she switched to novels and has released over two dozen titles, including two *NY Times* Bestsellers and a handful of *USA Today* bestsellers. Her audiobooks have won APA Audie Awards and Earphones Awards.

She resides in Hollywood in a house that's just big enough for her two children, two cats, her long-suffering husband and her massive ego.

To find out when her next book is coming out, sign up for her mailing list here or at cdreiss-dot-com.

Printed in Great Britain
by Amazon